Emerald Glory

Vikings of Honor, Book Two

RENEE
VINCENT

EMERALD GLORY
Copyright © 2017, Renee Vincent
Trade Paperback ISBN: 9781944484088

Digital ISBN: 9781944484071
Hardback ISBN: 9781944484163

Cover Art Design by Renee Vincent
Stock Images by BigStock.com
Edited by Linda Ingmanson
Digital Release: May, 2017
Trade Paperback Release: May, 2017
Hardback Release: March, 2022

Publishing History
First Edition of revised work published by Turquoise Morning Press
under the title *Mac Liam*
Copyright © 2010 by Renee Vincent

Second Edition of revised work published by Renee Vincent under the
title *Mac Liam*
Copyright © 2015 by Renee Vincent

For God.
You never left my side when I needed you most.

And for my two beautiful daughters,
Madeline and Jolee.

Praise for EMERALD GLORY

"I was blown away! Ms. Vincent surpassed all of my expectations with her impressive writing abilities that will keep readers coming back for more. Readers should be warned of the emotional turmoil they will face once again while reading this incredible story. I eagerly anticipate the next story in this series, yet already mourn the finality."
—*Night Owl Reviews*

"This is one fantastic historical. The story is vivid and the historical detail so impressive without bogging the plot or action down. It comes alive and winds its way into your heart. This is a must-read for anyone who enjoys historical romance and I cannot wait to read the final book of the trilogy as this story has stayed with me days after I read the last word."
—*The Romance Studio*

"I have to admit, while I was exceptionally fond of Daegan in Book 1 of this series, Breandan held a special place in my heart from the time he entered the story. As with the first book, action, adventure and soul-melting romance abounds. Another double thumbs up for Renee Vincent."
—*Coffee Beans and Love Scenes*

"…this is a story you will hate to see end!"
—*Romance Junkies*

"I will admit I was leery about reading this. After all the hype, I was worried I would end up being let down, as is often the case, especially with great historical romances. Boy, was I wrong this time! I am very impressed with this series and can't wait for the next book."
—*Marissa's Sizzling Hot Reviews*

"Renee Vincent weaves another beautiful, intriguing, and mesmerizing tapestry of a tale. The steadfast, true love Ms. Vincent creates takes one's breath away. A memorable, satisfying story!"
—*Long And Short Reviews*

"The twists and turns of book 1 continue along in this installment. Not once was anything given away, you know how when you read a book and say . . "ah, I saw that coming." That isn't going to happen here!"
—*Romancing The Book Reviews*

"I loved this book! There were many nights where I could not put the book down!"
—*Knights of the Round Table*

EMERALD GLORY
Vikings of Honor, Book 2

For seven long years, Breandán Mac Liam has been haunted by the memory of Mara. The Connacht princess captured Breandán's heart but married a Northman and traveled far from the lush forests where first they met. Now word reaches Breandán that the Northman is dead, and a perilous charge has been assigned him: escort the princess through war-torn lands to her dying father's side.

Mourning her husband and struggling to raise their troubled young son, Mara does not know she's the object of the Irishman's longing. Heartbroken over the loss of her husband, she is totally unprepared for the feelings Breandán awakens in her.

As their worlds collide, Breandán not only finds himself wrapped in the arms of Mara's embrace but forced to defend his honor. With Mara caught between the family she loves and the father she knows, can Breandán uncover the mystery of her past and still protect her from a secret that threatens them all?

*Previously published as *Mac Liam*. (This new edition has been partially rewritten and professionally edited, along with a new title and new cover.)

Chapter One

Iceland, AD 923

The door of the longhouse burst open, and seven men, outfitted in conical helmets, snow-dusted wolfskin cloaks, and swords, rushed in. They hastened to surround the boxbed where two entangled bodies sat up in complete surprise, the covers drawn to their chins to hide their nakedness.

Before the master of the house could utter a single word of protest about the rude intrusion—not to mention the seven swords now pointed at his heart—an eighth man entered, taller and broader in stature but with more of a casual arrogance than his comrades. He too was helmeted. But as he strolled closer, he removed it, revealing a headful of dark blond hair.

The master of the house swallowed hard and somehow gained his tongue for speaking. "How dare you burst into my home!"

The Norse intruder only stared, as if to collect his thoughts after the long tiresome journey he'd endured before this moment. His breathing was not heavy or labored, and his face showed no signs of emotion. It was difficult to say why his words failed him, but there was no doubt the tension in the room grew as the silence lengthened. Finally, he spoke, but not to the master. He looked at the woman.

"Are you his wife?"

"Of course not! She's but a whore!" the man answered for her. "And what matter is it of yours?"

The red-haired woman's lips pursed tightly, and she slapped her master's face. In the heat of her anger, the linen sheets she'd been holding to her chin dropped and revealed an ample blessing of youthful breasts for all to see.

For the first time since his entering, the Northman smiled. "Be not angered, woman. The insult this man delivered has just saved your life. Get your clothes and leave."

"And where must I go on a cold night like this?" she asked, seemingly unafraid of the eight towering men surrounding her.

"Wherever you choose. But know this, I shall never insult you should you decide to leave with me, *my lady*."

A slight grin eased across her rosy cheeks upon hearing the noble title the bearded stranger flattered her. Likely no one had ever called her by a dignified name. And it seemed enough to convince her that tagging along with the man—whose name she'd yet to learn—was a better idea than wading in knee-high snowdrifts toward the next warm longhouse owned by a man she'd already lain with countless times.

She stood up from the boxbed and approached the handsome Northman. She looked at him with seductive eyes, and he gazed over her firm stark-naked body, blushed pink from the warmth of the room's fire.

The Northman reached out to the nearest wall and swiped her master's fine bear cloak, then wrapped it around her shoulders. "My langskip awaits you outside. Go on," he said with a subtle jerk of his head. "This is no place for a delicate woman."

She slowly walked away, dragging her hand across his armored chest before bending down and gathering the rest of her clothes. The Northman didn't catch sight of her provocative stoop, for his eyes remained fixed on her master, whose face now fumed with rage.

Once the Northman heard the door close behind him, he stepped forward, this time in a quicker fashion. "Get up," he demanded.

The man stood as he was told and locked eyes with his aggressor, the very man who stole his woman property right out from under him with barely an effort. "Who do you think you are?" he growled.

As if thankful the man finally asked, the Northman smiled callously and introduced himself in a monotone voice. "I'm Gustaf, son of Rælik, son of the man you slaughtered in Hladir twenty-three winters ago…in his own home…his wife to watch. I've come to avenge my father. There were ten of you sent by Harald Fairhair. I've traveled through rain, snow, and bone-chilling north winds in search of each one. You're the ninth, Ragnar, son of Thorsteinn."

Gustaf watched as Ragnar's eyes widened. Not only had he burst into this man's home, threatened him with a show of swords, and taken his harlot, he'd also traced Ragnar's lineage and proved that the rumors of Fairhair's involvement in the other eight deaths were all untrue. Fairhair had not paid a group of thugs to eradicate those who knew any of his past treacheries left hanging in the wind. It was one man's vengeance—an avenging son.

Ragnar scoffed. "So 'twould be you who have forced us all to leave our families and homelands to live in exile—"

"Give me the name of the tenth man," Gustaf cut in, "and I swear your death will be swift. Give it not, and you'll die in the same manner which you had once deemed necessary for my father—drawn and hanged by your own entrails."

It did not take long for the man to decide his fate. "I'll not give you his name, as I'm neither a coward nor a traitor. What I did, was by order of the king." He spat at Gustaf's feet. "Long live Harald Fairhair."

"So be it." Gustaf unsheathed his dagger for the punishment at hand.

Chapter Two

Ireland, AD 923
Seven Years After Dægan Ræliksen's Death

Breandán Mac Liam rested his weary bones against a select tree trunk in the forest of the Clan Rourke hunting grounds. He was an adept hunter of both large and small game, and his talent for doing so brought him a considerable amount of wealth in the trade market despite his tender age of twenty-seven years. The livelihood of red deer, hare, and fox fur trading in Galway afforded him much freedom and independence, but he didn't particularly enjoy the solitude. The unfortunate result of loneliness was often having too much time to think. And all he could think about was the Connacht king's daughter.

Though it had been more than seven years since he'd seen Mara, his love for her hadn't lessened. He was chained to her memory and the hope that one day they could be together.

When he'd first laid eyes on Mara, she was a teenage girl, riding her horse through the meadows of his father's land. Had it been anyone else, Breandán would've put a swift stop to it. But with Mara, he didn't mind that she occasionally disturbed his hunting.

Her natural beauty and grace caught his eye first. The more he'd seen her lingering in the fields and lounging near the River Shannon, the more he came to appreciate her freeborn spirit and gentle kindness, traits he assumed she hadn't inherited from her pompous father, Cathal Mac Conor.

Mara was nothing like him. She was lighthearted and nimble as she sang and danced in the wildflowered fields. She was elegant and agile as she raced her horse through brooks and briars. And above all, she hadn't an arrogant bone in her body. She'd greet and welcome anyone who came into her life without ever looking down on them.

Despite her graciousness, Breandán had never felt comfortable enough to approach her. In his eyes, he was naught but a common man with common needs, and—given her noble status—he couldn't give her what he thought she deserved.

When he finally had made himself known to her, she was already in love with and married to a Northman named Dægan Ræliksen. To add to his misfortune, Mara no longer lived near Breandán, but on Inishmore, an island off the west coast of Ireland.

Since that time, Breandán had desperately tried to move on. Tried to forget her. But it proved useless. Each passing summer, when the ports brimmed with gossip, he'd hear tidbits of information regarding her current state of affairs. One summer, it was news about her husband's tragic death. The next year, it was how she'd given birth to the Northman's son the following spring.

While most of the chin wagging was usually hearsay, the thought of Mara being all alone and raising a son on such a harsh island as Inishmore pulled at his heart. Much of his desire to see her again was driven by the deep love he'd always had for her and the sincere need to make certain she was all right. He'd mulled the idea of going to her a thousand times over in his head. But the one time he'd finally convinced himself to visit her, he'd learned there was talk of another marriage between her and another Northman.

Again, he'd missed out on his opportunity to be with Mara.

That was the final stake driven through his heart, and since then, he could hardly bring himself to step foot in Galway. Instead, he relied on his childhood friend and hunting partner, Marcas, to trade his goods. He stayed clear of everything that would or might remind him of Mara. He even went as far as hunting farther north to avoid familiar landmarks she used to frequent.

None of his efforts or the changes he'd made to his routine mattered. Nothing, not even time, could lessen the pain or water down the vivid image of Mara's face. She haunted his thoughts and his dreams.

"I suppose you expect me to build the fire tonight," Marcas grumbled as he dismounted from his horse and found Breandán already relaxing against a tree.

"I snared more rabbits than you this day, did I not?"

"You always do, but I didn't know it meant I had to wait on you hand and foot. Would you like me to cook your dinner as well? Perhaps even draw a hot bath for you?"

The sarcasm in his friend's remark was almost humorous. Almost. "Dinner will suffice."

Marcas scoffed at his reply and unsaddled his horse, tossing the heavy tack on the ground beside Breandán. "When are you going to get Mara out of your head?"

It was bad enough he had to cope with her absence, much less explain the reason why he couldn't let go to someone else. He wanted and needed her as badly as any man could want or need a woman, and trying to put it into words was beyond his capability.

"Or better yet," Marcas added, adjusting the cloak around his shoulders, "why do you not simply go to her. Perhaps her marriage to another was naught more than port gossip."

"The man I spoke to said he heard it directly from Tait's mouth. Why would Dægan's comrade say anything untrue? Besides, I cannot go to her without a relevant reason. Imagine the chatter my unsolicited visit would bring. I don't want that for her, nor do I want to appear desperate in her eyes."

"It's been seven years, *a chara*. I'm certain she's moved on, and you must do the same."

"I've tried."

"Isolating yourself in the hunting grounds is not going to help you forget her. You need to remove her from your mind permanently. And I know the perfect remedy."

Breandán let his head fall back against the tree, knowing his friend's antidote was probably either a drunken stupor or a wild romp with a practiced woman, neither of which interested him.

"What you need," Marcas said joyously as he slid to his knees beside Breandán, "is that fine woman your father has deemed worthy of you. Regan's daughter. What is her name again?"

"Sorcha."

Marcas's smile grew at the sweet sound of her name. He even reached out with both hands in a gesture that resembled mild groping. He shot Breandán a sideways glance. "Can you not see what gifts she has to offer you?"

Breandán cracked a smile at his crude companion. "My

eyes have seen, but…"

"But what?"

"She's like a sister to me."

"Ach," Marcas groaned. "Why must you resort to that?"

"Because she is," Breandán confirmed. "I've known her all my life. She used to meet me in the forest when her father and brothers were busy with their chores. She'd often keep me from mine, which in the beginning gained me a swift beating, but I found ways around it. Rising before sunrise to get a head start or simply working faster."

Marcas's interest was suddenly piqued, albeit for suggestive reasons. "Aye…go on."

"Nothing ever happened," Breandán amended. "We were merely children who got along well together. We fished, climbed trees, laughed at each other…"

"Naught more?"

Breandán furrowed his brow. "We were children, Marcas."

"Not forever. She grew up mighty quickly if I recall."

Breandán nodded and swiftly added, "And so lost interest in fishing and climbing trees, as most girls do."

Marcas shook his head in disappointment. "You're truly daft, *a chara*. There are other things you could've done in that forest to keep her interest."

"And have her three brute brothers, not to mention her very large father, after my hide? I think not."

Marcas raised a single finger, denouncing Breandán's logic. "But now you've attained their blessings. You could do anything you wanted with that voluptuous woman and have no ill will from any of her family because you'd be her rightful husband. You'd obtain a heavy dowry along with her, and your father would gain the alliance he desires with

Regan. Everyone would win, including me."

Breandán looked at his friend oddly. "*You?* How would *you* benefit from the union?"

"By getting to hear all the naughty details of your conjugal interludes. I relate all my interludes as they happen."

Breandán rolled his eyes. "Well, it's certainly not because I've ever asked you to." He became suspicious of Marcas's motives. "Did my father put you up to this?"

"You'd like to think that, wouldn't you? 'Twould be easier to dismiss altogether if others tried to involve themselves in your private matters. But rest assured, I'm the only one who matters, and I couldn't care less about your privates."

As Marcas walked away into the depths of the dark forest, laughing at his own joke, Breandán gave thought to the arrangement between him and Sorcha. It would be a good match considering they were already friends. Most often a man was married to a woman he barely knew, and love came, hopefully, thereafter. They, however, wouldn't have to endure that awkward part of the relationship.

I could love her, he thought. Sorcha was a beautiful young woman with long ebony hair and ice-blue eyes that looked straight into a man's soul. She was taller than most girls her age, and more endowed than most women who'd birthed three or more children. While she wasn't a promiscuous woman, a man would have to be blind not to notice her.

Aye, I could love her. He already cared deeply for her, given their childhood and the time they'd spent together. Learning to love her as his wife might come easier than he thought...if he tried hard enough.

Breandán pulled his cloak of gray hare tighter around

his shoulders as his breath misted the air. He started to feel the chill of the cool night and eventually the cold, harsh reality that even if he could love another the way he loved Mara, did he really want to?

****

Breandán woke to the sound of a twig snapping underfoot and realized he'd fallen asleep sitting up against the tree. The last thing he remembered was thinking about Mara as Marcas left to fetch wood for a fire.

He examined his surroundings with a careful shift of his eyes. Marcas lay a few feet from him, snoring quietly. A fire burned warmly at his feet, and his dinner—that Marcas must have cooked anyway—hung from a spit beside him.

Farther beyond his immediate surroundings, he noticed the horses had their ears perked high as if they too heard the sound. He peered in the direction they stared and unsheathed his dagger. He tried to awaken Marcas with a hard nudge of his foot, but Marcas only grunted and rolled over, muttering something about "get your own wood."

While keeping his eyes on the darkness ahead, Breandán frowned and decided to search the woods alone. He didn't bother with his bow, as it was too dark to make out a distant target. His plan was to sneak up on the intruders in the same manner as they'd sneaked up on him, while hoping he'd not be terribly outnumbered.

He rounded the horses and darted behind a tree. Cautiously, he looked again, allowing his vision to adjust from the bright light of the fire to the dim obscurity of the dense woods. Once his eyesight adapted and he could distinguish woodland objects, he scurried from tree to tree, taking a deliberate wide and circular path until he found refuge behind a vantage point of thick brush and boulders.

He scouted the area as he crept and caught sight of a single dark figure in a hood and cloak, moving closer to where he and Marcas had made camp. The stranger was not close enough to do any harm to Marcas yet, but it was obvious the person was advancing in that direction.

Breandán reached down and picked up a stone. He launched it distantly behind the trespasser and hit a tree to distract him. As planned, the hooded figure walked guardedly away from Marcas, but foolishly in the direction of the ricocheting stone.

The man was quite short in stature and apparently unskilled in stealth or hunting. Breandán could easily take him alone, bearing in mind he wouldn't get much help from his oblivious comrade. Taking a deep breath, he cut a path straight toward the stranger and pounced on him. With one arm around the man's forehead, Breandán stretched the hooded man's neck to meet a well-placed dagger. "Who are you? Speak your name."

"Please," a woman's whimpering voice proclaimed. "Do not kill me. I beg you."

Breandán's heart stopped, and his breath caught. He knew that voice but couldn't believe his ears. He spun the woman around and jerked the hood from her head, gasping at his find. His legs faltered and his steady hunting hands shook until he dropped his knife.

Breandán spoke Mara's name, but it came out so erratically, he sounded more like a stuttering fool.

She smiled after hearing it on his lips. "I feared perhaps you'd forgotten me."

Breandán gawked at her, thinking he was dreaming and she'd soon disappear. But he watched her step forward and heard the sound of the wet autumn leaves beneath her feet. He saw the few wisps of hair blow back from her face. He even swore he felt her light, warm breath on his cheek as she neared.

He swallowed hard, trying to pull himself together, but he failed. He recognized the fragrant oils she used from when they'd first met, like honeysuckle, only sweeter, and it made her presence that much more convincing.

This was no dream. Mara was real and standing before him.

An image of him pressing his dagger against her precious throat flashed in his memory, and his voice returned. "God's teeth, Mara, I could've killed you!" He cradled her jaw and tilted her head. To his relief, her skin hadn't even reddened from his blade.

Mara looked deep into his eyes. "You would never harm me."

Captured by her sensuous stare, he held it with his own. A slight grin tugged at his lips. "Aye, I would never harm you, Mara."

She melted against him and laid her head upon his chest. "I thought I'd never find you."

Reality smacked him in the face, and he gripped her shoulders, holding her from his body. "You came alone? Surely your new husband would not approve of such recklessness." He peered into the forest, searching for a spouse. Surely, not even a neglectful husband would allow her to journey this distance unaided. "Did you come alone?" Breandán demanded, "Answer me, Mara."

"Aye," she replied. "No one is aware of my travels."

Breandán couldn't believe she'd journeyed so far on her own without some sort of escort. Was she mad? "Mara, do you not know the risks you've taken in coming here, let alone the strains you may have placed upon your marriage? Your husband won't take kindly to this. We must get you home."

"Please, do not sent me back there." Mara gripped his arms. "I've come so far to see you. Please, do not send me away."

Breandán read deeper into her pleas. "Has he hurt you? Has anyone hurt you?"

Mara shook her head. "Nay, he is a good man."

"Then why are you here?"

"Because I love—"

"Mara," Breandán interrupted quickly. "Do not say that."

"But 'tis true. For so long, I've held it inside me, and I cannot anymore. I belong with you."

Her words opened a dam, and his emotions came rushing forward. Everything he'd ever felt—ever hoped for.

I belong with you.

But as soon as that little phrase echoed in his ears, he remembered the man who'd taken her as his wife. His heart deflated. "You married again before God and witnesses. What is done is done."

Mara's eyes welled with tears. "Did you not hear me? I said I belong with you."

"I heard you," Breandán replied, adoring those words. "But 'tis not something you should say to me. Do you not know how difficult 'tis to stand here and look at you, and not greedily take what is rightfully another man's?"

"Then you still love me as I've always believed."

"Aye, but my undying love for you does not make this just." She burrowed closer to his chest, looking at him in a way that matched his own lustful feelings. "Please, Mara,"

Breandán begged halfheartedly. "I cannot resist you in this way."

For years, he'd dreamed of this moment and now, when it was actually upon him, he was pushing her away. Was he out of his mind? Marcas would call him an absolute imbecile.

"Kiss me," Mara encouraged.

And her little request stole his last fiber of strength. "God forgive me," he muttered before he threaded his hands in her hair and took her lips with a slow, hesitant kiss.

"Breandán," was all he heard, but it did not come from Mara. It was male and very stern. As he whirled to face the voice behind him, a solid fist walloped him square in the jaw.

Breandán gasped, and his eyes flashed open to find himself sitting by the fire, against the tree, with Marcas now looking at him oddly. Everything was as it had been before he fell asleep, and the figure of another man was nowhere in sight.

"Are you all right?" Marcas asked. "You were talking in your sleep. At one point, you were asking God Almighty for forgiveness. What were you doing?"

Breandán finally allowed himself to breathe. "I dreamt Mara came to me. And she was there in my arms, in my very possession."

Marcas sighed and rolled back under his warm animal pelt. "And I suppose you're gathering meaning from this now."

Breandán pondered the actual difference between this dream and the ones from his past. He could still feel the remnant sensations of Mara's lips on his, and he could smell the distinct aroma of honeysuckle when it was far too early in the season for blossoms. How could he not gather meaning from this encounter?

Though he had no idea if they were destined to meet again, he prayed that fate, or chance, or even God would somehow bring them together.

Chapter Three

The next morning proved to be just as cruel for Breandán as waking from a dream in the middle of a heated kiss with Mara. The breeze came off the Atlantic harsh and forceful, blowing vindictive, rain-filled clouds across the sky. What showers he'd hoped wouldn't fall until late evening threatened to arrive on the tail end of his long journey to his father's homestead.

Leading the pair of horses that drew a cart brimming with venison, hare, and assorted pelts, he crested the hill and admired the valley below. A rush of familiarity and nostalgia came over him as he gazed upon the large fortified man-made island positioned strategically in the shallow end of Lough Allen. The crannog accommodated his childhood home and the many circular houses of his clansmen, each constructed of wattle-and-daub walls and thatched roofs.

Weeks had gone by since his last visit, and he hated that his livelihood often determined the frequency of his returns. If hunting was scarce or the market demanded more hides and meat than he could supply, it wasn't unusual for months to separate him from his family. To make up for present lost time, the surplus of game and furs he toted along would be a fitting gift for his father and the clan that resided there.

A gust of wind cut across the peak and sliced all the way down to the marrow. He gathered his cloak under his chin and held firm to the horse's bridle, soothing the skittish animal with a string of Gaelic words. When Marcas joined him at the top, slightly out of breath, he regarded his friend with a worried glance. "'Tis very quiet."

"Sure 'tis! God Himself couldn't hear anything with this bloody wind howling in His ears."

Breandán scowled. "That's not what I mean. 'Tis much too quiet down below. Where is everyone?"

Not a single person moved about between the small thatched houses of his father's crannog. Felim's three sons should've been out splitting wood, or at least arguing about who split more in less time. Declan's young twin daughters should've been furtively chasing the geese around the back of the storage house. The women of the lake dwelling should've been busy tending the large cauldrons of food at the numerous hearths—which also lacked the necessary fires. And above all, his father should've been out tending the distant fields. Nothing was within the realm of normal.

"I don't like this one bit."

Marcas grunted. "I agree. Your undue suspicions are getting rather annoying."

"I'm serious, Marcas. What if Duncan Mac Flann has decided to return for another go-round? He didn't take kindly to his defeat at Ath Luain a few years ago, and we've known for quite some time he'll stop at nothing to gain more territory. He blinded one brother and killed another, for heaven's sake. With the health of our Connacht king deteriorating, we'd be foolish men to think he graciously turned his back on us."

Breandán could hardly stomach the idea of a ruthless man such as Duncan Mac Flann forcing his expanded reign here. It was a peaceful place of rolling hills and tranquil lake waters abundant with fish and wildlife. The nearby woodlands provided both a colorful palette in any blooming season and a much-needed supply of timber for sustaining the *crannog* and its defenses. While he hated to imagine his childhood home under attack, it was more insufferable to think of his family enduring it.

His father was getting to the age where simple actions such as climbing this very hillock had become increasingly difficult. Chores, once finished by midday, took more time and more exertion, both of which his father had little to spare. And then to think of his dear sweet mother and his two younger sisters coming face-to-face with heartless men who cared only for the victory at hand and the spoils they could salvage from a fire-engulfed village in the name of Duncan Mac Flann made him ill.

His gut twisted as he pored over the valley. Then something caught his eye just outside the wooden causeway of the *crannog*. Five mounted men against one man on foot stood conversing with one another. He assumed the solitary man to be his father, but feared the others might be Mac Flann's men since everyone else had taken to hiding.

Breandán grabbed his bow from the cart and tossed Marcas's to him. "Be quick and mount up," he commanded as he unhooked both horses from the confines of the shafts. "Father's in danger. I could only count five. There may be more." He led his horse into the open, turned it about, and leapt upon its back. He waited only long enough to confirm that Marcas had mounted as well, then dashed down the hillside. With his heart pounding, he reached over his shoulder and plucked an arrow from his quiver.

****

"I understand the message you bring is urgent, as 'tis from the Cathal Mac Conor himself, but I can no more rouse my son from the vast lands of the Uí Briúin Bréifne than I can a dead man deep in his grave. You're more than welcome to search for him in the mountains. But I should warn you, he won't take kindly to it after his hunting is disturbed."

Liam Mac Rourke stood bravely before the Connacht king's messengers and didn't much care about their growing agitation. By right, he should've allowed them passage, and provided them with food and shelter until his son, Breandán, arrived. But his return could be weeks from now—as he tried to explain. He never knew when Breandán would descend from the hills, nor could he predict it.

"Like I said, should you seek him out in his own hunting grounds, you're sure to find him." His white hair swept across his stern brow as the vibrant woad-dyed cloak at his shoulders waved wildly beside him. And even though his weathered face and crooked posture confessed his near-elderly years, he wasn't a man to underestimate. There was still enough strength in his back and arms to yank a few men from their horses and inflict several fatalities before someone could stop him.

None of the five seemed willing to take that chance. They didn't budge from their stance on the matter, until an arrow whizzed by them and pierced the wooden post directly in front of their horses. Liam, undeterred by the sudden assault, merely smiled.

Immediately, the five turned their spooked horses in the direction of the unknown archer, and a few more arrows sank into the ground at their horses' feet. In the commotion of it all, one horse even reared and toppled its rider.

Liam unsheathed his sword and prevented the fallen man from gaining his feet, resting the point of the blade beneath the man's chin. Breandán and Marcas came sprinting closer to the group, their bows tightly drawn for the next targets—ones that would bleed.

"Speak your names and your purpose for being here," Breandán demanded sternly.

Once the horses settled, the largest of the men chose to speak, causing Breandán to take aim at him. "My name is Angus Mac Farrell, and we're messengers of the king."

Messengers of Mac Conor or Mac Flann, Breandán wasn't taking any chances. He kept his bow taut. "What message do you bring?"

"I'm to speak only to Breandán Mac Liam. I've tried to explain that to this old man, but he refuses to comply."

Breandán nudged his horse closer, putting more pressure on the messenger with an inescapable mark upon his chest. "That old man, Angus, is my father." He waited for the revelation of his identity to sink in, then appended his statement with "So, did you come here to insult my father or deliver a message?"

Angus swallowed hard. He gave a quick glance at his men and back at the arrow marked for his heart. He drew a careful breath. "Cathal Mac Conor is on his deathbed."

"News of his failing health has already reached us," Breandán stated matter-of-factly. "Your long journey is in vain, I'm afraid."

"The king wishes to see his daughter, Mara," Angus added.

The king's message sounded utterly trivial, and Breandán couldn't help but be sarcastic in his reply. "If 'tis my permission he seeks, I shall grant it. Now be off."

"Cathal also wishes for you to bring her to him," Angus said, undiscouraged by the remark. "She is without her Northern husband, and since Duncan Mac Flann is threatening these parts, the king trusts only you to make certain her journey is safe. I now can see why."

Breandán stayed focused. "Why can't Mara's present husband do the honors? I've never met the man, but I assume her father wouldn't have given his blessings to a less than advantageous match. Surely he is better suited than I."

Angus glanced at his men with a befuddled expression and spoke in a tentative voice. "Forgive me but...of what husband do you speak?"

Breandán lowered his bow and felt a twinge of hope pull at his heartstrings. Was it true Mara had not taken another husband after Dægan? Was the port gossip about her second marriage simply a rumor? He wanted to believe it, but secured his heart behind a protective wall of skepticism.

"Two summers after Dægan's death, I was told she was to be married to another." He clenched his jaw. "Gunnar...I believe was his name."

Again, Angus exchanged glances with his men before addressing Breandán. "I assure you, the king would know if his own daughter had taken another husband."

Marcas cleared his throat. "Did you not hear what the man said?"

Breandán heard the man but ignored the upshift of his own heartbeat. "Are you certain the king wishes for me to provide her protective escort?" Marcas groaned at his insistence, but Breandán continued to press the king's messengers. "Perhaps you're mistaken in the small details of Cathal's demands."

"I've four witnesses," Angus said, gesturing toward his group, "who will account for my accuracy."

Breandán looked at each man and read each one's confirmation in his face. He then gazed long and hard at his father, presuming his answer would affect him most. "And if I refuse?"

Angus's mouth turned up in a quick smile. "Cathal thought you'd ask that." Breandán didn't find it funny in the least, and Angus soon amended his grin to a straight line, almost stuttering. "If you don't agree to his wishes, then Cathal will have to assume he hasn't the majority alliance of the Connacht men and will be forced to ally himself with Mac Flann."

"A bit drastic…" Breandán muttered, raising a single brow.

"Aye, but Cathal's choices are limited. He is near death and claims he'd rather side with the devil to keep peace than make war with the devil and lose it all. Moreover, if he allies with Mac Flann, that would mean—"

"I know what that would mean," Breandán interrupted. An unexpected flash of anger suffocated the little bit of excitement inside him. He'd rather die than see the lands of the Uí Briúin Bréifne fall into the tyrannical hands of the enemy; lands that his father, and his father before him, had bled to keep. Then he thought of seeing Mara after all these years. No matter how many times he turned it over in his head, he could barely imagine such a grand moment. And how could he be so fortunate? Had his prayers actually been answered?

He tamped down his emotions and squared his shoulders. "I'll give you my decision by sun-up. I've made a long journey myself, and I aim to fill my belly with the red stag I've brought with me. I'd imagine the lot of you could stand a good meal as well. Your horses will be given the proper food and water, and I give my word there shall not be any threats made upon you as you stay here. However," Breandán said as he replaced his arrow in the quiver on his back and threaded his arm through the bow. "None of this will be granted you until an apology is given unto my father, and then accepted." He nodded out of respect to his father and waited for Angus to do so.

Angus crowded his brows as if to ponder his degrading request for pardon. Before he could open his mouth, Liam rolled his eyes and waved it off. "Save your breath. Let's all take cover before this rain soaks us to the skin."

Breandán winked at his father and turned his horse, trotting back up the hill to retrieve his cart, Marcas following. The two men made their way up the steep incline, silently at first, until Marcas noticed Breandán's face.

"Is that…a smile I see?"

No answer.

"You look like a grinning fox who stole the egg right out from under the goose."

"Why should I not smile? An opportunity to see Mara has come my way, and I've never been so fortunate."

Chapter Four

"So, my prodigal son returns," Liam jested as he and Breandán entered his thatched home.

It was large in comparison to the other eight on the crannog, but quaintly built nonetheless. A substantial fire burned in the central hearth, and several beds lined the circular perimeter walls, each boasting an assortment of animal furs and thick woolen blankets for the cool nights ahead.

His mother, Aoife, looked up from her embroidering, happy to see her husband and surprised to see her son. Grania, his youngest sister, immediately left her mother's side and ran to her brother. "Breandán, you're home!"

He bent down and opened his arms, preparing to catch her midleap. He swung her from the ground and embraced her warmly. "Oh, my little Grania. Have you been a good girl whilst I've been gone?"

Her tiny-toothed smile was bright and honest. "I have."

A single scoff from the back of the room interrupted the cheery air. Breandán glanced up at his other sister, also embroidering, who'd barely acknowledged his presence. "Clodagh," he said with a humored smile. "I trust you've behaved as well."

Clodagh rolled her eyes and didn't miss a stitch as she sewed.

Breandán carried Grania on his hip to meet his

mother's embrace. He kissed her forehead. "'Tis good to be home, Mother."

"You stayed away so long this time, I began to worry you forgot where home was."

"Never," Breandán assured her.

Aoife glanced at her husband with dread. "Have those men left?"

"Fear not, wife. All is well," Liam replied. "They're Cathal Mac Conor's men and will be staying until the morn." He gestured toward the outskirts of the room, though privacy was hard to come by in the open space. "Let us talk, son. It seems we have much to discuss."

Breandán set Grania to the ground and did as his father bid him. He knew his father was referring to the journey he was about to embark upon in favor of their king, but he was more inclined to broach the matter of his father's safety, something he knew his mother had often worried about.

"You shouldn't have been standing against those men alone, Father," Breandán reprimanded lightly. "Felim and Declan should've been with you."

"I agree," his mother chimed in from across the room. "There was absolutely no reason to purposely outnumber yourself."

"I'm not an invalid, you two," Liam said, retrieving a simple earthenware mug of mead from the table.

Breandán noticed the slight tremble in his father's hands. "Aye, but you're long in the tooth."

"I prefer the term 'venerable.'"

Aoife scoffed and quickly turned her back, pretending she wasn't listening anymore.

Liam handed the mug to his son, but Breandán refused

it with a quick shake of his head. "You're ignoring me, Father."

Liam raised the cup to whisper behind it. "I've gotten pretty good at it since you left me to fend for myself with your mother and sisters. 'Tis the only way a grown man can survive around here."

Breandán enjoyed the jest, but returned to the seriousness of the subject in spite of it. "Your survival is relevant to the point I'm trying to make. Mac Flann is ruthless—"

"Every king is ruthless if you're on the opposing side," Liam declared, drowning that thought with a long drink.

"Even so. Perhaps 'tis time for me to come back home—for good."

"But not before you make your way to the king's daughter, aye?" Liam took a seat on one of the beds, and when Breandán fell silent, he motioned with a twitch of his head for Breandán to sit as well. "I know why you hide yourself away. And I know you're very anxious to see Mara again. But I warn you, just because she's not taken a husband does not mean she's waiting for one to come along. Seven years is a long time for a woman—a highly valuable young woman such as herself—to be without the company of a man. You may not like what you find when you get there."

Breandán hung his head, knowing there was so much to consider that he hadn't had a chance to think of. "I know. And you're right. Seven years is a very long time."

"All right, enough of her," Liam interjected. "Let's talk of her father. It seems Cathal has not forgotten how to twist the arm of his supporters. He's always made it difficult for the Connacht man. Clever coercion is the way of our king, and his deathbed hasn't changed that. He is just as cunning and ruthless as Mac Flann, but Cathal's alliance, as it stands, is crucial, and we cannot afford to lose it."

"So, I've no choice but to go."

"A man always has a choice, Breandán, no matter what he's faced with or how far back he's cornered. But if I had to decide between Duncan Mac Flann and Cathal Mac Conor, I'd rather choose the lesser of the two evils."

His father spoke sensibly, and he was a great man with a natural air for leading. People, even from the widely dispersed clans, respected him as a man to whom they should listen. Venerable, Breandán concurred, was an ideal word to describe his father.

"Don't let Cathal scare you," Liam said before downing his drink. "He learned at an early age that fear is a great motivator, and that's what he wants. You do what you think is best. And no matter what you decide, I'll always stand by you."

Breandán inwardly breathed a sigh of relief. Though he longed to make the journey toward Mara—one his heart had already decided upon—his father's approval ultimately determined the course of his actions.

****

Another arrow sank deep into the heart of the hay-stuffed burlap sack that resembled a human torso, where four other tightly settled arrows had already found their marks. Pleased with the consistent accuracy of his newly strung bow, Breandán lowered his weapon and leaned it against the closest tree, then crossed his arms over his chest.

It was later that evening, after he'd excused himself from the dinner meal to find solace in the woods where he could be alone with his thoughts. His few quiet hours of solitude, however, were disappointingly short-lived as he felt the prying presence of another. Without setting eyes on the person, he had a feeling it was Sorcha, and he wished the rain had confined the flirtatious girl to her home.

"If you're trying to hide, you're doing a horrible job of it," Breandán announced.

Sorcha stepped out from behind a distant oak, wearing a very surprised look on her face. "How did you know I was there?"

He bypassed her question. "Does your father know you're here?"

"Nay," she crooned as she batted her sultry eyes.

For most men, that look would have spurred numerous indecent and suggestive thoughts, but to Breandán, it did absolutely nothing. "You shouldn't be in the forest alone."

Sorcha sauntered over, leaving little room between them. Her large breasts nearly spilled over her tunic as she lifted her hand to touch his cheek. "I'm not alone."

Breandán caught her wrist and held it away from his face. "Why are you here?"

Sorcha glanced at his hand. She seemed to take immense pleasure in the warmth against her skin and that he was actually touching her. It wasn't often he'd allow himself to get near her, much less boldly grasp her.

"I heard talk amongst my brothers you were home. I had to see for myself."

He released her and leaned back against the tree. "I'll not be staying long. I leave again in the morn."

"So soon?" she asked, closing the distance once again

between them. "Can you not put your hunting off for a few more days?"

"My leaving is not due to another hunt. And I haven't much say on when we depart."

"We?" Sorcha's brows lifted. "Who is 'we'?"

"Cathal Mac Conor's men and myself."

Sorcha leaned against him and started to draw imaginary circles around his chest with her finger. "The king? Hm…sounds important indeed."

Breandán ignored her and spoke directly. "He wishes to see his daughter one last time before he dies."

Sorcha's finger froze where it was, and her eyes altered from lazily lustful to envious and severe. "The princess? The one you cannot—"

"Have" was the word he knew she meant to say, but skillfully, she changed it to "forget." He nodded.

"You know…" she said, "I can give you what you need, Breandán." She dragged her hand slowly across his chest. "I can give you what you desire."

The eyes that undressed him spoke volumes, and he doubted she truly knew what he wanted. He plucked her hand from his chest again and held it away. "Your father will be worried if you're not home by nightfall."

"I can make you forget all about her," Sorcha whispered, trying another approach. "Stop dreaming of what can never be, and take what you want from what is real—flesh and blood. Mara, by her own vows to another man, denies you what you long for. I'll never deny you, Breandán."

His first instinct was to argue the point of the princess's marriage, or lack thereof. But he went easy on her, knowing his next words would probably crush her anyway. "You're a beautiful woman, Sorcha, and any man would consider it an honor to lie with you. But you deserve better. You deserve a husband who'd love you with all his heart. I cannot love you the way you should be. I'd only hurt you." Sorcha opened her mouth to speak, but he drew his face closer to hers. "I *would* hurt you. I wouldn't mean to, but I would. My heart already belongs to her." He didn't want to use Mara's name, as that would have been more cruel. He merely continued his tender reasoning with "I was asked to retrieve the princess and protect her whilst she makes her journey through these lands, and I'll do whatever is asked of me when it comes to her."

Sorcha's shoulders relaxed. "If you've only been *asked*, then you can surely *refuse*."

He admired her persistence, despite his enormous desire to end the conversation. "'Tis not as simple as you think, Sorcha. Now, come on. I'll walk you home."

Before he could even pick up his longbow, she'd turned around and started to make her way through the forest. He could see the disappointment in the way she walked and the sadness from the position of her head.

Damn fool. You hurt her already.

Breandán caught up with her. "If it makes you feel any better, you and I are one and the same. We both have longed for things we cannot have."

Sorcha recoiled in distaste. "And that is supposed to comfort me?"

Breandán frowned, knowing his words sounded idiotic. He stepped in front of her, trying again to gain her attention. He put his hands on her shoulders and stopped her from going farther. "I'm trying. You know I've never been good with words. Look at me," he demanded, gently lifting her chin. "I do love you, Sorcha. You and I have always been friends, much before anyone ever took notice. And I'm honored you would still, to this day, hold me in such high regard. But that is as far as I can love you. Do you understand?"

A tear slipped from her eye, which nearly brought Breandán to his knees. His heart sank with pity, and he wished there was more he could do than wipe it away. Lord knew words failed him again.

He pulled her into his arms and held her against his chest as she sobbed. It was the first time he'd ever physically embraced her, and he hoped she could feel his sincerity, since his ability to verbalize it proved ineffective.

Chapter Five

Dark Atlantic water lapped against the sides of Gustaf's longship as they sailed southeast from Iceland to the Faroe Islands. The wind was brutal and swift, sufficient to carry the ship to its destination by morn.

All eight men huddled within the shallow hull with their wolfskin cloaks wrapped tightly around them, eagerly anticipating a brief stopover at the isles for at least one good meal and a long night's sleep next to a roaring fire before continuing their search for the last man involved in Gustaf's father's slaying.

Twenty-three years ago, when this manhunt had begun, they were as driven as Gustaf was. But no one could've predicted the amount of time and determination this single task would require, as each assassin seemed to be further and further from reach. In the beginning, the first few were easy to find. But as word spread about their peculiar deaths, so did the remaining murderers—some taking refuge in places not even fit for man or beast.

Regardless of the dangers and difficulties of tracking down each assassin, Gustaf's men remained loyal and vowed to be until the last man was found. Most times, they did so without complaint, but starvation and sleep deprivation made for a thin veil where secret grievances were concerned.

"You should've pushed Ragnar harder for the last man's name," Jørgen criticized. "Instead, we're left to search the ends of the world again. It took us four winters to find Ragnar. Who knows how long we'll be searching for this next bastard."

Gustaf kept his composure. "The man hung from the rafters by his own bowels and never uttered a word. What else could I've done to persuade him?"

"You could've tortured him more."

Gustaf snorted at the remark. "What could possibly be worse than the fate he already faced? Better yet, let's hang you by your entrails, and you can tell me what would be more torturous."

Jørgen held his tongue as if he feared his chieftain might actually do it.

Everyone was famished, exhausted, and homesick. They'd forgone a great deal for Gustaf, and since he understood the reason for their short temper, he offered a suggestion. "We've been at this for quite some time, and I cannot be more pleased with the sacrifices you all have made on my behalf. You've made my vengeance your vengeance. You've bled with me, starved with me, nearly froze to death with me a time or two," he said, then pointed to nine notches of his sword. "And most importantly, you've celebrated each success with me. The last man is yet to be found, but we're so close. So close I can taste it. That said, I'm willing to rest my head and my weary bones over the coming winter. As a token of my gratitude, I shall bestow your freedom upon you, my loyal comrades. To do whatever 'tis you want. Sleep for days; drink for weeks. Go home to your women—if you have any left." Gustaf glanced at Øyven, the youngest of the group at age twenty. "Or find yourself some accommodating livestock. I've heard the ewes this time of year are relatively docile."

A roar of laughter erupted, and the men continued to make jibes at Øyven for his extensive abstinence, through no fault of his own. It had been an ongoing jest, smoldering for several years, but now that Gustaf had relit the fire, they spared Øyven no sympathy in their ridicule.

Øyven had joined the group at the tender age of seventeen after his entire family was murdered. Rage and retribution filled his heart so that he had no room for sympathy and affection, missing out on the merriment young men often experience during that postpubescent time.

Gustaf waved his hand to settle the joyous chatter. "All right, men. Once we land on the Faroes, you can all go your separate ways and we'll reconvene at the first sign of spring. Here," he added, kicking his wooden chest forward at their feet. "There should be enough in there to gain you a boat to Gokstad and back."

"But what will you do?" Jørgen asked.

For such a long time, the men had gone everywhere with Gustaf. It didn't seem right that he'd not accompany them now. He glanced at the woman sitting at the prow of the ship. Her face was red from the cold and her eyes drowsy from lack of sleep. Her hair tumbled over her shoulders in a tangle of auburn and gold, and the cloak she wore was three times too big. Despite her weary and untidy appearance, he believed she still looked as beautiful as the goddess Freyja.

Admittedly, Gustaf was hard put to imagine anything else but spending time with the redhead as soon as they ran aground. Like Øyven, he'd gone far too long without a woman's delicate touch and her soft curves in the palms of his hands. But he didn't think that was what Jørgen meant by his question.

"I plan to stay on the Faroes. The isles swarms with rogues and gossipers. Someone is bound to know something about our last little coward."

After he stated his intention, he took little part in the following conversation where others prattled on about future plans and frivolous amusements. They couldn't wait to see their wives and families, they looked forward to spending long summer afternoons at work with their sons in the fields, and their mouths watered for the taste of fresh breads, hot boiled meats, harvested greens, and creamed tarts. Each proclamation got louder and louder as they thought of better things to indulge upon.

Gustaf was glad to have appeased his loyal men, for as vengeance goes, there wasn't much to be had except satisfaction, and even that wears away rather quickly. For the first time on his ship, excitement and joy filled the hull. Everyone wore a smile, including his female guest.

He caught sight of her staring at him with a look that stole his breath away. When he smiled back, she stood up and made her way across the deck, meandering through the unmindful, noisy men.

Gustaf let go of the steer board to take her hand, and he steadied her until she could sit beside him. "Why were you smiling?" he asked. "'Tis not as if there's anything upon this wretched langskip a woman would find worth smiling about."

She contemplated his remark, then reached up to smooth his beard. "I would beg to differ."

"Is that so?"

She answered him with a slight nod of her head, never taking her eyes from his.

Gustaf could feel the weight of her beautiful stare as if she bore a hole into his soul. Her eyes, up close, were even more entrancing than he remembered. They were thinly rimmed in the darkest shade of cobalt, and by the time the lustrous flecks of her irises reached her pupils, they'd blanched an icy blue. He had to will himself to look away.

He took hold of her hands and cupped them between both of his, blowing warm air inside. "May I have the pleasure of knowing your name?"

She watched him tend to her cold fingertips as if the act itself was unheard of. It was obvious to Gustaf that she'd never known kindness or consideration.

"My name is Æsa."

"And I'm Gustaf, son of Rælik," he declared. "By morning, we'll have reached the Faroe Islands, at which point you can stay with me, or if you'd rather, you can accompany Øyven. He'd no doubt enjoy your companionship as well."

Æsa flicked her gaze between Øyven and Gustaf. "He is but a lad."

"Aye, he is. But a brave lad, nonetheless."

She crowded her brows at him. "Are you giving me a choice?"

"Aye, m'lady. I am. Though I must admit, I'm hoping your choice leans closer in my favor."

Æsa looked deep within Gustaf's eyes, holding his gaze for a time. "No offense to Øyven, but I prefer to be with a man."

He inhaled deeply, trying to settle the excitement she stirred in him. "I suppose he can't take offense to anything he didn't hear, now can he?"

She bit her lip. "You won't tell him, will you?"

"Of course not. What good would it do to shame his

virility at such a young age? He's got plenty of time to do that on his own."

She giggled and turned a lovely shade of pink. Gustaf brushed back her hair from her face and regarded her natural beauty. It was easy to see why she'd fallen victim to such a degrading profession among disreputable men, and it pained him to imagine how many had violated her.

Her past life was nothing she could help, and nothing he could ignore. He fixed his gaze on her eyes and leaned in for emphasis. "Should you stay with me, know that I will not tolerate you rewarding favors to others. I will not share you with anyone. Do you understand?"

It seemed Æsa wasn't the least bit affronted by his strict demand and was perfectly content to give up her promiscuity. She placed her hand on his knee, then asked, "How soon before we land?"

Not soon enough, Gustaf thought.

****

Mara stood alone in her longhouse and stirred a pot of boiled meat for the coming evening meal. It was a large home for her and her son, but Tait had insisted upon it when he rebuilt their settlement on Inishmore. What's more, he custom-constructed her longhouse to replicate the way Dægan had once built it—complete with carved wood entrances, a huge storage area off the main room, and a private closet-enclosed bedchamber that held a beautifully carved boxbed and silk tapestries.

Mara didn't need all those amenities, but she didn't object to Tait's fanatical devotion. She understood it as his way of keeping Dægan's memory alive.

He and Dægan had been inseparable. They had a strong connection to each other, which was born the day they swore a blood oath as adolescents. In slicing their palms and clasping a symbolic ring, their blood ran together, establishing them, from that moment on, as brothers for life. Not even Domaldr, Dægan's departed twin, could equal that bond.

Even after Dægan's death, Tait never let anyone forget about the late chieftain. He'd tell grand stories, which may have been a bit exaggerated, of Dægan's bravery and skillful combats with challenging opponents. It was nice to hear them, even if they were a little biased.

Mara recalled the many times Tait would begin his tales and the utter silence around the elongated mead hall as he'd narrate the story in such an absorbing poetic fashion. He even mesmerized the small children of the group with his elaborate discourse.

Like the people of the village, she was always fascinated by the stories of her late husband, so she memorized every little detail and passed them on to their son, Lochlann. The more she knew about Dægan, the more it helped her to heal during her most difficult time.

Losing Dægan was the hardest thing she'd ever had to endure. Having his child grow inside her enabled her to stop dwelling on the past. Instead of reliving that horrible moment when he died in her arms, she'd looked forward to the moment his child would come forth from her womb.

She named the boy Lochlann, after the first word she'd uttered to Dægan upon meeting him. At six, he was a spitting image of his father with golden hair, a fiery temper, and stunning blue eyes that lit up like sparks in the night.

A slamming door brought Mara's meandering thoughts to a sudden halt. She turned to find her son stamping past her at the hearth. He made his way toward the table behind her, slumped in his chair, and crossed his arms—a normal day's ritual.

"Good afternoon, Lochlann," Mara said with a sideways glance and a motherly smile.

"Is it?" he spouted off. "I wouldn't know."

Mara went back to stirring her pot and ignored her son's irritation. "Did you finish your chores?"

"Aye," he sighed. "As I have every day, Mother."

Mara knew that *As I have every day, Mother* didn't translate to *You needn't doubt I finished my chores.* What it really meant was *I'm perfectly capable of finishing them, despite my smaller size compared to the other boys my age.*

"You know you shouldn't worry so much about what your friend Alfarinn says about you."

"He's not my friend."

By her son's proclamation, she got the impression the frequent minor teasing might have gotten out of hand—as it easily could between two rambunctious boys. "What happened?"

"The same as every day. Alfarinn kicked my arse in swords again."

"Let's clean the mouth that kisses me, son," Mara corrected lightly. "And were you not supposed to be gathering seaweed?"

Lochlann rolled his eyes. "We were—I mean, we did."

"Did you now? How many baskets?"

"Five."

"Don't lie to me, boy. I don't want to have Tait breathing down my neck like last week when you failed to gather all the cattle. We lost a good calf in that storm because of you."

"I know."

Mara stopped abruptly. Her son had taken enough punishment for his mistake, and he didn't need anymore. "Five baskets?"

Lochlann nodded.

"Look at me, son. Look me in the eye, and tell me how many baskets you alone gathered."

Lochlann looked up at her, his face as innocent and sweet as the day he was born, his eyes, big and pleading. "I carried five full baskets of seaweed to the field."

Mara's smile grew with motherly pride, and she tousled his hair. "Good. I believe you. Now eat your meal. You don't want to be late."

"I'm not going."

"What? You've been waiting for months to go to Veigsfjordr. 'Tis your first time on the langskip—"

"I've been on it many times."

"But not when 'tis sailing across the ocean," Mara argued.

"Is Alfarinn going?"

"Of course, he is. You honestly think Tait would take you and leave his own son behind?"

Stiffening his bottom lip, Lochlann said, "Then I'm not going."

Mara crossed her arms. "What about Brondolf? He would be very disappointed if you didn't go along. He needs you. You know this."

She couldn't help but pity Lillemor's son. Brondolf had talked all the time when he was younger, but soon after the death of his grandmother, Svanhild, he never spoke again.

Many attributed it to the trauma of the ordeal, as he was one of the first to come upon her in her bed that morning. But two years had passed, and Mara thought he should've come out of it by now. She'd never known a boy of this age with so little to say.

"You're the only one who knows what Brondolf means to express. He needs you to be his mouth for him."

Lochlann rolled his eyes. "He has to learn to use his own mouth someday."

"And with you encouraging him, one day I believe he will."

"I'm still not going."

Mara tapped the wooden ladle against the iron pot and set it upon the hearth. She thought about what could make her son happier. What would cheer him up enough that he'd forget all about the swordplay and Alfarinn's big win.

She wiped her hands on her apron and made her way to a chest at the foot of the boxbed. She paused, feeling a grim sense of longing, and knelt to keep from trembling.

She took one look at her son, staring at his cold food and lost somewhere between two hard biscuits, last night's cheese, and his defeat. She opened the heavy lid and smiled. On top, neatly folded, was a bear cloak of deep brown fur. A cloak that had once belonged to Dægan.

It had kept him warm and dry on many occasions, and she remembered how noble and strong he looked with it draped across his shoulders with the wind blowing in his hair.

Mara laid her hand upon it and lightly petted the fur with one long stroke. It was soft against her palm, flattening beneath her caress. With reverent hands, she unfurled the cloak, and its length nearly touched the floor at her knees.

Lochlann took notice and watched her lift it to her nose. She drew in a deep breath and, with an exhale, folded against it as if Dægan were still wearing it. When she opened her eyes, she met Lochlann's curious gaze. "Would you like to hear a story?"

For the first time in a long time, Lochlann grinned with anticipation as if he knew a tale about his father would unfold—as only a six-year-old boy could earnestly hope.

Mara thought of Dægan and how he'd jump headfirst into a grand narration, much as Tait had done in the past years. A talented skald, he was, and Mara fancied to be half as good as he. She took a deep breath and led her son into a day when Dægan was just a gangly teenage lad.

"Your father set out one early brisk morning to venture through the sharp inclines of Hladir's mountainous terrain—the hunting grounds. Food was scarce that year since Rælik, your grandfather, and many able-bodied men of the village hadn't returned from their long merchant journey with the necessary wares and supplies for the fast-approaching winter. Gustaf, your father's eldest brother and the finest hunter of Hladir, was also on that ship. So, it was up to your father to bring back the much-needed venison."

Lochlann, still immersed in the story, picked up a biscuit and bit into it without taking his eyes from his mother. "Go on," he encouraged as he chewed.

Mara stood to give more emphasis on the next part.

"Your father was in the middle of tracking a sizeable stag after spotting a series of impressive tree rubs, but he soon found a bigger prize—a brown bear." Mara swung the heavy cloak around her shoulders, imitating the massive creature.

"Knowing the bear would feed more of his people for a longer time, he decided to forget all about the buck and instead made plans to bring down the beast."

Mara watched her son take another bite as he sat

entranced, and continued.

"Your father never forgot what it took to be a successful hunter—or warrior," she pointed out specifically. "Rælik had told him, at about your very age, that a man who slights caution presumes his death. And in keeping his advice, your father carefully plotted the way in which he'd kill the bear, leaving nothing to chance. He even had a way to escape should his plan fail."

Lochlann inched to the edge of his seat and shoved the rest of the biscuit in his mouth. Mara ignored his lack of manners and walked toward him, acting out the careful footsteps Dægan had taken to close in on the animal.

"Your father crept downwind from the bear...and when he was close enough, he threw a rock at its snout."

Lochlann's eyes widened in surprise.

"The bear immediately stood on its hind legs, growling first at the pain and then at your father, who'd jumped out of the brush, waving his arms. The bear, rightfully angry, charged your father, and he ran as fast as he possibly could." Mara reenacted the scene, running around the table and past the hearth. "He never looked back, as he could already feel the bear gaining on him. The weight of its paws thundered upon the ground behind him. Just when the bear could've reached out and clawed him, your father darted across a log suspended between two cliffs and jumped to a short ledge below where he'd left his spear.

"Of course the bear followed and, just as it lunged forward, your father thrust the spear up through its heart and killed it instantly."

Mara let the ending sink in before removing the cloak from her own shoulders. "This, Lochlann, is the hide from that very animal, taken by one small lad who possessed the willpower of ten men. Your father was no bigger than myself when he brought down this bear, but the size of his determination was what made him successful."

She wrapped the esteemed fur around her son's shoulders proudly and watched as his face brightened. "It looks good on you," she praised.

Lochlann straightened his back and pulled the cloak closer under his chin. It was far too long for his small stature, and she probably should've waited until he was big enough to wear it. But she made an exception and hoped this gift would help Lochlann gain self-confidence.

"Look at you." She winked. "You look exactly like your father."

"I do?" he asked in disbelief.

She tapped the tip of his nose. "There's no denying it."

His face beamed with joy. No better compliment could've been given him, as he'd longed for so many years to be like his father.

Mara turned away as tears of both joy and sadness welled in her eyes. It had been years since she'd seen that bear cloak on Dægan, and once she'd placed it on her son's shoulders, she remembered how much she liked the sight of her husband in it. He was an impressive man no matter what he wore, but that particular cloak represented the kind of man Dægan was.

"Mother," Lochlann called, oblivious to his mother's emotions. "Aren't you going to tell me the rest of the story? How Father dragged the bear from the hunting grounds down to his village?"

Mara swallowed her sorrow and hid it with a grin, determined to keep the grief away from her son. "Well," she said, facing him slowly. "I hesitate to tell you the rest. Your father failed to use his head amidst all his excitement."

"Please…"

Mara picked up the ladle and stirred as she spoke. "Your father packed the animal in snow and ice until he could get some of the elders to help him bring the carcass down the mountain. He nearly lost his hands to frostbite for doing so."

Mara looked at her son and dithered over whether to say much more to such an impressionable boy. "Always remember, Lochlann, even the smartest of men—or young boys—can lose their wits. Everyone has a weakness. Even Alfarinn."

Lochlann approached and hugged her around the waist. "I'll treasure this cloak always."

Mara knew he would. He had a keen sense of worth and a high regard for sentiment at such an early age, much like his father.

"Does this mean you're ready to face Alfarinn?" Mara asked.

"Aye, but I'm still not going with Tait to Veigsfjordr."

"Why not?"

"I've more important things to do now."

"Such as?" Mara probed.

"Such as going to the keep," Lochlann stated. "After Alfarinn left me sitting in the field, Nevan offered to give me sword lessons."

"He did, did he?"

"Aye. And I want to show him my new cloak."

Mara clasped his cute little face and leaned forward. "Very well, but—after you finish your meal and the rest of your chores."

Lochlann sighed.

"Not a moment before, understand?"

As he nodded, she rubbed his nose with hers. He was the one joy in her life, the little gift that half-filled the hole Dægan had left in her heart. The other half was void of something only a husband could provide, and she certainly didn't intend to marry again just to fill it.

Chapter Six

"May I speak to you before you leave?" Mara asked as Tait loaded the last chest aboard the *knarr*. "'Tis about Alfarinn."

Tait spoke a few commanding words to those upon the large cargo ship and then descended from the gangplank. She watched the way he strolled across the pebbled shore, his thoughts in full speed while his eyes were distant and slow to look at her.

"You mean, 'tis about Lochlann," he amended.

Mara grimaced slightly, twisting her hands within the folds of her tunic.

Tait approached her, his arms defensively crossed. "What has my son done this time?"

"You know Lochlann is a troubled boy," Mara began.

"I know. And I've tried to remedy that, but you refuse to accept my offer. Gunnar would make a fine father for him—"

"Tait, we've been through this," Mara interrupted. "I'm not marrying out of convenience. And besides, Gunnar is not the sort of man I want raising my son."

"Why not?"

Mara clenched her jaw. She didn't want to insult Gunnar as he'd been nothing but loyal and kind since he first joined Dægan's army years ago to defeat Domaldr. And even after Dægan's death, when Gunnar had left his hired-soldier lifestyle behind and stayed on the island with

Tait, he'd been the perfect substitute for all things missing.

The loss of his best friend and chieftain had crushed Tait, and Gunnar was the right sort of man to rebuild not only the many longhouses destroyed by the fire, but Tait's will to carry on and prosper. Even Gunnar's humor helped to make the gruff Northman smile through the difficult and trying times of restoring all that had been lost. Gunnar was a godsend for Tait, but to Mara, he was still a stranger in the midst.

"Why is he not good enough for you?" Tait repeated. "Have you forgotten the sacrifices he's made in leaving Havelok and his own men to join us? Or that 'twas he who helped rebuild this entire settlement when all was in ashes? He's even gone above the call and taken Brondolf under his wing, and God knows the boy needs it. Has Gunnar not proved himself time and time again?"

Mara didn't care for Tait's tone. "I've not forgotten Gunnar's loyalty and selflessness. But just because a man is loyal, does not make him—"

"I know, Mara. He's not Dægan. No one is, or ever will be."

Mara heard the pain in Tait's voice. "I had no intention of saying that."

Tait scrubbed his hands down his face. "It matters not anyway. I know where you stand when it comes to Gunnar, and I cannot force you to see him as I do. All I can say is you're doing your son no good by being overly particular. Lochlann needs a father."

"What he needs is a little time from you. He looks up to you, Tait. You're the closest thing he has to his father, and if you'd give him a small portion of yourself, a smidgen of the man who knew and loved Dægan, 'twould mean so much to him. 'Twould mean so much to me. Please. You knew Dægan better than anyone—better than myself."

Tait's eyes bore into her, and she saw guilt rise within him. He dropped his head and sighed. "What exactly do you want from me?"

Mara bit her lip before saying, "I want you to teach him how to beat Alfarinn in swords."

Tait's brows went skyward and a quirky smile lifted one corner of his mouth. "You realize the boys are only six years old?"

"Lochlann is six. Alfarinn is five, a full head taller, and more skilled with weaponry. Do you not know what that does to a lad's confidence when someone younger gets the better of him?"

Tait staring at her as if struck by her unusual request. "They are boys. They'll have the rest of their childhood to build their confidence, and 'tis nothing you can force. Lochlann is smarter than that. If Alfarinn lets him win, Lochlann will know it."

"I don't want Alfarinn to lose on purpose, but for you to teach Lochlann to beat him squarely. You know Alfarinn's strengths and weakness, and you can teach Lochlann how to use them to his advantage."

"So, at the expense of destroying my own son's confidence, you want me to help build Lochlann's?"

"I want him to feel proud of himself, to feel as if he is worthy of being Dægan's son. My words are not enough for him, Tait. He needs to feel it."

Tait looked past Mara and saw his pregnant wife, Thordia, coming toward him with his excited son. "You ask much of me, but I'll do it. As soon as I return, I'll make certain Lochlann has his day. Satisfied?"

Mara smiled and nodded.

"Everything loaded and ready for your departure?" Thordia asked upon reaching them.

Tait immediately grinned and tossed his son over his shoulder. A fit of boyish giggles escaped Alfarinn as his father locked an arm around his neck and tousled his hair. "I believe everything is loaded save for this sack of—"

"Tait," Thordia scolded before her husband could spout off a jocular slur ill-fit for young ears. "Need I go along so that my son doesn't come back with as coarse a tongue as his father?"

Tait winked at Mara and let the boy slide off his arm to the ground. "Go on, son," he said, swatting Alfarinn on the rear. "Get to the ship before your mother puts an end to our fun. Hurry!"

Tait watched him run for a moment, then turned back to his wife. Ignoring her scowl, he pulled her into his arms and buried his face in her neck, whispering things not meant for Mara's ears. Whatever it was, Thordia blushed and hid her face in the crevice of his shoulder.

"Tait, you're incorrigible."

"'Tis about time you appreciate it too," Tait said, biting her neck playfully.

Thordia squirmed but couldn't escape his strong arms. He was mindful of her overly round belly and cradled her body where it would not harm her or the baby within.

Mara thought it was endearing the way Tait acted around his wife. Only a handful of people got the pleasure of seeing that side of him, and most wouldn't believe it anyway. Tait was typically a serious man with too much responsibility for one man's shoulders. But when he was with Thordia, a whole new man emerged. She preferred his playful side, despite the fact that it often reminded her of Dægan.

Tait leaned down to kiss his wife, and Mara gave them their privacy, looking away.

"Take care of my wife, Mara. And, don't let her have this babe before I get back."

"I shall do my best," Mara promised.

Tait released Thordia as Lillemor, Brondolf, and the rest of his men came down the shoreline. His face fell. "I assume Lochlann is not coming."

Mara shook her head. "He's getting sword lessons from Nevan."

"His choice," Tait murmured. "We'll talk about it more when I return."

"How soon can I expect you?" Thordia called to him.

Tait turned around, and, as he walked backward, he winked and said, "Fear not, wife. I'll be back before you've had a chance to miss me."

Mara glanced at Thordia and knew, by her own experience, the woman greatly missed him already.

****

"Must you leave so soon, brother?" Grania asked, her tiny voice breaking the peaceful silence of the valley. "You just returned, and I miss you greatly when you're gone."

Breandán looked out across the Lough Allen. The sun gleamed in the water with the reflection of the nearby trees shimmering amid the light. Mornings like this were not too common and, regardless of his sister's whining, it was a good day for a long journey.

He hugged his baby sister tightly as she sat upon his horse with him, her little legs dangling over the left side of the saddle. "I miss you as well, but I must do as our king demands."

Grania held the reins as Breandán had taught her and led the horse around the lake, more times that he'd counted on. He knew it was the only tactic she had at stalling and allowed the detour, enjoying the fact she thought she was clever.

"I heard you and Father talking," Grania admitted, "about protecting the princess."

"Aye."

"Is she a real princess?" Grania asked as her voice tapered off to an excited height.

"Indeed."

"I imagine she is beautiful."

Breandán smiled to himself. "She is."

Grania's tone suddenly changed, and her little head dropped. "I wish I were a princess."

Breandán grabbed the reins from his little sister and pulled the horse to a stop. He picked her up and turned her in his lap so she faced him. "The way I see it, princesses are simply born of great men, and our father is the greatest man I know."

Grania grinned brightly. "Do you love her?"

Breandán recoiled, unsure how to answer her question. He barely spoke of his feelings to anyone, much less a child.

"'Tis all right, brother. You needn't answer. I already know the truth. Your eyes tell me. And…you speak of her in your sleep."

"I do?" Breandán tried to wrap his head around his stunning lack of prudence.

Grania giggled. "Aye, you do. Last night as you slept, you called her *a thaisce*."

Breandán settled deeper into the saddle, troubled by

her words. It was true he referred to Mara as *his treasure*, but he thought it only in his mind. Never had he ever used that endearment openly, and to know his feelings had escaped beyond his control was rather disconcerting.

"Don't worry yourself, Breandán. I won't tell a soul. I promise."

Breandán chuckled aloud. "You're too smart for your own good, Grania."

"Sister says I poke my nose where it doesn't belong."

"Does she now?" Breandán looked her over keenly. "Let me see for myself. Bring your nose up here."

Grania naively lifted her nose high in the air for Breandán to examine. With one careful finger, he moved her nose to one side and then the other, nodding and humming upon each new feigned discovery. "Your sister may actually have spoken wisely for once," he said finally. "It seems your nose has been in places it shouldn't have. Perhaps...behind the storage house with the twins...chasing geese?"

Grania's anticipatory face melted, and she averted her eyes to hide a growing wry grin.

"Thought I had not noticed, aye?" He tipped her chin to gain her full attention. "Do you not know what Father would do to your behind should he catch you toughening up his fowl?"

"You'll not tell, will you?"

He had no intention of tattling, but let her sweat a few seconds. "It seems we both possess a secret of the other. Shall we call it even, then?"

Grania swung her arms around his neck and hugged him. While Breandán reveled in the love his little sister offered him, he imagined the unconditional love of his own child—one fine day—to be twice as grand, near indescribable. He was certainly at the rightful age to be a father, and looked forward to a day when his son or daughter would come into the world and embrace him in this very manner.

Although his mother's pregnancy and the resulting healthy birth of Grania had been a complete shock to his aging parents, it had brought an unforeseeable joy to Breandán, another reason why he and Grania had gotten along so well.

"Please don't leave me, brother," he heard her whisper in his ear.

Drawing back, he saw her tear-filled eyes. "I promise I'll come back very soon," he said as he wiped the trail of wetness from her cheeks.

She sniffed and forced a smile. "Will you bring the princess with you? I'd love to meet her. I shall even make her a gift. Mother is teaching me embroidery."

Breandán face lit up in a genuine smile as the word "embroidery" came out with a slight impediment. "I cannot promise that, but I'll certainly extend the invitation to her."

"Thank you, Breandán."

"Now, you best take me back before Father sends out a search party for us."

"May we go fast?"

Breandán lifted her easily from his lap and turned her back around in the saddle. He slipped one strong arm under her arms and held her close, taking the reins with the other. "Hold tight," he warned and, in a split second, they sprinted across the meadow.

Chapter Seven

Æsa stared at Gustaf from across the fire pit of the simple longhouse he'd acquired for their stay in the Faroes. It was small and relatively unfurnished, save for the necessities of boxbeds for sleeping and a hearth for cooking and warmth. She wasn't sure how he'd acquired it so quickly, nor did she much care. Her concern involved the long-term issue of what was to become of her now that she'd been rescued from Ragnar, and the role she'd fill under Gustaf's custody.

He'd been considerate and kind from the moment he first called her *my lady*, but aside from that, he didn't pursue her as she would have thought, especially now since they were off that wretched longship and alone.

He was different from the others. He never ordered her around or pawed at her like most men she'd known. Even after they bathed and ate well beyond contentment, he never made a motion to satisfy his other primal needs. She knew he had them. All men did. But instead, he sat a distance from her, sharpening his dagger upon a small block of stone.

She watched him with intent as each stroke of his knife scraped against the gray whetstone in a rhythmic fashion. His hands were large, strong, and masculine—something she admired on a man as they often indicated a similar inner strength.

His hair, newly washed and damp, was a beautiful

combination of blond and reddish-brown hanging slightly above his broad shoulders. *Perfect for running my fingers through.*

His face was equally pleasant to look upon, with eyes of the clearest blue she'd ever seen. His brows and closely trimmed beard were darker than his fair-colored mane, and they accentuated the well-defined structures of his nose, cheekbones, and jaw. His mouth was perfect and enticing, with lips at the right fullness and curvature.

Beneath his tunic, though she'd only her rampant imagination to assist her, was probably a well-muscled torso with a thin layer of blond chest hair and a flattened stomach. Most men she'd entertained were often wealthy men who hadn't a care in the world, and their sagging, plump physiques corroborated their overindulgent ways of life.

Gustaf was far from lazy, and she expected his body to represent his active lifestyle. In truth, she desperately longed to discover just how energetic he was when with a woman. Right now, he didn't seem interested at all. He only appeared content to hone his dagger.

"How old were you when your father was killed?" Æsa asked, hoping to bait his interest with casual conversation.

Gustaf looked up from his sharpening implements, but he never missed a beat as his knife continued to skate across the gritty stone. He gave the question thought before answering. "I was in my nineteenth year."

Suspecting he was over twice that age now, she widened her eyes in disbelief. "You've been avenging your father all this time?"

His hands halted, but the even tone of his voice remained. "I've a duty to him until the last man falls."

"And what of your family?" Æsa asked curiously. "Where are they?"

Gustaf looked down at his hands, and a look of guilt washed over him. "I know not where they are."

Her heart swelled with sympathy as she heard the sorrow in his words. "Have you searched for them?"

"When my father was killed, I left in haste. My rage kept me from seeing anything beyond revenge. After several summers, I returned to Hladir, only to find everyone gone—not a trace of them anywhere. I can only assume...and hope...my brother, Dægan, led them away to a safer land."

Æsa sensed the tiny strand of hope Gustaf held on to and dared not sever it. In her own cruel past, she'd learned all too often what a man was capable of doing when all his hopes were shattered. Fortunately, she had only a few minor scars to prove it.

After a few moments of silence, Gustaf returned to sharpening and spoke as if he anticipated further questions about his family. "I know my brother well, and Dægan wouldn't allow anything to happen to Father's people, nor would he give one ounce of homage to the man who commanded our father's murder. I'm certain he left as soon as it was feasible. But where? I could not begin to guess."

"Have you not tried to find them beyond Hladir?"

Gustaf's hands slowed, and eventually he put his dagger and stone aside before answering. "I suspect by now they all think me to be dead. Everyone else has, including the families of the men I've killed. 'Tis better that way. And safer for my family. With one man left to find, there will always be a threat to them should anyone know I'm alive. I cannot bear to put them in harm's way." He paused as if to convince himself of his own words. "One day, we shall be reunited."

Æsa sat in silence, not thinking her original question would have led them down this path. The sharp turn from casual to serious left her with a sense of uneasiness as she sat across from him, bewildered. It seemed he'd been through much in his life, and she didn't know how to comfort him. She began to second-guess her grand idea of enticing him with idle talk.

"Where is your family?" Gustaf inquired as he arose from his seat and took a new one beside her on the boxbed.

His large presence made Æsa's heart skip. "I've no family left," she explained, finding it difficult to look him in the eye.

"What happened to them?"

"After Harald became king, there was a huge revolt. My family was slaughtered, and I was taken as a slave. I was very young and had no one." Her next words were hard to admit. "I would go where I was needed. Until they'd tire of me."

Gustaf's voice softened. "I'll never tire of you, Æsa."

His words allowed her gaze to meet his. "You say that…they all say that. There's not much I haven't already heard."

"Indeed," he said agreeably. "But I imagine the kind of men who've pined for your attention and cajoled you with eloquent tongues were naught more than wretches and cowards who found amusement in passing you around like a frivolous good. You're in my home now. What you hear from my lips will always be the truth. I've no desire to waste my breath on falsehoods."

A smile gathered on her lips. "If naught else, you're certainly charming."

Gustaf made a sound resembling a low hum. "I'm pleased I'm at least something in your eyes."

For Æsa, Gustaf was more than something. He was more than she ever thought possible of a man. She felt safe with him and, for once in her life, didn't wish for better. She was undoubtedly in foreign territory, and she'd no idea how to behave or what to offer without offending.

Normally, for the food and the warm bed provided for her, she would have been expected to impart sexual favors. But Gustaf acted as though he counted on reaping nothing more than a harmless conversation.

"You've done so much for me," Æsa said timidly. "And I've naught with which to repay you."

"I need not reparation," Gustaf replied steadily as he lifted her chin with a hooked finger. "Nor do I expect it."

He stood from her company, and before she realized what she was doing, she reached out for his forearm. "What if I want to?"

Gustaf flicked his gaze between her and her grasp. "You needn't think like that anymore. You're free to come and go as you please without having to first please another."

Though his words were the most gracious she'd ever heard, they also came as a kick in the teeth. Did he not want her? Was she not good enough for him because of the past life she'd led?

How could she blame him, though? She was a whore and had been for most of her life. But to think he was so repulsed that even her touch disgusted him wounded her more than if he'd backhanded her. She released him and hung her head in shame.

Gustaf saw this and sat back down beside her, bringing his hands up to her face. "That was not a rejection, my lady. That was me granting you free will. No longer are you a thrall."

Æsa felt the warmth of his hands upon her cheeks and shivered. His straightforward contact sent her heart aflutter and her wits scurrying to the farthest part of her brain. She had no words.

"You're trembling," Gustaf said softly. "Why do you shake like a scared rabbit? Do I frighten you?"

She shook her head. "N-nay, 'tis just that—" She struggled for the right words. "'Tis your touch.

Gustaf stroked his thumb across Æsa's cheek, wondering how a woman, who once had little to no modesty, could suddenly turn timid in the palm of his hands. He knew this wasn't the first time she'd felt a man's touch. If anything, the stroke across her face was probably the most innocent contact she'd ever felt.

"I don't understand. Do you not like my touch?"

He heard her swallow. "I like it very much. Very much indeed. But I'm not accustomed to men such as you. You're gallant and honorable, and though I want more than anything to—" She stopped abruptly. "I'm not worthy of you."

He slid his hands from her face into the thickness of her hair, holding her so close, she had to tilt her head upward to look at him. "Worthy, you say? Woman, have you forgotten what I've done all my life? I've killed many men and will kill more before I'm through. How do my actions make my worth more than your own?"

"Your actions are righteous."

"Only to some," Gustaf confessed sardonically. "I believe nine others would argue differently."

"Even so," Æsa insisted. "Your past dealings, at the

least, have furnished you with a sense of satisfaction."

"Is that how you see it?"

"I do," she replied. "Everything I've ever done has been disgraceful."

"Disgrace comes only when the choice itself is disreputable," Gustaf sympathized. "You were never given the freedom to choose, lest it meant your life. But with me, you'll always have a choice."

Æsa swallowed again and looked as though she wanted something from him, but hesitated to open up in light of their conversation. Eventually, it seemed she found some courage. "As choices go, I would like very much to kiss you."

He smiled. "I would like very much to kiss you as well. I've wanted to ever since I laid eyes on you." He paused, allowing her time some time to think. "Are you sure this is what you want?"

She gave him a look that expressed her undeniable desire for doing so, and he obliged. By degrees, he tilted his head and pressed his lips to hers. He breathed in, relishing the smell of her soft, freckled skin. In her eyes, he saw an untamed ocean trapped behind crystalline glass, and beneath his palms, she burned like fire. His body reacted to the sweet torture she inflicted upon his senses, and yet he'd only begun to kiss her.

She moved to his lap and straddled him, hiking her skirts as she sat on his thighs. "Now 'tis you who trembles."

What she called trembling, he called arousal. He laid her down and settled himself between her legs, burying an involuntary moan deep in her mouth.

Æsa heaved a long sigh and drifted into transient recollections of the night. Nothing could've been more perfect than lying within Gustaf's arms. He was the most amazing lover she'd ever had and selfless to the very end. Even now, when most men would have succumbed to a deep sleep, unable to be roused or moved, he was awake, stroking the length of her arm ever so lightly. She could certainly get used to his way of fornicating. His way was sensual and deliberate, as if every touch and kiss had a purpose and a meaning.

As he shifted, she tensed, then heard him chuckle as he dragged the animal furs from the bottom of the boxbed and over their bodies.

"You thought I was going to leave your side, didn't you?"

Æsa relaxed and snuggled into the protective bow of his body. "Forgive me. I didn't mean to think that. Old habits, I suppose."

"Look at me," he commanded. He rolled her body to face him and brushed the back of his hand across her cheek. "Close your eyes and may you never worry again, my lady. When you wake, you'll find me right here beside you. This I promise."

Chapter Eight

"You're beginning to worry me, Mara," Nevan stated as he scanned the mead hall at the many people enjoying the closing meal of the day. "Since Tait has left, you've been quite reserved. I assure you, Lochlann is doing well in my charge."

Mara offered her best smile to the handsome king sitting beside her. He was the chieftain of the Uí Bhriain on Inishmore and had been an ally of Dægan for many years. Both the long-established Irish and the newly settled Northmen of Dægan's family shared the isle peacefully, and it was within this mead hall where everyone gathered.

Mara sipped her wine. "I know I put you at an inconvenience, but I'm grateful for the time you've worked with my son."

"'Tis a pleasure. Lochlann is like a grandson to me, you know this. He gets frustrated easily, which I assume most lads his age do when feeling the need to prove themselves. But I dare say, he's quick to learn. Would you not agree, Ottarr?"

Ottarr, an elder Northman and Dægan's former advisor, quickly chimed in from Nevan's right. "Aye, he is indeed. And that, m'lady, cannot be taught. He's well on his way to being a warrior's son."

Nevan patted her hand reassuringly. "See? You've naught to worry about."

Mara found a little consolation with those words, but

not enough to matter.

"Something tells me there's more to your fretting than Lochlann and his progress."

"I always worry when Tait is abroad," she admitted.

"He's in Veigsfjordr trading goods, naught more."

Mara glanced discretely at Thordia across the table. "I worry for his wife."

"All will be well in a few days. And if I know Tait, it may be sooner."

A roar of laughter from the left side of the table erupted after one of Nevan's men told of his hilarious bout with a stampeding sheep herd and one aggressive ram in rut. There was an incredible amount of amusement in the mead hall that night, even though many were missing from the festivities and accompanying Tait on his merchant route. Lively music filled the room as women sprang into dance, and enthusiastic men raised their tankards and voices over the collective noise.

As Mara sipped the last of her wine, she saw the king's watchman briskly enter the hall and weave himself through the crowd of dancers. Once he reached Ottarr, she could see a thick layer of concern on his face, but was unable to hear his whispered words.

Ottarr quickly glanced at Nevan and back at the watchman. "Are you certain?"

"Aye, m'lord."

"Sire," Ottarr said. "We have visitors. A *currach* of seven men, sailing toward our shores."

Nevan thought briefly on the news, then addressed Mara. "It seems we have guests approaching. I'll not be long. Please," he insisted, touching her hand. "Enjoy the rest of your meal."

Mara nodded respectfully, though she was curious as

to who was coming ashore. It was not as if Inishmore was a busy port like Limerick. In fact, very few cared to visit the rock-infested isle, save for a few ascetic monks who chose, on their own accord, a hard life. Assuming the small number of men approaching was, indeed, a group of harmless religious men, she didn't let it compound her present worries. "I shall be fine."

Nevan smiled and stood, absentmindedly touching his sword at his hip. He and Ottarr left the hall, followed by a handful of summoned Irishmen.

****

The leather-clad *currach* caught a riotous wave of the unmerciful Atlantic and skated along the shallow depths of the shore until its bottom ran aground. Breandán and his companions leapt from the small boat before another wave accosted them, and dragged the vessel through ankle-deep waters. Before they could make it to dry land, the surf shoved the boat against the back of their legs and knocked a few men down in its wake.

Curses rang out as the water retreated, and Ottarr and Nevan ran to help. They grabbed a few helpless amateurs by the back of their cloaks until they gained their footing. Ottarr hid his smile as best he could, while complaints about the angry sea continued in their struggles.

"I'm afraid the sea holds no compassion here, gentlemen," Nevan said apologetically.

Once they were out of the sea's reach, they all stood together on the rocky shore, regarding each other warmly. One by one, the islanders took notice of their visitors' faces, and soon the hospitable mood flipped. Ottarr unsheathed his sword and pointed it at Breandán. The rest of his crew flinched and stepped back. Before Nevan could question the Northman's hasty rationale, Ottarr uttered Breandán's name as though it had left a bitter taste on his tongue.

Breandán stood undeterred by the threatening sword. Quite frankly, he expected it, though he assumed Tait would be the one to draw the first weapon as they'd never gotten along. Yet, Tait was nowhere to be seen. "Ottarr," he said calmly in reply.

Nevan looked between the two men as if waiting for more words to follow, but neither spoke as they sized each other up. "What is the meaning of this?" he asked.

Ottarr scoffed as if he suddenly found humor in Breandán's presence. "This is Breandán Mac Liam."

Nevan eyed the young man as the name didn't register. "Should I be familiar with him?"

"Aye," Ottarr sneered. "You should. He was once an ally of Dægan's cowardly twin, Domaldr."

"Prisoner," Breandán corrected.

"I saw no tethers around your ankles or wrists as you fled toward Domaldr's langskips that fateful day with Mara as your captive." Ottarr kept his eyes fixed as he filled Nevan in on the facts. "Sire, Breandán is the very man who brought Domaldr to your shores seven years ago. He was the cause of several of your men's deaths and the reason we had to rebuild our entire settlement, as all was burned to ashes by the time he left."

Nevan narrowed his eyes, but not in a way that showed anger. A sense of contemplation, perhaps. "Is this true?"

Breandán shifted his gaze to Nevan—privately noting he was in the presence of a king, based on Ottarr's reference—and then back at Ottarr. "Aye, but I no more set fire or killed your men than Mara did. I was merely trying to rescue her after she'd been taken from her land. I was never an ally of Domaldr, but a servant of Mara's father, Cathal Mac Conor—as I am still."

Upon Breandán's words, every islander drew their sword and stepped forward, waiting eagerly for Nevan's command. The tension grew between the men, but no one moved from their positions.

Marcas's eyes widened. "Perhaps you shouldn't talk anymore, Breandán."

Nevan stretched his arm in the direction his men stood. "I'll not have further bloodshed on my isle for a grudge held upon a dead man. Domaldr and his torment are no more upon us. Nor will I stoop to Cathal's level and take a man's life out of mere suspicion. Put your weapons down." When no one responded to his command, he raised his voice above the ocean's roar. "Sheath them now!"

Reluctantly, each man lowered his sword and slid it slowly into the scabbard at his hip, save for Ottarr.

Nevan waited a few seconds more, taking notice of the Northman's indomitable stare and his irregular breathing. "Ottarr," he said sternly.

"Forgive me, sire, but my grudge is larger than yours. Dægan was both my chieftain and brother-in-arms, and he's no longer with us due to this man's," his next words rolled from his tongue in callous sarcasm, "service to his king. If Tait were here—"

"He isn't here," Nevan interrupted. "He's not here to make decisions nor give commands. Thereby, in his absence, you heed my words. Sheathe your sword, Northman."

"Or else what?" Ottarr challenged. "Going to turn on

me, are you?"

"I've no such intention. However, I don't condone eye-for-an-eye reasoning. If you run him through, there are four of his men who have swords and one with a bow strapped across his shoulder. Would you be so foolish to think they don't know how to use them? Is it worth your life to find out? Is it worth mine, knowing the position you'd force upon me should you strike him dead?"

Ottarr regarded Breandán as he mulled Nevan's warning through a clenched jaw. Breandán hoped the king's words would be enough to settle the Northman's temper, but put his hand on his dagger at his hip just in case.

Ottarr exhaled in frustration and shoved his sword into its sheath with the force of what he would have used had he thrust it into Breandán. When Ottarr looked away distantly, Breandán gave Nevan his full attention.

"I apologize, Breandán, for the reception you and your men have received," Nevan began. "Though seven years is a great span of time, 'tis with a heavy heart we still mourn the loss of our friend Dægan as if it were yesterday. Surely you can understand."

Breandán was also accustomed to dealing with loss. Though his bereavement had been losing Mara to another man, it hadn't hurt any less than if she'd died. His heart wouldn't have known the difference. "I hold naught against anyone here for their loyalty to Dægan. He was a great man, and few men deserve that title."

A thin reflective smile ran across Nevan's lips. "Indeed. You speak as though you knew Dægan well." He cleared his throat before adding, "It seems you also know his men and the hostilities they hold against you. So, my next question is, why are you here?"

"I've been sent to deliver a message to Mara from her

father."

Nevan glanced to his left as if to remind his men to stand down.

Breandán noticed this and couldn't understand why both monarchs held such an interest in Mara's well-being. Twice now, the islanders reacted over the mere mention of Cathal Mac Conor, yet his own daughter was welcome among them. The more puzzling question was why would Cathal allow Mara to stay with a clan he was at odds with?

"What message do you bring?"

Breandán spoke curtly despite the tension of the close-quartered group. "Cathal's not well. He's on his deathbed and has asked to see his daughter."

Nevan was overcome by Breandán's statement and lost all sense of speech. No one present understood the magnitude of Cathal's request. It was such a simple request really, but he knew both his worst fear and his greatest joy were about to unfold.

His mind drifted back in time to a profound discussion he and Tait had had soon after Dægan's passing.

"I know this is very hard for you, to find out you have a daughter, born of the only woman you've ever loved, and that it must not come to light. But think it through. Right now, Mara has three men who love her. If you tell her, she'll hate you all. She'll hate Cathal for keeping the secret, she'll hate you for bastardizing her, and she'll hate Dægan for knowing the truth and taking it with him to his grave. Do you really want to hurt Dægan that way? Dægan made this all possible. He made it so you can be with your daughter, and he gave his life for it. Do not tarnish his memory over details of little worth. All that matters is that Mara is yours, and you know it to be true."

With Cathal requesting to see Mara on his deathbed, Nevan could only assume he was ready to right the wrongs from his past. He came out of his reverie and gathered his wits. "I suppose you're here to see that Mara accedes to his request. I imagine Cathal didn't offer you a choice in the matter."

Breandán smiled. "You know him well, then."

"Quite. You could say he and I have had a long…" He wanted to say feud, but in light of his company, he chose to be vague. "We'd had a long history together. But I'm afraid I cannot allow Mara this journey. Tait is not present at the moment, and out of respect for him, a decision like this cannot be reached without his knowledge. In light of that and the long journey you've made, you and your men are welcome to stay here on the isle until Tait's return. Together, we shall all come to a decision."

Ottarr looked even more disconcerted. "Surely you jest, sire."

Nevan gave Ottarr a sideways glance. "To send these men back without a resolution would be rude and unproductive. Need I remind you a man's life hangs in the balance of his last wishes."

"And where do you suggest they stay?"

"The most sensible place would be Mara's longhouse, as hers can accommodate all seven," Nevan said, but then interrupted Ottarr's next protest. "Without Mara, of course."

****

Breandán's heart nearly stopped. He and Ottarr seemed to have shared the same look of surprise, though Ottarr was more vocal about it.

"This is your idea of sensible?" the Northman muttered.

"If you've a better suggestion, Ottarr, by all means, speak."

Ottarr stepped into Nevan's space. "Do you not realize the ramifications you face once Tait gets word of your excessive generosity?"

"I'll deal with Tait when the time comes," Nevan said frankly.

Ottarr scoffed. "I'm not sure what I'm going to enjoy more. Tait's wrath upon *you*…or Breandán. Both will be equally gratifying."

Breandán watched the two men carefully. Nevan stood unruffled beneath the Northman's glower. Any other man would have taken offense at Ottarr's statement, but the king remained levelheaded and tolerant.

"I can understand your discontent, Ottarr, but your criticism is premature. You lack the knowledge of what this day has brought me, and I assure you, Tait will understand."

"Tait will have your head on a spit!"

Nevan crossed his arms and tilted his head. "I presume that means you're short of a better suggestion?"

"What I'm short on is patience, Nevan. Why do you insist upon appeasing these men? You shall gain naught by it."

"On the contrary. When was the last time you saw Mara smile?"

"What?" Ottarr's face shriveled like a prune.

"Cathal has denied Mara for many years," Nevan explained as he put his hand on the Northman's shoulder. "Even after Lochlann was born, Cathal refused to see her.

She'd been practically disowned by her own people. And with Dægan gone, she's been utterly lost. Now, for whatever reason, Cathal has come to his senses and asked for his daughter. Do you not think that news alone will excite her to her very core? For once, I want to see her happy again. To make her feel as if she belongs. That, my friend, is what I shall gain. Now if you'd be so kind as to send for Mara—"

"I'll have no part in this," Ottarr interjected. "You want her? Then fetch her yourself."

The grizzled old Northman walked away and, to Breandán's best guess, to where the mead supply was plentiful enough to inebriate himself.

Nevan stood there as if contemplating his next actions, until one of his men spoke up.

"Permission to speak frankly, sire."

Nevan glanced over and assessed the look on the loyal islander's face. "Please, by all means. Speak your mind."

"While we all trust your judgment, Breandán is still one of Cathal Mac Conor's men."

"Noted," Nevan said with a nod, then looked at Breandán. "Show me your heel."

Breandán narrowed his gaze, not fully comprehending the king's strange request. "I'm not sure I understand."

"Remove your shoe and show me your heel," he repeated. "Mara and I once talked about that fateful day when Domaldr had come here and done the unspeakable to his own brother. She told me if not for a certain man, Dægan would have been murdered on the spot. And the man who spared Dægan bears a deep scar across his heel."

Compared to Dægan's heroic measures, Breandán couldn't fathom Mara remembering the sacrifice he'd made on her behalf. Nor did he expect her to share it with others.

It was such a long time ago, and until now, he'd nearly forgotten about the out-of-sight scar on the bottom of his foot.

He reached down and pulled off his boot, turning around to lift his foot for all to see.

"As you can see for yourself," Nevan declared, "this man was Dægan's ally. And if Dægan can trust this man, then so can I."

"But, sire…"

"I'll hear no more on the subject. Send for Mara and have her meet us at her longhouse. That is an order." As the islanders straggled one by one back to the mead hall, Nevan looked at Breandán and his companions who stood before him, apprehensive and drenched. "You all must be cold. Come, let's get you settled for the night."

Chapter Nine

The thought of staying in Mara's longhouse thrilled Breandán no end as he and his men walked up the shoreline. The cream-and-sable-colored pebbles beneath his feet were as numerous as the questions in his head.

How would Mara react when she saw him?

How would he feel sleeping in her home?

How would she feel knowing he was sleeping in her home?

And how long would this streak of luck last before Tait returned and spoiled it all?

Taking into account the cold reception he'd gotten from Ottarr, he half expected Tait to outright kill him when he got back. And given the number of years that had separated him and Mara, she might be just as bitter as the others.

He couldn't deny that he was the reason Domaldr had landed upon their shores and brought death and destruction to Dægan's family, as Ottarr had argued. Nothing he could do or say now would ever make up for that. But at the time, he was barely a score and hardly a man. He was too naïve to have known the consequences of his actions and too proud to have thought the daughter of an Irish king would fall in love with a Northman. If he could relive those days, he would have certainly done things differently. He could only hope that with the time Mara had to reflect on his involvement, she hadn't grown resentful.

Against his better judgment, he followed Nevan inside Mara's longhouse. The warmth of the room was a blessing with a roaring fire in the central hearth. The main room was spacious and eerily identical to how Breandán remembered it seven years ago. From the woven tapestries hanging on the walls to the intricate carvings etched into the massive doorframes, every last detail had been carefully considered and replicated. But what caught his eye was the chest at the foot of the perimeter boxbed. He'd never forgotten its significance at a time when he stood head to head with Dægan.

"Why would you even care to save this chest from the fire? You had a purpose, and it had naught to do with selflessness. Come on, tell me. Why would you bring this?"

The silent deadly stare between Dægan and Breandán was long and barbed with jealous animosity. Neither blinked nor flinched as they gazed deeply into each other's souls, until realization struck Dægan. "You love Mara. You brought this in hopes to win her heart should I have died. To begin where I left off."

Mara stepped forward and touched Dægan's forearm, his fist clenched at his side. "That is absurd, Dægan. He pulled it from the fire so that I might trust him. Tell him, Breandán."

Dægan scornfully coaxed the Irishman, "Aye, Breandán. Do tell."

"Fine. I love her. But what good does it do to proclaim it? My heart's longing will never be satisfied. At the least, you might find consolation in that, Northman. Be that as it may, I'll protect her with every beat of my heart, and there's naught you can do about it."

"Breandán? Is it really you?"

Breandán shook the vivid memories from his mind

and turned in the direction of the female voice behind him. Nothing could've prepared him for this moment. He was completely and absolutely stunned by the breathtaking sight that was and always would be his *a thaisce*, Mara.

Chapter Ten

Mara's long, flowing hair trailed her back in one thick braid. Loose strands fell in silken tendrils over the smooth, creamy skin of her face. Her eyes, the color of glorious emeralds, reflected golden flecks of fire behind dark feathery lashes. For a brief moment, time suspended as he stood in her presence. Then her perfect lips parted and spoke his name again, yanking him back to conscious reality.

He blinked and stammered on his reply. "M-m'lady." A prickling heat rose from his chest and up his neck as he humbly bowed before her. It was then that he noticed how ridiculous he must have looked in his dripping wet attire. "'Tis a pleasure to see you after all these years."

Mara's face lit up like a flame, oblivious to the others beside him, and she hurled herself into his arms. He stumbled backward a step but recovered quickly as he enveloped her delicate body in an embrace.

When he looked up, all eyes rested on him and he became painfully aware of his actions, which might or might not have been appropriate. He released his arms from around her back and offered his sincerest apology. "I should've warned you I was soaking wet. I'm afraid your gown is ruined."

Mara smoothed her hands over the bodice and waved him off. "'Tis only water." She regarded his face more thoroughly now, and a giddy laugh escaped her. "I cannot believe you're here." She then realized he wasn't the only man in the room. "Angus, please, forgive me. I didn't see you there, else I would have greeted you properly."

Angus bowed deeply. "Trust me when I tell you that your greeting has surpassed all others we've received thus far."

Mara regarded the rest of the men in her company, and her smile slowly faded. "What brings you all here?" Initially, she directed the question to Angus, but soon turned her attention to Breandán when the pieces of the puzzle didn't fit into place. "Breandán?"

He felt the ground wobble beneath his feet. He hated to be the one to tell her about her father's failing health. Why couldn't Angus do it?

Nevan stepped forward. "It seems your father would like to see you."

Mara's attention fluttered back and forth between the men. "Why does my father want to see me?"

Breandán noted the acidity in Mara's voice. Why wouldn't a father want to see his daughter? From what he remembered years ago, Mara had reciprocated his love. He'd seen it with his own eyes. Had things changed between them?

"Your father loves you," he said, hoping he wasn't too presumptuous.

Mara shot a quick look toward Angus. "Does he? I fail to see it."

Breandán eyed Cathal's messengers. Judging by the way they fidgeted like sinners in a church, he knew that something significant enough to leave Mara heartbroken had occurred. "Forgive me, Mara, but I'm ignorant to anything that has transpired between you and your father since we parted ways. What I do know is that he's not well and wishes to see you."

A single tear slipped from her eye, but she quickly wiped it away. "Is he dying?"

Breandán glanced at Nevan for support. Or perhaps some answers. "He is."

Nevan stepped forward and clutched Mara's shoulders from behind. "Cathal has refused to see his daughter, despite the loss of her husband and the birth of her son."

Breandán recoiled. "Why would he do that?"

"I cannot speak for Cathal. You would have to ask him."

To deny his own daughter without reason was utterly spineless. Though, in truth, it didn't surprise him much. Cathal Mac Conor might have been a king he was supposed to serve, but he never cared for the man or the lengths to which he'd gone to get what he wanted.

Breandán kicked himself for being so blinded by his own desires that he didn't see the scheme behind Cathal's request. His king not only threatened to side with Mac Flann, but he used Breandán's emotional attachment to Mara as a pawn to further his purpose. Once she found out what Cathal held over Breandán, she wouldn't likely refuse.

Coward.

Breandán remembered what his father had told him before he left. *"A man always has a choice, no matter what he's faced with or how far back he's cornered. There's always a choice.* And he was making his now.

No one would manipulate Mara, especially her own father. No matter what strategic vise Cathal had placed on him, Breandán was not going to choose the wrong side again. He'd already done so once in his life with Domaldr, and it proved to be his biggest mistake. He wouldn't play the ignorant fool again.

"I'm sorry that Cathal has treated you this way," Breandán began, no longer referring to the deceitful, crafty king as her father. "I can only hope, since he's on his deathbed, he's come to his senses. However, if you decide you don't wish to see him, I'll not hold you to it."

Angus flinched. "But, you have orders to bring her to him."

"In light of what Cathal has done to Mara, those orders are no longer mine to carry out. Nor will I allow anyone to force her. This is her choice, and I stand by her decision, whatever that may be."

"But she's his daughter. She should know what her father has planned should you refuse his command."

"You mean, what he has threatened to do, naught more."

"However you choose to see it, Mara has a right to know."

Breandán drew in a breath and adopted a commanding voice. "Angus, hold your tongue."

"You've no authority over me, Breandán,"

"He may not," Nevan interrupted, "but I do. Speak one more word, and I shall have you thrown from this isle before your next breath. You're a guest in Mara's home, and I remind you to act like one."

Mara's gaze lifted to meet Breandán's, and she grasped his arm. She looked pale and unstable on her feet. Breandán reached for her and steadied her by the elbows. "Are you all right? You don't look well."

She touched her hand to her throat as beads of sweat clung to her skin. "I need some air."

Nevan leaped forward and helped to stabilize her. "Indeed, you look quite distraught. Come, let's step outside." He flashed a stern look toward Angus before ushering her out the door.

Breandán, however, was not as merciful.

Chapter Eleven

As soon as the door closed, Breandán confronted Angus. "You best tell me what you know about Cathal and why he turned his daughter away when she needed him most."

"I know naught more than you."

"You're a liar."

"Breandán, if I may," Marcas interrupted.

"You've hardly said a word since we landed," Breandán said sharply. "I suggest you continue to do so." He glared back at Angus. "And, as for you—"

"I swear to you, Breandán, I don't know why Cathal refused his daughter. The only person who'd likely know would be his advisor, Fergus, as he was the one who turned Mara away."

Fergus turned her away? Breandán didn't see that coming. He thought better of the king's advisor—until now. Breandán squared his shoulders. "Then I suppose your services here are no longer needed."

Angus crowded his brows in surprise. "What is that supposed to mean?"

"It means you're getting back in that boat and heading for the mainland."

"You cannot be serious," Angus protested "We're all soaked to the bone already."

"A condition that will only worsen when you board the *currach*."

"And what do you expect me to tell the king when I return without his daughter?"

"I care not what you tell him," Breandán barked. "With any luck, Cathal will be dead before you make it back. But you can inform Fergus I'll be coming for him, with or without Mara, and he'd better have answers for me."

Angus stood dumbstruck. "That is the message you want me to take to the king?"

Breandán crossed his arms. "Aye."

"Have you no concern for your own people? The risk you put them in for forcing Cathal to ally himself with Mac Flann?"

"His threats do not frighten me. No matter with whom he's allied, we'll fight Mac Flann and we'll win."

Angus shook his head. "You've lost your mind."

"And you're putting a strain on my patience." Breandán stared until Angus finally realized he had neither the pity nor the intent to change his mind.

Reluctantly, all five of Cathal's men walked around the hearth to keep from having to pass Breandán on the way out, but Angus lingered at the door. "You will regret this one day, Breandán. Mark my words."

"And there will come a day when Cathal will regret that he ever hurt Mara. Mark mine while you're at it."

****

Breandán sat down on the boxbed behind him and squeezed his head between his palms. He didn't regret his decision concerning Cathal as Angus proclaimed, but he was more troubled by how upset Mara was when she left.

He couldn't shake the look she'd given him or the tears that had welled in her eyes.

He removed his bow and quiver from his shoulder and set them beside him, before he felt obliged to apologize to his friend. "Forgive me, Marcas. I had no right to speak to you that way."

"Are you granting me permission to speak now?"

Breandán rolled his eyes, knowing his friend would speak his mind regardless. "What is it you want to say to me?"

"You actually have to ask?" Marcas paced the room and flailed his hands about. "My life has been threatened, on several occasions mind you, and you've the gall to sit there and ask me what 'tis I want to say? We nearly died tonight!"

"You knew well where we were going and the Northmen that have occupied this territory. I never hid that from you. In fact, as I recall, I warned you."

"You said the Northmen might be a bit belligerent. There's quite a difference between holding a grudge and wanting vengeance. Did you not see the look in the old Northman's eyes? Two more breaths and I swear he would've run you through and paraded your head around the isle on the end of his sword."

Breandán glanced nervously toward the door. "You might want to keep your voice down, then. Ottarr might have been mad, but by now, he's likely mad *and* drunk."

Marcas flopped down on the boxbed opposite Breandán and closed his eyes as he rested his head on the wall behind him. "I could certainly use a drink myself."

Breandán detached the drinking pouch from his belt and tossed it to his friend, who then glanced at the pouch in his lap. "You call that a drink?"

"I call it the best I can give you at the moment."

Marcas's eyes lit up, and a grin tugged his lips. "Speaking of giving, I saw the look you gave Mara. Especially when she wrapped her arms around you."

Breandán wasn't impressed. "You've always known how I felt about her."

"Aye, but does *she* know how you feel?" Marcas sat up and braced his elbows on his knees, rubbing his hand together in front of the fire. "She's widowed and hasn't yet taken a husband."

"Marcas, we've just arrived. Could we take one day at a time, please?" He blew warm air into his cupped hands and extended them out toward the fire, trying to thaw out his fingers as he warmed up to Marcas's suggestion. The idea of telling Mara how he felt about her sounded great in theory, but no matter how many times he ran it through his head, the scenario never ended well. He either came across as too forward, or Tait came at him with intent to kill. Right now, his main concern was for Mara and how she was dealing with the news he'd brought.

A few minutes later, her door opened. Hoping that it might be Mara returning, Breandán politely stood but was disappointed when only Nevan entered. "Is Mara all right?" he asked.

"She will be. She's staying with Tait's wife, Thordia, for as long as she needs to." Nevan gazed around the room. "Where are the others?"

Breandán almost forgot. "I sent them on their way."

Nevan quirked his brows. "You sent them away? And Angus agreed to this?"

Breandán shrugged. "Not exactly. But I didn't give him much choice. He'd caused Mara enough distress."

Nevan seemed pleased with Breandán's forthright decision, but he didn't say anything to confirm it. Instead, he smiled and offered the stack of dry clothing he'd come in with. "I believe you two are in need of these."

Breandán accepted them, humbled by the king's graciousness. "I'm sorry my presence here has caused quite a stir."

Nevan clasped his hands in front of him and rocked on his heels. "Sometimes a little excitement is good for everyone. Let's hope the rest of your stay is pleasant."

With Tait due to return, Breandán didn't hold his breath.

"Is there anything else I can get for you?" Nevan asked. "You're welcome to join me in the mead hall once you get settled. There's plenty to eat…and drink."

Breandán gave Marcas a sideways glance, knowing Nevan's latter mention sparked his friend's attention. As good as it sounded, he worried that Ottarr was steeped in mead by now. "I think 'tis best we stay here. At least until some tempers have cooled."

A wide smile crossed Nevan's face, and he nodded deeply as if he too brought a drunk and bellicose Ottarr to mind. "Perhaps you speak more wisely than I, Breandán." He turned toward the door but stopped as he opened it, waiting. Finally, he faced Breandán with a serious look. "Thank you," he said, bowing his head, "for making Mara smile again."

* * *

Breandán did not expect those words to fall from the king's mouth. It seemed Nevan had a personal interest in Mara, almost as a father would. But why?

"Give me those," Marcas demanded as he snatched the pile of leines and cloaks from Breandán's hands. "I've stood in these wet clothes long enough." He searched through them aimlessly until he found a pair that suited him, and threw the rest on the boxbed behind Breandán. "Are you not going to change?"

Breandán regarded his friend. "Aye. I was just thinking."

Marcas ripped his clinging wet tunic over his head and replaced it with a dry one. "About what?"

"About Nevan and Mara. Their relationship goes beyond king and villager, almost as if they are family. Perhaps he's Mara's uncle...mayhap Mara's mother and Nevan were siblings."

Marcas scoffed. "Nevan and Cathal as brothers-in-law? With the hatred they share between them, I doubt it."

Breandán peeled his own wet leine from his body and over his head as he eyed his friend askance. "Stranger things have happened. Look at Dægan and Domaldr. They were twins and yet they hated each other." The more he thought about it, the more he felt he was on to something. "There has to be a common thread that ties Mara to both Cathal and Nevan...but what?"

Marcas rubbed his temples. "You're hurting my head with this."

Breandán stared into the dancing fire, unaware of anything around him or that he'd fallen into deep thought in the nude. While Marcas rummaged through her home unbeknownst to him, he mulled over every possible connection he could think of linking Mara and Nevan.

Sparks jumped from the fire and floated upward, startling Breandán and forcing him to step back. He shielded his vulnerable genitalia as Marcas continued to throw new logs of turf on the blaze.

"Could you please dress yourself?" Marcas insisted, blocking his view with the back of his hand.

Breandán snagged a leine from the pile behind him and raised a curious brow at the amount of turf Marcas had thrown on the fire. "Where did you find all that?"

Marcas motioned behind him. "Whole storage room full."

"You've no right to go searching through Mara's house."

"'Tis turf. I don't think she'll mind."

"Whether she minds is irrelevant—" Breandán's words were suddenly cut short as the longhouse door opened. In walked Mara and two other women, carrying a grand display of meats, breads, and cheeses on trays. They froze, eyes wide, as he dropped both hands to his groin to cover himself with the wadded-up tunic.

Chapter Twelve

Had Mara's eyes deceived her? Was Breandán truly naked?

Lillemor's murmur of *Oh, my…* behind her confirmed he was indeed very naked.

Mara averted her gaze and shuffled her feet, embarrassed that she'd stared at his hard-muscled shoulders and arms, brawny chest, rippled stomach, and…oh, yes, that too. She couldn't even let herself think she'd caught a glimpse of it. She wanted to run from the room, but couldn't as her two friends, not so willing to budge, blocked the entrance.

"I-I'm sorry," she stammered. "We thought you'd be hungry. Please, take it."

Breandán, who had already fed his arms through the sleeves of the leine and pulled it down over his hips, handed off the trays one by one to Marcas. By the time he'd taken the third, the three women had clumsily turned and disappeared out the door, slamming it shut behind them.

Marcas looked at Breandán on the brink of laughter. "Did you see the look on Mara's face?"

"Keep your impure thoughts to yourself," Breandán growled as he grabbed his belt and raced out the door. "Mara! Wait. Please." His heart sped up as he approached her. When he stood in front of her, he released a sigh in place of words. He had no idea what to say. "I didn't mean to be...I mean, I was unaware you were coming back...with food. Nevan said you were with...well, that you had..." Breandán stopped himself and tried to gather his wits. "I truly didn't mean for you to walk in and—"

Mara's bright smile beamed, cutting him short. "I should've knocked first."

He glanced over his shoulder at the longhouse. "'Tis your home, not mine. I'm merely a guest." He bowed slightly. "A humble guest. And I'm so sorry." As he leaned forward, Mara's green eyes caught him by surprise. He hadn't expected her to hold his gaze with such intensity and wonder. Quite frankly, he hadn't expected her to stare at his bare-naked body for as long as she had either. Somehow he felt both self-conscious and fearless, if that were possible.

Thordia cleared her throat, breaking the trance between them.

"Forgive me," Mara said, stepping aside to introduce the others. "Breandán, this is Lillemor," she directed, "and this is Thordia, Tait's wife."

Breandán bowed again. "'Tis a great pleasure to meet you both."

Thordia and Lillemor each smiled, tickled, even, by his presence.

"And thank you...all of you," he added, "for the food. 'Twas very thoughtful."

"Is there enough?" Mara asked. "We can certainly fetch more if—"

"Please, do not trouble yourselves any more than you already have. There is more than enough. Would you care to join us?"

Thordia spoke up first. "Lillemor and I have already had our fill earlier. But I'm certain Mara would like to."

Mara clumsily stepped forward as if she'd been discreetly pushed from behind and scolded Thordia with wide eyes.

"You barely ate," Thordia reminded her. "You should eat. 'Twould do you good."

Mara slowly faced Breandán and bit her lower lip as she rocked back on her heels. He could see her apprehension and wondered if it was due to guilty feelings of unfaithfulness to Dægan. "Are you certain you won't join us?" Breandán offered to the others in an attempt to alleviate Mara's discomfort. "Thordia, you *are* eating for two."

"Thank you ever so much, Breandán, but I couldn't eat another bite." She and Lillemor smiled in agreement and walked away together, their whispers and suppressed giggles trailing behind them.

The last thing he wanted was for Mara to do something she wasn't comfortable doing. "If you'd rather not—"

"Oh, please, that's absurd."

"What I mean is," Breandán rephrased, "would you rather share a meal in a place less private so as to limit the talk of the isle? The mead hall, perhaps?"

"How very considerate, but it would be an honor to eat with you. Besides, we have much to catch up on."

Mara admired the lengths to which Breandán was willing to go to save her good name, although her reputation was hardly worth the concern seeing she was no longer a delicate maiden. Eating in the privacy of her own home shouldn't cause any alarm amongst her people, especially since it was Nevan's idea to offer the food to begin with. If he didn't want her to dine with Breandán, then he shouldn't have sent her. He should've delivered the food himself.

The meal they shared was a quiet one. The only time Breandán had spoken at all was when he was spoken to. And even then, he was short on details.

By her recollection, he looked the same as he did years ago—lean and tall with the same boyish handsomeness. Yet, some things were noticeably different about him. His hair was much shorter than before, cropped nearly to his scalp, which now accentuated a strong jaw she'd never noticed when his hair was shoulder-length. And he carried himself with an undeniable confidence in his face and posture.

Marcas, on the other hand, talked extensively and made jests from time to time, though Breandán often looked hard put to appreciate them. It wasn't until Marcas had poured himself a third tankard of mead that Breandán finally felt the need to reprove his friend's nonchalant behavior beyond the usual grimaces.

"Do you not think you've had enough to drink?"

Marcas shrugged, then winked at Mara. "I'm catching up on the days I lost voyaging across Mother Erin with you."

Curiosity suddenly emerged within Mara. "Why have you come, Marcas, if you don't mind me asking? I understand Breandán's reasons for making the journey, but yours are lost on me."

Marcas's expression turned serious, and he drew an uneasy breath. "Breandán needs me. If I weren't here to accompany him, he'd walk around in a constant state of nakedness. To say 'tis embarrassing is putting it mildly."

"Marcas," Breandán cautioned.

"I have to remind him to keep his clothes on."

"That's not true," Breandán insisted. "He's making jests about—"

"You've seen him, m'lady," Marcas badgered. "I think 'tis a condition, not contagious, mind you, thank the Almighty. But someone's got to watch over him lest he goes out of doors with his co—"

"That will be quite enough, Marcas!" Breandán shouted. "You must forgive him. He has no idea how to behave in front of a lady or how to conduct himself in appreciation for all that's been given to us this evening. As you can see, he's an ungrateful dolt."

"Cutting me down to size won't make you the bigger man, Breandán. She's already seen what little you have to offer."

Mara covered her mouth to keep from laughing aloud with Marcas, and did her best not to encourage him. She had to look away from the men as their exchange of raillery and ridicule continued to amuse her.

Breandán eventually gave up and apologized once more. "Again, I'm so sorry…"

"Please, don't apologize." Mara waved him off. "In fact, Marcas reminds me of Eirik, Dægan's brother."

"He was an ungrateful dolt as well, aye— Ow!"

Judging by Marcas's howl and the sharp contortion of Breandán's face, Mara assumed Marcas had been kicked beneath the table. This time, she couldn't hide her laughter if she wanted to.

"So, you've a son," Breandán interjected with a change of subject.

It was the first time he initiated a conversation, and she

was doubly glad the focus was on something she never grew tired of talking about. "I do. His name is Lochlann."

"A name very fitting from the father who sired him, no doubt."

Mara agreed with a nod. "He resembles his father in many ways."

"How old is he now?"

"Six," she said proudly. "Though he wishes he were a score and six."

"Since I've yet to meet him, I assume Lochlann has joined Tait in his travels?"

Mara sighed. "Nay, he is staying at Nevan's fort, learning the ways of a warrior."

Breandán looked at her askance. "And this troubles you?"

"'Tis not the lessons in warfare that trouble me," Mara explained. "He's a boy, and skills of that nature are to be expected. In these times, a man must learn at an early age how to defend himself, but..." She hesitated, looking down. "He's lost, and I cannot help him."

"Lost?"

Mara looked up from her lap. "Aye. He desires to be exactly like his father, yet..." Her words failed to come forth. It pained her to speak of her family's hardships, especially with Breandán, who, in all honesty, she'd rather make believe they were doing quite well.

He smiled sympathetically. "All young sons go through this, Mara."

"They do?"

"Of course. Six is a very tough age for a boy. They have so many aspirations and so many elders to please, and when the meager strength of their arms fails to succeed in a task otherwise effortless for a man, 'tis a direct strike against their very pride. Even Lochlann's warrior father fought against those things in his youth, I'd imagine."

She knew she shouldn't beat herself up for things she couldn't help, for things that happened beyond her control. But she was left a widow, Lochlann was left fatherless, and she was forced to take on the responsibility of both parents. "As hard as I try, I can't be the father figure he needs."

Breandán leaned across the table toward her. "Lochlann would feel this way with or without his father in his life. 'Tis nothing you're lacking, trust me. This shall pass as he grows stronger."

"How do you know that? You've yet to meet him."

"You forget, I was once a boy myself. And only time can remedy this."

Mara inhaled deeply, letting Breandán's supportive words blow through her heavy mind like a gentle breeze. "Would you like to meet my son?"

Breandán straightened in his chair and smiled at the invitation. "I would be most honored."

"Marcas?" Mara asked, realizing he'd been held out of the conversation. "Would you like to join us?"

He exchanged a look with Breandán, then cringed. "Hm…more strangers to meet in the dark? More swords to be drawn? I believe I'll stay right here."

"Suit yourself," Breandán replied. "I shouldn't be gone long."

As Mara and Breandán arose from their seats, Marcas tipped his tankard to his lips and called out before they shut the door, "Keep your clothes on, *a chara*."

Chapter Thirteen

Mara led Breandán to the stable behind the longhouses. It was a meager building compared to the rest, but large enough to house an assortment of precious livestock. There were separate stalls for the horses, though most were empty save four, and a large area where the sheep congregated for the night in a bed of hay. One massive dairy cow stood in its own compartment, chewing her cud without much concern. The horses, however, showed a great deal of interest as she and Breandán approached the stalls. They perked their ears and nickered, hopeful for a treat.

"Whose horse would this be?" Breandán asked of the stout, muscular draft horse poking its head out of the stall.

Mara grinned nervously at the dun. "'Twould be Tait's."

Breandán reached up and stroked its muzzle. "What breed is it, might I ask?"

"A Fjordhest," Mara answered, intrigued by Breandán's strange regard for the ornery beast. "They are only found in the western part of Norway. Why do you ask?"

"Because I fancy one."

Mara wanted to laugh. "You want an obdurate, ill-mannered steed?"

Breandán finally took his gaze from the horse. "He is not ill-mannered."

"Presently, he's not. But place a saddle upon him, and you'll wish you hadn't."

Breandán narrowed his eyes at her. "You've ridden him?"

Mara shook her head. "I favor my neck unbroken. But I've seen his temperament, and he would just as soon throw you as let you put one foot in the stirrup."

Breandán stroked up into the horse's forelock and around his dark-tipped ears. Contrary to her description, it lowered its head as if to encourage more. "May I?"

Mara's eyes widened a bit as she read the excitement in Breandán's voice. "Ride him?"

"I don't think Tait would take kindly to that. I only want to pull him out of his stall to get a better look at him. Maybe mount him."

"Did you not hear what I said?"

"Oh, I heard you," Breandán insisted. "But this horse isn't temperamental."

"So, I'm a liar?" Mara joked.

"Hardly. I'd rather wager Tait is simply too stubborn to take the time with such an impressive animal."

"You remember Tait well, then."

"One does not forget a man like Tait."

Mara couldn't agree more on both accounts. On many occasions she'd seen the wild spontaneity of this horse and the trouble Tait would go through to mount up, often getting bucked off or roughed up. And never did he once use patience to break the high-strung animal—only an *exhaust the horse enough to ride it* mentality.

"Are you sure you know what you're doing?" she questioned as Breandán slipped a halter and lead rope, hanging nearby, over the animal's ears. He led him out of the stall and into the open, admiring everything from its upright mane to its thick frame.

"Every horse is rideable, Mara. But not everyone is able to ride the horse."

Mara loved this hidden side of Breandán. The side of him that was confident and certain—and, to her surprise, a bit daring. She crossed her arms and cocked her head. "And what if he tosses you on your backside right here in this stable?"

"'Twould only hurt my pride, I assure you."

Mara shook her head and sighed. "If you feel you must…"

Breandán's smile lit up the darkened barn like a torch. He walked the horse in a circle and talked to it in a voice too low to be deciphered. Mara watched with reservation, silently praying he'd not get hurt in the process.

After he slowed the horse to a stop, he approached it, palm prone in an unaggressive manner, but the beast snorted and pinned its ears back flat against its head, warning Breandán with wide eyes and flared nostrils.

Breandán allowed the reaction, where Tait by now would've corrected it, and eased a hand up to its withers, petting and praising the horse as it began to put up with his presence. In time, the horse relaxed and licked its lips, a sign of contentment.

Mara wanted to close her eyes with Breandán's next attempt, but didn't dare. His quiet horse-handling skills mesmerized her to the point that she wondered if this was Tait's horse at all.

Breandán leaned on the horse and soothed it with his voice. She didn't bother to make out his words as it wasn't what he said as much as how he said it that kept the horse calm and accepting. Once the animal tolerated the angled weight, he applied more, this time directly upon its back with his feet dangling over the dirt floor. The horse hardly flinched and gave an audible sigh, at which point Breandán gripped its roached mane and swung his leg up over its back.

Mara smiled, pleased he'd mounted the horse without incident. "If only Tait were here to see this."

"I doubt he would've trusted me as you do."

The look in Breandán's eyes all but made her stomach flutter. She did trust him, but how to respond to such a statement was another matter altogether. She found herself tongue-tied as he patted the horse's neck and slid off its back, landing on both feet with a thud. The only thing she was able to say was the obvious when the horse followed on his heels. "I think you've made a friend."

Breandán looked over his shoulder as he approached her. The horse nuzzled once at his cheek, shoving Breandán's head to one side. "Perhaps I have." He laughed and returned the gesture with a good scratch around the horse's cheeks and muzzle.

"I believe he'd follow you anywhere."

He slowly stopped petting the horse and turned toward her. "I'd follow you anywhere."

Mara smiled and looked down at her feet, words failing her again.

Breandán closed his eyes. "That was entirely too forward."

It had been a long time since she'd heard affectionate words from a man, and despite the restlessness that settled in her chest, she liked the way those words sounded on his lips. But Breandán was right. It *was* too forward, or perhaps too soon. She needed more time to sort out her thoughts, and, more importantly, the decision pertaining to her father.

He was on his deathbed and wanted to see her one last time. The woman she was seven years ago would've crossed mountains of fire to get to him in time, but he, through his dismissal, and Dægan, through his death, had carved a hole so great, she honestly didn't know if she had any heart left for either Cathal Mac Conor or Breandán Mac Liam.

It was all too much. All of it was. Every thought about either man swam in her brain and in no apparent order. Yet...here Breandán stood before her, resolute and unwavering, during a time when so much in her life had changed, and most of it not for the better.

She finally looked up and realized she'd shot him down with her awkward silence. "Breandán," she began sympathetically.

"Mara, please," he interrupted. "You don't have to say something to spare my feelings. I'm a grown man. I should've known better."

"Known better than to what?"

Breandán's shoulders rose high through a deep breath and fell. "I should've known better than to think you were ready to hear that."

There might have been a foot between them, but Mara imagined the heat of his body had to be as hot as hers. She was burning up from the inside out. "Well," she began to say as her words balled up in her throat. "'Twas a bit of a shock, I'll admit, but at least I know exactly where you stand."

Breandán fixed his gaze on her, and she couldn't look away. The dual colors of blue and green in his eyes twisted together in a brilliant fashion behind a dark rim of thick lashes, and it was there she saw a reservoir of emotions he'd kept hidden. Was she really prepared to know what lay deep inside his heart?

She felt his hand take hold of hers. Her first reaction was to pull away, but the comfort of his touch stopped the shaking within her.

"You've always known where I stood when it came to you, Mara. Naught has changed in my heart since we last saw each other. And it never will."

Her heart swelled within her, but her head pounded at this revelation. *No, I'm not ready to hear this.* But she wasn't quite ready to reject him either. As her heart raced, she swore she would've felt his rapid pulse as well if her fingers rested a bit higher on his wrist, and somehow, that simple notion stirred something familiar within her. Was her touch doing to Breandán what his was doing to her?

Dægan had been the only man incited by her touch, and it had been so long since she'd experienced it that she nearly forgot how it felt to know a man was incapable of controlling certain involuntary bodily responses. With Dægan, it was easy to feel—easy to fall. But with Breandán, so much was at stake; her son, for one, and then her extended Norse family, Nevan, the islanders... So many could be hurt by one wrong move. One impulsive decision.

Even so, she still couldn't help but like the way Breandán's hand felt in hers. The way the warmth of his skin spread like wildfire up her arms. The way he looked at her at this very moment.

Mara squeezed his hand warmly. "It took a great deal of strength to say that to me. And I'm glad to know how you feel, but..."

"Listen to me, Mara. I didn't come on this isle to upset you or to force anything upon you—that includes both

Cathal's wish and the longings of my heart. I'm simply here to see you, and be with you as long as I'm allotted. Beyond that," he said, cupping her chin with his free hand, "I don't wish for more."

He held his fingers ever so lightly on her face, a touch that contradicted the words echoing in her ears, *I don't wish for more.*

At an ill-timed moment, Tait's horse snorted forcefully and blew a clear slimy spray of snot on the back of Breandán's neck. He closed his eyes, and Mara tried not to laugh, but the appalled look on his face was too humorous for her to hold back.

He reached up and wiped the wetness from his skin. A thin smile lessened his look of disgust. "That's rather foul. And completely uncalled for, I might add."

"Here," Mara said, pursing her smiling lips as she took a kerchief from her apron pocket. "Let me help you."

He stood motionless as she reached up on tiptoes and cleaned the remainder of mucus from his nape. Being that close, she could smell a light masculine aroma emanating from the dampness of his skin. Her mind wandered. She imagined how good he'd smell if she were pressed against his muscle-plated chest.

"You're enjoying this, aren't you?"

Mara froze. "Excuse me?"

"What Tait's horse did to me...you think it's funny."

Mara broke in a small fit of giggles. "I'm sorry..." she said, content to let him think her pleasure came the horse's mischief. She stepped back from him. "There. You're a new man now."

He lowered his head and looked right into her eyes. "Indeed, I am."

Chapter Fourteen

Silver moonlight streamed through the passing clouds as Breandán and Mara loped across Inishmore toward Nevan's stone fort to meet her son, and he swore he was right in the middle of another dream. With the feel of the powerful animal beneath him and the lingering scent of Mara's hair wafting past him on the breeze, he could only hope this was, in fact, a real occurrence.

She looked beautiful as she rode beside him on her dapple-gray horse. She wore a long tunic of light blue linen, hemmed with a fancy tablet-woven braid of darker blue, white, and gold. Her cloak was made of thick indigo wool and attached with two remarkable oval brooches boasting sapphire glass beads amid gold and silver filigree. Her hair hung as a heavy braid of silken rope to her waist and mildly patted her back at each suspended beat of her horse's gait.

Above all the dazzling adornments that embellished Mara, her smile was the most stunning. It was like a thousand suns sparkling with iridescent rays, and he had a very difficult time not staring. Lucky for him, Inishmore was a relatively flat and treeless island with an open plain of wildflowers, rock perimeter walls, and limestone.

Finally, after a long, playful run, Mara pulled back on her reins and slowed her horse to a trot once they reached the outermost defensive wall of the fort. Breandán did the same and rode abreast with her as their animals gradually cooled through a casual walk.

"You ride very well bareback," Mara said, her smile still at its fullest.

"My father taught me when I was young to ride the horse and not the saddle."

"Wise words. Speaking of fathers," Mara inquired. "How does yours fare? You seem to know so much about mine, but I know naught of yours—or the rest of your family, for that matter."

"You've never asked."

Mara reined her horse to the left so she faced him and their bent knees nearly touched. "I'm asking now."

Breandán didn't think she paid much attention to how close her leg was to his, but he did. He noticed many things about his surroundings. Directly in front of them was a relatively high rock wall with a well-built gateway, covered by a single massive lintel. Beyond that, about six-hundred feet inward, stood another rock wall, lit by torches, with several guards along the terrace who'd turned their attention to them the moment they stopped at the gate. He counted seven.

"What is it you want to know?" he asked.

"Everything. Do you have siblings?"

"Aye. Two younger sisters."

Mara's eyes widened with interest. "Younger sisters? How young?"

Breandán enjoyed her slight emphasis on the word younger. "Clodagh is six years under a score, and Grania is barely four."

"Five?" Mara said, surprised. "Your mother must have been quite stunned by her condition. Frightened at her age, as well, I'd imagine."

"That goes without saying. We all were. But Father took grand care of her and held his concerns to himself so as not to alarm her."

"Your father sounds like a wonderful man. Generous and perceptive," Mara added. "Traits you've no doubt inherited from him." She inched her horse closer so they were now parallel to each other. "So, tell me more about Grania."

Her leg brushed his, and every muscled stiffened in his body. He cleared his throat, hoping to clear his mind of her wonderful, feminine warmth. "She is a lively little one. Very curious. And often smarter than we give her credit for."

"I venture to say she looks up to you."

Breandán thought about his little sister. "You could say that."

"I would love to meet her one day."

"Grania dearly hopes to meet you as well."

Mara's brows rose high. "She told you that?"

"Oh, aye, she did."

He saw a sense of endearment on Mara's face as she inquired further. "And how does she know of me?"

Breandán wanted to laugh. "I think it rather difficult to find one person in Connacht who doesn't know of you. You are Cathal Mac Conor's daughter."

"I suppose you're right," Mara replied, seeming slightly dejected.

It might not have been the answer she was looking for, but it was the truth. She was the king's daughter, though nowadays it didn't hold much merit where Mara was concerned. Conscious of the disappointment in her voice, he added, "If it makes you feel any better, my whole family has talked about you. And they look forward to one day meeting the woman whose father was once very generous to them."

Mara contemplated his words. "Would I be too presumptuous, then, in thinking that was an invitation?"

Breandán smiled. "Not in the least."

She smiled. "I believe that might very well be a better reason for going to Connacht."

Any other man would've pushed the issue, hoping to convince her of that decision. Breandán, however, did not. He wanted her to meet his family because she desired it, not because he swayed her toward the notion.

"Shall we?" Mara asked, gesturing toward the fort.

Breandán dismissed his thoughts about family and took one last look at the distant guards eyeing him. "After you."

Mara dismounted and led her horse toward the narrow gateway. Breandán followed suit, and trailed behind her. He took notice of how the entrance wall strategically veered to the right so as to retard those who entered, and hesitated to pass through.

Mara glanced back beyond the lintel. "Worry not, Breandán. You're amongst friends here. Your own countrymen."

Despite her encouragement, Breandán was unable to forget the reaction he'd gotten from those fellow countrymen earlier that day. As they entered the gates, the impressive span of the outer wall and the large area it encompassed could truly be appreciated as it was now readily visible. Before them lay an open field of circular stone huts with thatched conical roofs and slow-burning fire pits in random places. A few men arbitrarily congregated between the houses, sharpened tools, and discussed topics of unknown debate, though he suspected his arrival on the isle had already been the main subject of conversation.

Breandán's eyes shifted all around him. He added the number of men he'd counted along the distant terrace wall with those he saw within as a precautionary measure.

"Come. This way," he heard Mara say.

He followed her through the maze of huts until it broadened into a field of haphazard vertical rocks. Upon seeing the impressive chevaux-de-frise, he realized why the ancient fort had long stood the test of time. The marvelous display of obstacles scattered about the base of the second wall would effectively prevent any enemy from attacking. Their usual means of rams, horse-drawn carts, and even the charge of foot soldiers could never get close enough to lay siege. It was certainly a remarkable sight.

To the northeast of the wall, he saw several men swordplaying with a small boy—Lochlann, he presumed.

Breandán watched intently as they came at the boy from all sides, jabbing and thrusting in a sequential dance. Lochlann turned and twisted, blocking with his shield and countering with all his might. He even thought he heard the boy grunt at times in his efforts.

Breandán smiled, thinking back to when he was a lad, learning the ways of the sword. He remembered his own struggles with the weight of the weapon and how he wasn't quite as graceful as Lochlann appeared to be.

Mara threw her reins over the horse's back and walked briskly toward the group. When the boy caught sight of her, he left his lessons and ran to her, weapon and shield still in hand.

"Mother! You came just in time!"

Mara tousled his unruly blond hair as she hugged him. "I did?" she said, feigning ignorance. "Why for?"

He stepped back from her arms and thrust his sword

forward as if she were the dangerous enemy, and then spun around on his toes, using his shield to protect his vulnerable little body.

Mara placed both her hands on her hips, watching her son's display with pride. "Extraordinary footwork, Lochlann."

But Lochlann dropped his arms to his sides in disappointment, his large wooden shield nearly touching the ground at his feet. "You're not supposed to be watching my feet, Mother. You're supposed to watch my sword. Ultan taught me how to thrust and then to use my shield to knock out Alfarinn's teeth!"

Mara frowned, though more of it was directed at Ultan, Nevan's brother, for teaching her son overexuberance. "I didn't agree to let you learn how to knock out Alfarinn's teeth. You're here to learn sword skills, though I'm not too certain why it must extend beyond your bedtime."

Lochlann rolled his eyes.

"Now come," Mara redirected as she put her arm around him. "I've someone I want you to meet."

Lochlann sighed and dragged his feet as he walked toward Breandán. A look of complete disinterest plagued his sweaty little face.

Breandán inhaled deeply. By the look of the boy, it was going to be a challenge to impress him, much less hold a conversation. He was disturbing something Lochlann enjoyed, and he knew that was the only thing the lad had on his mind.

Mara and Lochlann stopped directly in front of him. The boy was dressed in brown breeches, torn at one knee, and a common blue tunic. His dark blond hair was disheveled and dripping wet at his temples. What stood out from the typical, energetic lad's attire was the oversized bear cloak draped across his shoulders. It was far too big on the boy and nearly scraped the ground at his heels. He also noticed Mara still had her arm around the boy, a tactic most probably used to keep him from retreating.

"Lochlann, I want you to meet a friend. His name is Breandán." She gently nudged him forward.

Breandán dropped to one knee so the boy didn't have to look up to meet his gaze. "Hello, there."

Lochlann staked his wooden sword into the ground at his feet, more concerned with how far he'd driven it than talking with Breandán.

He tried another approach. "I see you're wearing your father's cloak."

Lochlann's eyes shot up from the ground. "You knew my father?"

Breandán glanced up at Mara and back at the suddenly eager boy, expecting her to be worried what he'd say. "I did. Unfortunately, 'twas very brief, but I can say I had the honor of knowing him."

"Did you fight alongside him?" Lochlann asked, his voice rising.

Breandán smiled humbly, still glancing intermittently at Mara. "I didn't have the opportunity to fight alongside your father. But together, we did save your mother."

Lochlann twisted his head over his shoulder and up at his mother. "Is that true? He was there?"

Mara smiled and nodded.

Lochlann frowned. "But I listen very closely when Tait tells that story. He never talks about Breandán being there. Why?"

Mara fidgeted uncomfortably, and a look of apology

spread across her face toward Breandán. He decided to help her out on this one. "Of course Tait wouldn't mention my name. Those grand stories are saved for the warrior heroes like your father."

Lochlann turned his attention back to Breandán with more questions swimming in his eyes. "You're not a warrior?"

"If the need arises…I wouldn't hesitate to be one."

Lochlann looked him over. "Where's your sword?"

Breandán knew where this was going. In a young boy's mind, every warrior needed to wield a sword, or he wasn't a real man. "I don't carry a sword. My weapon of choice is the bow."

The boy's face drooped. "You're not a warrior, then. You're only a hunter."

"Lochlann!" Mara scolded.

"'Tis all right. I am a hunter. And there's no shame in it. Without me, you…" he stated, poking Lochlann's belly, "would go hungry. And warrior heroes who fight with swords need twice as much food to sustain their strength."

Lochlann was still not impressed. "But I could kill you with one slash of my sword and seize the deer you hunted."

Mara eye's narrowed to slits. "Lochlann, where is your respect? And where did you hear such viciousness?"

Breandán stared at the boy now, accepting the child's inadvertent challenge. "You could very well kill me. I can see it in your eyes. But remember this…you first must get close enough to do it. With my bow, distance is both my advantage and my ally. Your sword would then be useless to you."

Lochlann thought hard on the scene Breandán had laid forth. It actually made sense to the lad, and lucky for Breandán it struck a chord. "Would you teach me the bow?"

Breandán smiled, happy to have finally gained the boy's regard. "If that is what you desire."

Lochlann looked to his mother for approval. "Can I? Can I learn the bow?"

Mara rolled her eyes. "You think you're disciplined enough to learn it? I shall have you know 'tis more difficult to hit a distant target with a bow than 'tis to strike down a close target with a slashing sword. You need patience and a keen sense of depth."

Breandán sat back on his heels, astonished by Mara's knowledge of bow tactics. He thought he knew a considerable amount about the spirited princess, but this certainly was new to him—and intriguing.

"I'll do whatever Breandán says, Mother. Please, let me."

Mara glanced at Breandán, clearly thinking her son imposed upon him. Breandán made sure to express that it didn't. She sighed. "I suppose 'twould not harm you to learn patience. In fact, it might do you a wealth of good." Lochlann nearly jumped out of his short-ankle boots in excitement. "But...not at this hour," she reminded.

The boy sagged again in disappointment.

"Your mother is right, Lochlann," Breandán said. "The moon doesn't give as much aid as the sun. We can start in the morning."

"You'll still be here?"

Breandán caught the lad's surprise and inhaled deeply. "It appears that way."

Lochlann smiled. "First thing in the morning, then."

"Not so fast," Mara said. "Your chores must be completed before you delve into your lessons."

"Aye, Mother."

Breandán rose to his feet, and his gaze found and held Mara's. There was something different from just a simple prolonged look in her eyes. But what exactly, he wasn't sure.

Eventually, Mara tore her focus to the little boy standing beside her, her thoughts still seeming to tumble around in her head. "'Tis very late, Lochlann. Are you staying here with Nevan at the fort or with me?"

Lochlann glanced back at Ultan standing around with the others. "I still have to learn to beat Alfarinn before he comes home. I'll stay here."

"Very well, but not too much longer. Now give me a hug."

Lochlann reached up to meet his mother's embrace with a lack of enthusiasm. Afterward, he pulled his sword from the ground and ran back toward the Irishmen.

Mara smiled at Breandán and then said, "Come. I'll introduce you to Nevan's brothers, and then there's something else I want you to see."

Chapter Fifteen

As Breandán and Mara walked around the southwest corner of the fort, a strange sound arose. It grew louder the farther they journeyed, and, if his sense of direction served him well, they'd soon be nearing the edge of the isle. He could only assume it was the crash of the sea below the isle's cliff, but he'd never heard such a roar.

Mara glanced over at him as they walked, their horses following behind them. She locked eyes with him again, and this time, longer, even more intense. So much so that she paid no attention to the uneven ground beneath her feet and tripped. Breandán instinctively let go of his reins and caught her around the waist, hoisting her back to her feet.

"Are you all right?"

Mara glanced over her shoulder with a look of embarrassment. "Thank you, Breandán. I'm fine."

He realized that his hands fanned across the flat of her stomach, and removing them from her delicate waist would prove more difficult than he ever imagined. She was tiny within his grasp, soft in places where his fingertips rested. With as much reluctance as he would have severing his arm from his body, he released his hands and stepped back. "Are you sure you didn't hurt yourself? Twist your ankle, perhaps?"

Mara giggled. "My ankles are fine. 'Tis my heart that concerns me."

Breandán shot her an odd look. "Your heart?"

"Aye," she admitted, touching her hand to her chest. "We're very close to the edge."

Breandán glanced over his shoulder and saw the sheer cliff all but a few feet away. He'd been so engrossed by Mara and catching her that he hadn't even noticed the proximity of its edge. Curiously, he walked over and leaned forward, peeking over the side. Below him, the angry Atlantic broke against the distant rocky bottom in a daunting and beautiful spectacle of sea foam and spray. He inched closer for a better look, but felt her grasp on his wrist.

"Please," Mara begged. "You're frightening me."

Breandán regarded her hand, her touch provoking the incessant ache within him. "Why bring me here if I'm not permitted to see?"

Mara let him go as swiftly as she'd taken hold and fumbled on her next words. "I want you to see the beauty of this isle, but...perhaps 'twould be better if you saw it lying down."

Mara lowered herself to the ground and lay on her stomach, waving for Breandán to do the same. Her pulse skipped when she saw the muscles in his arms flex as he supported his weight on the way down. Even if she'd denied observing his prone, muscular body, she couldn't negate how it made her feel to lie so close to a man that space between them was virtually nonexistent.

She slowed her breathing one breath at a time and tried to settle the giddy feeling in her chest that had nothing to do with the dizzying height of the sea below. She drew her attention to Breandán, whose hands clutched the rocky edge for stability. His reaction to the breathtaking sight below was a feeling she understood well, and no matter how many times she came here, the sea still had the ability to draw her in. She breathed in the clean scent of sea salt wafting up and exhaled at length.

"'Tis beautiful."

His comment compelled her to look over at him, and his gaze no longer beheld the ocean. "Aye, 'tis. I love it here."

"I assume Dægan once brought you here."

For a split second, she felt guilty. That perhaps Breandán didn't take kindly to being in a place she and Dægan once shared. "I merely wanted you to see it. I thought—"

He touched her hand with just his fingertips. "This is a place that's very special for you, and I know it holds many memories. I'm honored that you wanted to share it with me."

Mara looked away. "I like to come here. Sometimes 'tis the only place I can find peace." She swallowed, fighting the urge to tear up. "'Tis the only place I feel close to him, where I feel like he's still present."

Breandán slid his entire hand over hers and squeezed. "I'm so sorry Dægan is no longer with you. If I could, I'd gladly change places with him." His gracious words caught her by surprise, and before she could ask why he'd do such a thing, he added, "Because I know 'twould make you happy. Your happiness is all I've ever cared about."

Mara's heart melted. She'd never known a man to be so selfless, so willing to sacrifice his life in place of another man's so she could be happy. Not that it could ever happen, but the thought astounded her. She could tell by the look in his eyes that he meant every word.

"I don't know what to say," Mara admitted.

"What is there to say? You loved him. You still do. Some people live a lifetime without ever feeling that kind of compassion. While others…can only hope for it."

Guilt again climbed within Mara. "I suppose 'twas thoughtless of me to bring you here."

"On the contrary," Breandán insisted. "Considering what you told me, I assume you thought enough of me to bring me here. Any man would deem himself most fortunate. 'Tis a grand place. Probably one of the most beautiful places I've ever seen. In truth, I can now understand why one would stay on this godforsaken isle for years at a time." He stared deeper into her eyes. "It holds many hidden treasures. And some not so hidden."

Mara's cheeks warmed with his compliment. "Are you saying one could get used to living here?"

Breandán narrowed his eyes in thought. "'Twould not be difficult—if one were to imagine such a thing."

What am I doing? Until her question came out and his answer followed, she hadn't realized what she'd asked. The tiny hint of a smile on his face told her he was drawn too far into the subject to let it go now.

She gave thought to Breandán living on the island, and though she couldn't say for sure if she welcomed the idea, she felt a strange feeling inside her when she thought of his departure. Something would truly be missing if he were to leave.

"May I ask you something?"

His deep voice broke the momentum of her thoughts, and her eyes fluttered as she came back to reality. "Of course."

"This, again, may be too forward," he warned.

Mara drew in a slow breath and prepared herself. "If

'tis, I'll let you know."

"Fair enough." He broke his gaze and looked out into the moonlit sea. "'Twas rumored you were to be married...years ago. Gunnar, I believe. Why did you not marry him?"

Mara stared into the distant horizon as he did. "I suppose I hadn't the heart for it. Tait really wanted me to. He thought it was a good match. But my concerns were with my son."

"How so?"

She took another deep breath before she explained. "Gunnar is a very loyal man, and he would've made a fine husband, but I couldn't convince myself he'd be a good father." She imagined every bone in Breandán's body wanted to ask why, but he didn't.

"So, Tait has dismissed the arrangement altogether?" he asked.

"For now. I can only hope if there ever is a decision to be made about a suitable husband, he'd allow me to make that choice myself."

"In other words," Breandán said lightly, "'tis not Tait I must impress, but you."

Mara smiled. "Is that what you were doing in the stable when you climbed upon his wild horse?"

Breandán shared the same wide grin. "Did it work?"

Immensely.

Before she could answer, he lifted a single finger to her lips. "Don't tell me. I only ask that you keep that smile."

His masculine scent filled her head with thoughts hardly becoming of a lady. It amazed her how one simple touch of his finger had such a profound effect on her heart and mind, and how disappointed she felt when it was gone.

He rose to his feet and held out his hand. "I should get you back to Lillemor's before they start wondering about us. We already have the fort talking."

Mara glanced up and saw a few guards gathered along the terrace and could only imagine the talk she'd created amongst them. She placed her hand in his and allowed him to help her stand. It was a comfort to feel her small hand in his and the strength and warmth within his firm grasp. She missed that simple pleasure very much.

"I want to thank you," she said, reminiscing on the evening's events, "for what you said to Lochlann about his father."

Breandán dipped his head to meet her gaze. "What I said about Dægan was not a lie. He was a good man, and I'm honored to have known him. No doubt we had our differences, but we also shared a common ground—your welfare. Even between the many years that have separated us, I still care for you as much now as I did then. It pains me to know you've been alone all this time. But rest assured, you're no longer alone. As a friend, I'll be here for you…for as long as you'll allow me."

Chapter Sixteen

Mara closed the door to Thordia's house ever so quietly, in hopes she'd not awaken anyone, but when she turned around, she saw Lillemor and Thordia staring eagerly at her from the perimeter boxbeds. She sighed and rolled her eyes. "Why are you two still awake?"

"You know very well why," Thordia replied, patting the edge of the bed beside her. "Come, come. Tell us all about it."

Mara pushed herself from the door and strolled past the hearth, wringing her hands. "I'm afraid there's naught to tell."

"Oh please, Mara, you've never been a good liar. Don't think you can start now."

"I've not the slightest idea what you're talking about. I shared a meal with a friend…"

"A handsome, gloriously endowed friend," Thordia added.

Mara scolded her with a look. "I then introduced him to Lochlann, and that was the end of it. Naught more happened."

Thordia frowned as Mara opened the chest where her clothes were kept. "You wouldn't keep Lochlann up at this hour. What else did you do?"

Mara opened the lid and pulled out a linen shift, hesitant to say. "We…went to the cliff."

Lillemor smiled at Thordia with an air of

condescension. "I told you so."

"I never doubted you, Lillemor. I only wanted to hear it from Mara's lips."

"And what is so wrong with taking Breandán to the cliff?" Mara asked as she removed her tunic and slipped into her bedclothes.

"'Tis not wrong," Thordia corrected. "Merely interesting."

Mara ignored Thordia and refused to even look at Lillemor, who sat smiling like a sly fox. All she wanted to do was sleep—or at least think in peace. There was so much to ruminate over, so much to sort out. And unfortunately, she wouldn't get much accomplished with these two nosy hens.

Mara unbraided her hair and ran a bone comb through her tangled tresses. Perhaps taking Breandán to the cliff was wrong. It had been a place she'd often go when she was lonely or when she wanted to be close to Dægan. Most times, it was a private place where she was left alone as a courtesy. No one on the isle disturbed her when she went there. What made her want to share it with Breandán? She didn't really know.

"Mara," Lillemor said in a gentle voice. "Why are you troubled?"

The comb in Mara's hand halted. She hadn't even realized she wore a frown as she tended the knots in her hair. She brought the comb down and nervously fingered the carvings on the comb. "Oh, Lillemor. What am I doing?"

Lillemor cocked her head. "You're being a good host to a friend."

"A handsome, gloriously endowed friend," Thordia chimed in again.

"Thordia!" both women scolded in unison, though eventually they all giggled as they recalled the splendid moment of surprise.

"Anyway," Lillemor readdressed. "You were saying?"

"I cannot possibly remember now," Mara said, reflecting on Breandán's lithe, muscular body. "Even as I stand here, my heart jumps out of my chest at the thought of him."

Lillemor rose from her bed and joined Mara, taking the comb from her hand. Kindly, she began combing where Mara had left off. "There is nothing wrong with what you're feeling. Breandán is a fine man, and you're still a young woman with needs. 'Tis only natural for you to think of him in intimate ways."

"Lillemor, please."

Lillemor stopped combing. "We both may be widowed, but we're certainly not blind. We'd have to be to not see what a…fascinating…" She swallowed hard. "Virile body…that man possesses."

Mara snatched the comb away from Lillemor. "We were not supposed to see him in that way. And if Nevan or Tait ever finds out—"

"Oh, don't worry about Tait," Thordia interjected, chuckling at Mara's fretting. "If anyone has to worry over Tait finding out, it should be me. I was there as well." She laid her hands on either side of her swollen belly as if to cover the ears of her unborn child. "And thank goodness I didn't missed it."

Again, the women giggled.

"He's quite beautiful," Mara admitted.

Lillemor took hold of Mara's upper arms and turned her. "And what was more beautiful was the way he looked at you. Did you not see it?"

Mara couldn't answer. She was afraid.

"Mara, don't worry so much about what you're feeling. Enjoy it. It has been seven years, and I think you're entitled. I know Dægan is still very close to your heart. He should be. You loved him. You bore his son. But I also know he'd gladly step aside and make room in order for you to be happy."

Mara stared at her sister-in-law, confounded that Lillemor knew exactly what she'd been struggling with all along. And Lillemor should know. She too had lost her Northman husband and had been living her life alone, raising a son without him. "But what if I cannot put Dægan aside? To even think it seems nigh impossible."

"I'm not telling you to forget him or force feelings you don't have," Lillemor instructed. "All I'm saying is don't let your feelings for Dægan get in the way. As much as this pains you, you know he's never coming back to you."

Mara hung her head, trying to keep her tears from showing. She knew Dægan wasn't coming back, but to hear it so bluntly felt like a knife stabbing her heart. As if she felt the pain of his death all over again.

"Mara," Lillemor said softly. "Follow your heart. If you find Breandán there, don't be alarmed. And by all means, don't push him away or think you have to. You may find he's exactly what you need."

"But how will I know what I need?" Mara pleaded. "And what if what I need is not what is best for Lochlann?"

Lillemor laughed and guided her toward the boxbed. "I believe as a mother, they're one and the same." She gestured for Mara to lie down and then covered her as she would her own child. "Now try hard to find rest. You'll feel much better in the morning."

Mara sank low in the boxbed mattress made of fleece and drew the fur blankets up beneath her chin, wanting to believe everything Lillemor had claimed. Especially the last part.

****

Breandán entered Mara's longhouse as quietly as he could so as not to awaken Marcas, who was fast asleep from being deep in his cups. His friend was right where he'd left him, sleeping like a babe—or, in this case, passed out with an empty tankard in his hand. He wished Marcas would give up the drink but understood why he often resorted to it. He couldn't blame him. His mother had killed herself after his father had been caught up in a torrid affair with another clansman's wife. He fell into the drink at a young age and had stayed there ever since.

Breandán tried hard not to be too judgmental, but he feared the drink had now become such a part of Marcas that the man couldn't let go.

He carefully slipped the cup from his hand and froze as Marcas stirred. After a few unintelligible burbles, Marcas went right back to snoring. Breandán shook his head. "Sometimes I think you need a woman more than I do."

He squatted down and picked up a few logs of turf beside the boxbed and placed them in the fire to keep his friend warm throughout the night. Once the fire took hold, he looked around the familiar home for a place to sleep for the night. He could've chosen the boxbed immediately across the fire from Marcas, but where Mara slept was far more enticing.

He slowly opened the heavy double doors to Mara's private quarters and stood in awe. The walls were draped with tapestries, probably bought in a far-off land. Intricately connected designs engraved the wood face and sides of the boxbed, and within it lay silks and linens fit for a princess.

He smiled, imagining the immense trouble Tait had gone through to make it as Dægan had once designed it. If he could say anything good about Tait, it was that he was tenacious.

Breandán took great care in sitting upon the bed, almost as if it would break beneath his weight. The mattress beneath him was soft and stuffed to the gills with fleece. The feel of the crimson silk against his palm was cool and slick. He'd never felt anything like it before. He imagined Mara's skin felt quite similar to the foreign fabric against his callused hand. Reverently, he lowered himself to the full length of the boxbed, breathing in the scent left behind on the plush textiles.

He thought back to when she'd first seen him standing in her longhouse, and the immeasurable delight he felt in seeing her smile and feeling her tight embrace. The faint smell of her reminded him of the summer sun, of honeysuckle and lavender. As he lay on her bed, he could distinctly smell those same fragrances.

Then his mind wandered to the cliff's edge where she'd lain beside him, and how her scent had no qualms in drifting in his direction. He drew in another breath and kicked his boots to the floor, pulling the thick linens over his body. He settled himself within the swath of the blankets infused with her aroma and closed his eyes.

Chapter Seventeen

Breandán felt the presence of someone standing beside the boxbed and opened his eyes. A faint smile twitched at his lips.

Mara.

He noticed there was no expression of surprise on her face when she'd found him lying in her bed. He, on the other hand, couldn't hide his disbelief.

Dreaming, he reminded himself. *I'm only dreaming…*

He watched as she slid beneath the covers. As if paralyzed, he stared as she rolled to her side and curled her body into the concavity of his. An immense heat gathered beneath the covers, and his heart thumped in his chest.

"Hold me, Breandán."

Her sweet words slammed into him. If he held her as she asked, he'd finally get to feel what it was like to hold the love of his life and press her close. He swallowed hard and stretched his arm across her body beneath the blanket. But he couldn't bring himself to lower it. A part of him still felt he hadn't the right to touch her in such a way—even if she did ask. By right, she wasn't his to hold.

Aye, he was dreaming. He had to be.

He closed his eyes and took a deep breath, preparing to feel her body disappear at any moment. Instead, he felt her slender fingers upon his hand. It was a light caress, but one that rocked him to the core as she guided his palm across the tender swell of her breasts beneath her shift.

She was soft and supple beneath his touch. The natural rise and fall of her breathing pushed her breasts further into his palm, and her taut nipple grazed the underside of his fingers. He heard her exhale, a long sigh he came to believe was the result of finding comfort in his embrace. She fell limp against him, though he lay poised and rigid.

He tried to relax as she did, but his mind wouldn't allow him. All he could think about was Mara's bare flesh and the urgent desire he had to pull her body closer.

"Breandán," she whispered.

He hadn't realized how dry his throat and mouth had become until he tried to speak.

"Breandán, wake up!"

His eyes flew open, and he found Marcas staring at him from the edge of the boxbed. He drew back in astonishment, then glanced down at his empty arms, discovering that he'd spooned a pillow in place of Mara.

He rolled to his back in disappointment and ran his hand back and forth along his scalp as if to erase the images lingering in his head. "That was a rude way to wake a man, Marcas."

"Oh, is it now? Well, at least you hadn't a knife stuffed beneath your chin like I had."

Breandán cocked his brow. "What are you talking about?"

Marcas leaned to one side and thumbed behind him at the small boy wearing an oversized bear cloak, standing in the doorway. Breandán sat upright and rubbed the sleep from his eyes. "Is it morning already, Lochlann?"

"Aye, 'tis."

"Did you not hear me?" Marcas griped. "The boy nearly ran me through."

Breandán laughed in spite of his friend's rebuttal. "It

seems he's a very good judge of character at such a young age."

Marcas scoffed. "He's fortunate I didn't break his little arm."

"I was protecting my longhouse," Lochlann defended. "No one said anything about him staying here. Only you."

Marcas crossed his arms and tapped his foot. "I see where I rank."

"Mara and I weren't gone long enough for your name to come up," Breandán said.

"I'm certain other things came up, though."

Breandán shot his friend a scolding glare. "Not in front of the boy."

"Ach, he's too young to know what that even means."

"Too young to know what?" Lochlann asked, his hands now resting defensively on his hips.

"Ignore him, Lochlann," Breandán said, climbing out of the bed and slipping on his ankle boots. "I do all the time."

"That can go both ways, you know."

Breandán ignored Marcas's warning and strolled past the young lad toward the hearth in the main room. "Have you seen to your chores, then, as your mother demanded?"

The boy fidgeted. "I was hoping you could help me with those."

Breandán turned Lochlann's request over in his head as he stoked the fire. "I don't see why I couldn't. What is it you must do?"

Lochlann neared him. "I have to gather seaweed and take it to the field. Five baskets."

Breandán glanced over the boy's shoulder at Marcas, who was exiting Mara's chamber at a casual pace. "I'm certain we can help. Isn't that right?"

Marcas plucked a hard biscuit from Lochlann's hands as he walked past. "I'm ignoring you."

"Hey! I brought them for Breandán," Lochlann protested.

Marcas dropped lazily onto the nearest boxbed in the room and reclined against the wall, taking his first bite. "Then I suggest you bring more tomorrow, else Breandán will not have any then either."

Breandán shook his head. "Don't worry about me, Lochlann. Your mother fed me well last night. I shall be fine."

Lochlann offered the single biscuit left in his possession. "But I brought it for you."

Breandán took notice of the boy's melancholy expression. Evidently he'd gone to his own amount of trouble to bring the small breakfast. Breandán accepted it. "I'll only take it if you've already eaten."

Lochlann smiled. "Nevan fed me. He always feeds me well."

"He's good to you, then?" Breandán asked, fishing.

"Oh, aye. He does things with me."

Breandán heard the slight inference that someone else didn't. "I imagine he's a good man to learn from. Not everyone gets to be chieftain, and remain so, for as long as he."

"My father was a chieftain," Lochlann added proudly.

"Indeed he was. A great chieftain, as I recall."

Lochlann hung his head. "My father didn't get to be chieftain long."

Breandán let out a quiet, lengthy sigh, pitying the lad for the father he never knew. "You're right, he didn't. But perhaps one day, you'll grow to be chieftain."

"Me?" he asked, as if the idea never occurred to him.

"Of course, *you*," Breandán said, crossing his arms. "You're Dægan's son, are you not?"

Lochlann nodded, but he still looked as if the notion of being chieftain was out of the question. Breandán came to him on bended knee and straightened the ill-fitting bear cloak upon the boy's narrow shoulders as he spoke. "You wear a chieftain's cloak. You've the blood of a chieftain pumping through your veins. And you're Lochlann, son of Dægan, son of Rælik. There should be no doubt in your mind as to where your destiny lies."

Breandán could see the slow change taking place in the boy. He stood a little taller and took in deeper breaths to fill his miniature lungs. Maybe it wasn't Breandán's place to say such things to Lochlann. Or maybe he just gave Tait another reason to hate him. Honestly, he didn't care about either. Lochlann needed a push in the right direction, and he took the initiative.

"Are you ready to take on those chores?"

"I am."

"Marcas?" Breandán asked, rising to his feet. "You ready?"

Marcas had his eyes closed and his hands folded neatly across his stomach as though refusing to acknowledge the call of duty. Breandán looked at Lochlann and frowned.

"He's ignoring you," Lochlann stated matter-of-factly.

"I wager he wouldn't ignore you should you unsheathe that dagger from your belt and stuff it beneath his chin again."

Lochlann accepted the dare. He took all but two steps forward and unsheathed the weapon from his belt before Marcas raised one eye open and caught the boy's wrist.

"Easy, now, you little rascal!" Marcas tickled Lochlann's ribs until the child released the knife and he was able to toss it to Breandán. "Keep that, will you?"

"Afraid of a boy less than half your size, aye?" Breandán ridiculed.

Marcas put Lochlann in a headlock and rubbed the top of his head with his knuckles, ignoring yet again the youth's objection. "'Tis not that I fear him, but that I've no trust in him. He *is* a Northman." He released Lochlann with a shove and laughed at the sight of the boy's disheveled blond hair.

Breandán caught and straightened him. "You better start giving Lochlann a reason to trust *you*. He'll be a chieftain one day, and you never know when you may actually need his alliance."

Marcas scoffed at the remark while Breandán winked at the grinning boy beside him.

Chapter Eighteen

Mara stepped out of Lillemor's longhouse and a fresh breeze met her face, carrying the scent of rain. She looked up into the ominous gray sky. Indeed, a mild storm was blowing in.

She drew the cool air into her lungs as she walked to her longhouse, trying to revitalize her drowsy self. She hadn't slept well last night, though it wasn't out of the ordinary. For many years she'd been unable to sleep due to grief and loneliness. But last night's sleeplessness was caused by something she wasn't accustomed to.

Excitement was the only way she could describe her unrest. Her mind was occupied with thoughts of Breandán, his valiant words, and his subtle touch that came on rare instances. Even upon waking this morning, he was the first person she thought of. Though he'd brought a great deal of mixed emotions with the news of her father's condition, and put many on the isle in an uproar, she was more than glad to see him again.

Aside from her son's birth, she couldn't remember a time after Dægan's death when she'd been this happy. This excited. From the moment she'd burst into her longhouse to see Breandán, she'd been on a strange high. A place where even the most depressing of life's tribulations, such as her father, couldn't bring her down.

It seemed Breandán had helped her to find a strength she long forgot she had, the part of her that refused to give up hope. The part of her that believed in small blessings.

Perhaps, Breandán himself was a small blessing...

She smiled, wanting to believe it. She wanted the freedom to rejoice in it as Dægan had always done with his windfalls. But then, she'd remember there were others involved. What would they think of Breandán? What would the islanders say behind her back? What would Tait do when he came home and found Breandán here? And above all, what would Dægan think about her feeling this way?

Dægan may have been gone from this earth, but she loved him and wanted to do things that would make him proud of her as if he were still physically here in her life. The cold, hard truth of it was that Dægan wasn't here to approve or disapprove. He was absent in every way. She couldn't touch him. She couldn't look at his beautiful face. She couldn't feel his touch upon her and grow weak with it.

And she missed it all. She didn't know she missed it until Breandán held her in his arms. Prior to that, she'd never given thought to a man's touch, nor did it keep her up at night. Now, because of one innocent embrace, one look of hunger in Breandán's eyes, she found herself craving more of those things. Those intimate things only a man and woman can share.

Oh, it has been so long. Years.

As Lillemor reminded her, it had been seven, and it was difficult to know what was natural and what was forbidden. She liked Breandán and had trusted him from the moment they'd met when Dægan's brother had taken them hostage. She knew her feelings weren't necessarily out of context, but she hadn't expected them to be so compelling, especially for someone who wasn't Dægan.

Was this right? Was it even appropriate to imagine Breandán in such a way? He was a man whose conduct seemed to conform to the standards of moral behavior, and her thoughts, by no means, came close—particularly the ones that involved the bare skin of his muscled chest, shoulders, arms, stomach, thighs....

She quivered as she reflected upon his strapping male physique.

Excitement.

No other word could possibly encompass the diverse emotions running through her. And Lillemor was wrong. She didn't feel any better this morning than she did last night about the things that had run through her mind about Breandán. Good heavens, she shouldn't have thought them at all.

She increased her pace to her longhouse and shook the images of Breandán from her head. As she reached the front door, she stopped to listen inside, wondering if she'd be interrupting Breandán's and Marcas's sleep. Or walking in on Breandán changing his clothes again.

For a split second, she smiled, then inwardly scolded herself thereafter. *Knock, Mara,* she told herself. She raised her fist to the wooden door and heard a distant fit of laughter from behind her.

She whirled to find her son with Breandán, carrying baskets of seaweed and Marcas on his knees, struggling with his share. They were too far away to notice her, but she could hear Lochlann laughing as Breandán helped his friend to stand. A few words were exchanged between the trio, followed by more easy laughter.

She smiled, for it wasn't a familiar sight to see Lochlann enjoying himself or to hear such gaiety. As a mother, it brought her great joy.

For a moment, she felt a compulsion to run to her son

and hug him, but thought otherwise, as she didn't want to disturb the bonding taking place between him and Breandán.

This was new for Lochlann and she was so happy he'd found gratification with some other adult besides herself, some other males besides Nevan and his brothers. They'd all been there for Lochlann, but Breandán wasn't bound by obligation. He'd made a deal to teach Lochlann how to shoot a bow, yet here he was helping her son with chores.

As she watched Breandán follow her son over the small crest of the hill, she also noticed that there wasn't the slightest hint of pity on his face. In fact, he looked as if he was actually enjoying himself.

"What's wrong?"

Mara flinched from the stern voice beside her. She found Ottarr looking out into the field as she was. "Not a thing," she affirmed. He grumbled under his breath and turned to leave, but she called to him, halting him in his tracks. "Why do you harbor such hatred for Breandán?" It was a simple question really, but Ottarr seemed to struggle with the right words, taking a moment to gather his thoughts.

"I should ask you why you don't."

His words cut deep, condemning her for the side she'd taken. "I realize many were killed because of me—"

"Nay!" he retorted loudly. "Because of Breandán."

She gathered her own thoughts on the matter, knowing she was making a stand on very shaky ground. "You're a smart man, Ottarr. I know this because Dægan put his faith in you on many occasions. And I know you held him in the same high regard."

He stared at her, his lips thin and straight between the long hairs of his gray mustache and beard.

"You trusted Dægan enough to make the right decisions."

He nodded once and looked away, almost as if he knew where this conversation was headed.

"And seven years ago, Dægan chose to ally himself with Breandán. He allowed him to escort me home to my father, and he also looked to him when he needed to breach my father's walls in secrecy."

Ottarr crossed his arms and waited impatiently for her to finish.

"If Dægan was man enough to let down his pride and trust in Breandán—even after Breandán had brought Domaldr to our shores—then why can you not do the same?"

"Dægan let down his pride then because all that mattered to him was you and your safety. I imagine if he were here today, he wouldn't be as eager."

"Why?" Mara asked, slightly outraged by the old man's accusation. "Because Breandán is being kind to me and my son?"

"Because Breandán has an ulterior motive, just as he did seven years ago."

Mara could feel her throat tightening. She didn't mean to take offense to any of this, but for some reason, Ottarr's grudge against Breandán rubbed her the wrong way. "Breandán cares for me. 'Tis no secret. He even proclaimed his love for me in front of Dægan and Tait."

"I know," Ottarr stated. "Tait told me what he'd done."

"Then all you've proved to me is Breandán is genuine, and you're selfish."

Ottarr furrowed his bushy brow. "Excuse me, m'lady?"

"Look at my son," Mara gestured toward the hillside. "Lochlann is happy because of Breandán's *genuine* interest in him." She purposely emphasized the word to accentuate her point. "Can you not see his happiness?" She knew Ottarr saw it, even though he'd never admit it, and continued to belabor her point. "If you continue to hold this ridiculous, groundless grudge upon a man who's done naught but put a smile on my son's face—Dægan's son— then you *are* the selfish man I pegged you to be."

Ottarr and Mara stared out into the field, watching as Breandán lifted Lochlann from his shoulders and knelt down before him. He exchanged some words with the lad, handed his bow to him, then moved to stand behind him. After some time of drawing the arrow together, they released it, paused, and reacted in joyous applause. Breandán praised him, and Lochlann drew another arrow from the quiver upon his back.

"Your bitterness will do no good except to surely break Lochlann's heart. Are you truly willing to hurt my son for the sake of your pride, Ottarr?"

"Dægan was like my own son. You know I'd never hurt his."

Finally, the old man softens. "Then help me," Mara said, placing her hand upon Ottarr's forearm.

He looked at where she'd touched him. "Help you do what?"

"Tait is supposed to return any day now. And you know as well as I, he'll not find Breandán's presence here appealing."

Ottarr cocked his brow. "And what makes you think I can make any headway with Tait? Nevan would be a better choice considering he was more apt to welcome the Irishman than anyone else on this isle."

"Tait has taken Nevan's advice into account before, but in the end, Tait does what he wants. You, however, he listens to. You were Dægan's advisor, and you're Tait's advisor now. Your long-standing relationship alone makes you more than competent to handle Tait."

"You flatter me well, my lady, but your words fail to convince me that I'll succeed."

"All I ask is that you try."

Her attention looped back to the distant hillside the moment she heard Breandán's cheers. She looked up in time to see Marcas standing beside her son as well, congratulating him for his superior marksmanship. "Wait until your mother sees," she thought she heard him say. Breandán then tousled Lochlann's hair and said, "Certainly. I'll go get her for you."

Her heart leapt at his approach. In light of her cantankerous company, she straightened her merry face and pretended that she hadn't heard Breandán or hadn't noticed him running toward her.

Ottarr eyed her inquisitively. "I see your interest in Breandán is not solely for Lochlann's sake, is it? Perhaps, you find the Irishman—"

"I find him sincere and dependable," she interrupted. "He's a friend, and no matter how you choose to see it, Ottarr, I cannot forget that he too had once put his life on the line for me. While in the hands of Domaldr, he would've given his life for me had it come to that. I saw it in his eyes."

Ottarr fed her words back to her as he stamped away. "Right. Because he's...*genuine*."

Chapter Nineteen

Excitement again vaulted in Mara's heart and shot straight up her spine, tingling the hairs on the back of her neck. She fell back against the door of her longhouse when she saw the broad smile on Breandán's face, and flattened her hands upon it for stability.

Breandán slowed his pace to a casual walk with a hint of a swagger to his gait as he drew near. "Good morning," he said pleasantly.

She exhaled at the delightful sound of his voice, trying to regain her composure. "A fine morning 'tis." She looked up at the overcast hovering about them. *What an idiotic thing to say.* The sound of a slamming door—Ottarr's, she suspected—erased Breandán's smile immediately.

"Is everything all right?"

"Ottarr and I were simply discussing Tait. He is due to return home any day now."

A quirky grin upturned the corner of his mouth. "And you fear this?"

Though Breandán never gave her the impression, she thought he too had some concern about Tait's return. "I think 'twould be wise for you to take caution with him."

He chuckled, and Mara noted it was the first time she'd ever heard him laugh.

"I appreciate the warning, but I'll be fine." Breandán glanced over his shoulder. "Have you a moment?"

She secretly pressed her fingertips against the wood of

the door again for support and could barely look away, or deny him, for that matter. His eyes could persuade her to put everything aside for this one span of time he requested.

"Your son wants to show you something," he added, ushering her up the hill.

Ah, Lochlann. She suddenly remembered his bow lessons. How could she forget? "Of course I have time for him. Has he made progress?"

"Lochlann has more than made progress this morning."

"Really," she said, at first pretending not to have any knowledge of it, but she couldn't keep it up for long. "I must admit...I was watching you." Heat flushed her face immediately as her words came out wrong. "I mean, I was watching you and Lochlann together. I'd heard his laughter from across the field and...and it was a beautiful sound." She looked down at her feet, counting the pace of her steps, feeling the weight of his eyes on her. "I'm grateful for the time you've given him today."

"He's a good boy. And he's not as lost as you think. He knows what he wants...and as he matures, he'll learn how to gain it—like his father."

Mara smiled. She doubted he knew how much his words of encouragement meant to her. To hear him commend Lochlann and measure him up to the larger-than-life warrior father his son aspired to be was quite gallant. Most men would've felt a sense of inferiority when speaking of Dægan. But not Breandán. He seemed very comfortable with Dægan's memory—*on many occasions*, she thought, recalling their conversation at the cliff's edge last night. What's more, Breandán's reason for saying such things wasn't for trying to win her affection, as Ottarr believed. It was because he cared, simple as that. And it was such a comfort to be with a man who wasn't out to gain something for himself through being with her.

"I'm simply here to see you and be with you as long as I'm allotted. Beyond that, I don't wish for more."

"You're smiling," he said with a cute little smirk. "Why?"

Her grin grew larger as she walked. "Why does anyone smile?"

"In my experience, it's because of happiness," he replied. "Are you happy, Lady Mara?"

The weight of his gaze pressed upon her, and she feared if she met his stare, she'd trip on her own two feet again and fall flat on her face. By the time she had the courage to answer, they had reached the crest of the small hill. Lochlann stood very still, his right arm bent with three fingers at his cheek, and his left extended in front of him. His legs were spread evenly with his shoulders. Everything about him was poised and patient. Without warning, he released his fingers from the taut string, and an arrow whizzed forward at great speed, hitting the makeshift target of hay and burlap dead center.

Mara's eyes widened in disbelief. She'd never given thought to her son being an excellent marksman. Especially so soon. *I'm very happy.*

Lochlann turned around to face her, a proud look upon his face. "Did you see, Mother?"

"How could I miss it?" she said.

"And that was only after a few tries," Breandán added. "Once I showed him how to properly hold the bow, he did the rest."

She flashed Breandán a look of gratitude, unable to hide her joy. This was a huge step for her son. He'd found a talent, a natural one. Something to help raise his self-esteem. Something to make him feel like he was a warrior's son. This was indeed a skill he possessed, and Breandán helped to bring it out in him.

"Now all he needs to do is grow into that bear cloak of his," Marcas jibed, shaking the boy's shoulders playfully.

She expected Lochlann to bristle at the ridiculing as that was his normal response to anything remotely negative in nature. But he grabbed Marcas around the legs and wrestled him to the ground in a fit of laughter. She appreciated that Marcas allowed her son to take him down, and that Breandán had made more headway with Lochlann than anyone else who'd ever tried.

"All right, you little Northman." Marcas grunted as he escaped the boy's grip and stood. "How about you show me that fish you were talking about this morning?"

Lochlann gathered himself to his feet, straightening his cloak. "You mean the water beast that could swallow you whole if he wanted to?"

"So you claim. But I'm not one to believe in fish stories. I have to see it with my own eyes."

"Do *you* want to see the water beast, Breandán?" Lochlann asked earnestly.

The two men exchanged that same peculiar glance as last night. "Perhaps later," Breandán replied. "I think your mother wants to try her hand at the bow."

Before she could argue, Lochlann shrugged and pulled Marcas along by his hand. Breandán had already begun to fetch the few arrows stuck in the target, and she crossed her arms. "I'm not shooting a bow."

"Oh, yes you are," Breandán said over his shoulder. He yanked three from the target and walked back to her. "I want to see if Lochlann comes by it honestly."

Her heart pitter-pattered in her chest. "I've never held a bow, nor do I think I can shoot one without hurting you or myself."

He stood directly in front of her, forcing her to look up. "You'll not hurt me."

She found it difficult to keep from glancing at the wide span of his shoulders and not think about the cords of long, hard muscle she knew were there beneath his leine. She tried to step backward, but her feet failed to budge. "And what if I hurt myself?"

"I'll not let that happen."

He reached for her hand, but it didn't occur to her what he was doing. All she could comprehend was the amazing warmth within his touch, the heat of his masculine fingers around her wrist. She barely realized he'd placed the bow within her grasp until he pressed her fingers around the wood with his own.

"Is it too heavy for you?" he asked, breaking the course of her thoughts.

She frowned at the absurdity of his question. "Of course not," she exclaimed and reestablished a grip upon the weapon. She assessed the distant target ahead and lined herself up with it, standing sideways, feet together. "Now what do I do?"

Breandán circled her slowly. He caught and held her gaze as he approached, his eyes gleaming against the darkened backdrop of gray sky. With the arrows still in hand, he clutched her shoulders squarely and wedged his thigh between hers.

"Spread your legs."

Aghast at his lewd command, she drew back. Then once he pushed his knee through the narrow space of her thighs and tapped his foot back and forth upon her ankles, she realized he was only adjusting her stance. She did as she was told, though she wished at this point she could've crawled into a hole. "Is this far enough?"

"Perfect."

Despite his positive reinforcement, she still felt inept. Her father had once taught her how to throw a dagger and how to use her forehead as a blunt object to break a man's nose, but it was so long ago. Shooting an arrow and hitting a target took skills she didn't think she had.

One try, she told herself. One arrow and then she'd be done.

"Now, pull back on the string as if readying yourself to release it. I want to see your form."

She exhaled deeply, knowing he meant to scrutinize her so he could correct her mistakes. "Must I?"

"'Tis important to hold the bow properly. These are fairly sharp, you know." He wagged the arrows in his hand before he set them on the ground. "Lochlann didn't fuss as much as you."

She was pretty sure Lochlann's heart didn't pound in his chest like hers did either.

Taking a deep breath, she pulled back on the string and held it. He reached up within the space of the open bow and turned her chin to face the target. "You have to look at your enemy in order to hit it," he joked.

She felt both of his hands now; one wrapped around her bow hand, clutching her fist with his own and steadying her, while the other pressed on her inner elbow. "And don't extend your elbow past this point, lest you hurt yourself when you release the string. Trust me, 'tis not pleasant."

Oh, but your touch is....

While he held firm to her bow hand, he raised her string fingers to the level of her cheek. "When you pull back, your fingers should come right to your lips and your elbow should be level." He laid his forearm across the top of hers to depict how parallel hers should be.

Her strength gradually diminished from holding the draw weight. It didn't help that he kept touching her on numerous parts of her body either. Her arms began to shake.

"All right, relax your arms," he directed. "You did very well."

She rested her cramping arms at her sides and felt both the burn of her muscles and the heat of her blush from his compliment.

"Are you ready for one of these now?" he asked, picking up an arrow.

To be honest, she wasn't. Her arms still ached, and she feared she'd only misfire.

He circled her slowly and stood behind her, lending a more enticing suggestion. "How about we shoot the first arrow together? Would that make you feel better?"

The only thing that made her feel better was that he couldn't see the sheer panic in her face. She clenched her jaw and reached deep down for an inkling of bravado. "There's less chance for me to shoot you if we do so together."

He laughed a deep, hearty laugh, and it branched out from behind her, titillating every nerve on the back of her neck. "There is that…" he agreed. "But more importantly, you wouldn't injure yourself." He wrapped his large palm around her fist. His grasp was solid as he lifted the weapon to its correct height. "Ready?"

"As I shall ever be," she breathed.

He directed the bow in front of her, flipping it at a horizontal plane so she could nock the arrow with ease. She felt his body press against her back as he reached around to instruct her. "Lay the head across the wood of the bow, and then take the tip between your index and middle fingers, affixing it on the string. There you go." His right hand took position with his three fingers lying directly over hers. He tested them first, making sure each knuckle sat comfortably within his fingertip grasp so as not to pinch her.

"Since we now have the arrow in place," he indicated in a quiet voice behind her ear, "we're going to raise and draw the bow at the same time. Understand?"

She nodded, unable to speak. Hot flashes and cold chills fluctuated throughout her body as she felt the sturdy wall of his chest at her back and the slightest hint of his breath upon her neck.

In one smooth motion, he brought the bow vertical and drew back the string, both of them poised in a fixed, rigid pose. If she thought his stance was indicative of a suggestive one before, this one had now tipped the scales. Heat radiated off his body and through her back, her arms, her cheek, and even the sides of her legs as he straddled her feet. To add to her torment, his whispered voice set her afire.

"Relax, Mara," he cajoled.

"I am."

"Nay, you're not. Look at your target. See it and don't be afraid of it."

"I'm not afraid of it," she defended.

She felt the corner of his mouth turn up into a smile. "Good. Now breathe in with me…then out…and release."

Together, they let the arrow fly, hitting the target near the top right corner. It wasn't a kill shot, but at least she'd made contact.

"All right, now your turn...all by yourself," he said, stepping back only inches.

She looked over her shoulder, still feeling his hovering presence. "I don't think so."

"I know you can do it. And you only injured the poor fellow. You need to put him out of his misery."

She laughed. "And what if I miss?"

He bent and picked up another arrow, reaching around her again to hand it to her. "You still have one more after this."

She sighed and snatched the arrow. "Fine. But this is the last time."

"Better make it count then," he teased.

She leveled the bow to a horizontal plane and nocked the arrow to the bowstring, linking her three knuckles around it.

"Remember, set your feet first, draw and aim in one motion, breathe, and release."

Right.

"Relax, Mara," she heard him say. But how could she? Even though he was no longer pressed against her, she could still feel him as though he were. The intoxicating smell of his skin, the silvery hum of his voice—they all distracted her.

Somehow, she found the initiative and drew the bow, finding an anchor point at her lips. She studied the target for a moment, took a breath in, and blew out slowly. As she released the arrow, she felt a gust of cool air blow past her earlobe, which caused her to flinch. The arrow, however, sank straight into its intended target, dead center.

"Well, look at that," Breandán said in surprise.

Mara whirled on her heel. "Did you blow in my ear?"

He winked. "I did, and you didn't let it distract you. Nicely done."

Didn't distract me? Little does he know....

Too absorbed in her archery lesson, Mara hadn't noticed that Ottarr stood behind them until he cleared his throat. When she peeked around Breandán, she saw a stern look of judgment on his bearded face.

"Tait's ships are approaching. You should take Breandán to your longhouse. 'Twould be best if he's not seen upon landing."

She nodded, understanding exactly what Ottarr was trying to do. "Have you sent for Nevan?"

"I have."

"What about Lochlann?" she asked. "He's with Marcas—"

"I'm not concerned about Lochlann or Marcas. Get to the longhouse, where Breandán will be safe."

Mara didn't push the old man or try to reform his ill manners for talking over Breandán as if he wasn't standing right beside her. She handed the bow to Breandán and motioned for him to follow.

Chapter Twenty

"'Tis going to be all right, you know."

Despite Breandán's words of confidence, Mara didn't feel at ease until they walked through her door and closed it behind them. And even then, she still felt anxious.

"I don't fear Tait's return," he tried again. "And there's no reason why you should either."

She gave him an odd look and paced deeper into the main room. "Perhaps you don't know him as well as you think you do."

"Oh, I remember him well. He roughed me up a few times when I first met him, but Dægan never allowed it to go much further."

She stopped in her tracks and glared. "Dægan is not here to protect you."

"Is that what Ottarr and Nevan are for? To protect me?"

Yes, Ottarr and Nevan were the very men she'd hoped would be able to talk Tait down, to make him see Breandán as a friend and not a foe. But even as she had total faith in their abilities to underplay Breandán's presence, and persuade the gruff Northman not to react hastily, she still feared Tait's anger would get the better of him.

She paced some more. When that didn't help, she sat on the closest boxbed and wrung her hands in her tunic.

Breandán studied her overwhelming apprehension and sat beside her. "Why do you fear Tait so much?"

She looked at him, her eyes soft and compassionate, far gentler than the severity of before. If he didn't know any better, he swore she might actually have cared about him—more than he realized.

"I fear what Tait will say…and what he may do."

Her words pulled at his heart. "The only way he can hurt me is if he harms you, and I suspect he'd never do anything of detriment toward his best friend's widow." He reached out and took her hand in his, a reaction he barely had control over. She closed her eyes as though she longed for his touch. "You're trembling." He gathered both her hands and cupped them in his own, squeezing gently.

She bit her lip.

Compulsion overtook him, and he reached up, cradling her face while he brushed his thumb over her bottom lip. "Don't hurt your lip over me."

The look on her face gave him the impression she was about to lean her cheek into his palm. He held his hand there and relished the creamy smoothness of her face and the delicate lines of her rosy lips. His head spun from gazing at her, and he tried to work out whether he was being drawn into this moment by her coercion or by his own desire. There was something in her expression that moved him. The way her lips parted. The way she glanced at his mouth in preparation for a kiss.

He swallowed hard, convincing himself this was not the time or the place, especially with the threat of Tait drawing near. The last thing he wanted to do was have the ill-tempered Northman walk into the longhouse and find him kissing Mara. He'd rather not give the man a legitimate reason to kill him.

The door of the longhouse was flung open, and there stood Tait, practically foaming at the mouth like a rabid dog. It was obvious that he'd ignored everything Ottarr and Nevan might have said to soothe his hostility, and looked as if anything could set him off.

Mara and Breandán dropped their hands and stood, neither willing to provoke him. Out of concern for Mara and her safety, Breandán slowly turned to face Tait head-on and protectively placed her behind his body.

"You bastard!" Tait growled and charged forward. His fist came out of nowhere and struck Breandán across the left eye.

Breandán fell onto the boxbed, feeling a warm wetness pour into his eye. He quickly wiped the slick blood from his vision and tackled Tait around the knees, bringing him to the floor. Tait was a powerful man, but Breandán had a clear mindset and agility on his side. His only goal was to keep Tait from striking out.

Though he struggled to outmaneuver the aggressive Norse brute, Breandán successfully rolled Tait facedown on the floor and seized his right arm. He bent it up behind him and laid it along Tait's spine, holding him in a secure position short of either breaking the man's wrist or popping his shoulder out of its socket.

"I don't want to fight you, Tait," Breandán gritted through his teeth. As he straddled the Northman's back and pinned him to the floor, his attention came to Mara. "Get out of here!"

Tait fought like a madman to get up, swinging, kicking, snarling. Breandán could've kept him down, but it would have required punching him in the kidneys or across the back of the head. He wasn't comfortable with injuring a man Mara deemed to be family. "Mara, I said get out!"

She didn't listen to him, and only added to his struggle. Finally, Tait exploited Breandán's limitations and surged to his feet, unsheathing his dagger.

Breandán jumped to his feet as well, knowing Tait had to be subdued. There was no other alternative. It was either that or someone was going to get seriously hurt. He feared it might be Mara.

With only a few seconds to decide, Tait rushed at him and slashed the knife across his midline. Breandán jumped back, and the blade missed its target. Fortunately for him, the crazed Northman had so much momentum that it carried his upper body forward face-down, allowing Breandán to feed Tait's head under his arm and in a choke hold before Breandán crashed to his back. The drive of their fall caused Tait's forehead to hit the floor, knocking him silly.

Breandán knew Tait wasn't finished. The man was stunned, for sure, but not at point of giving up. "Tait, if you don't stop this madness, I'll be forced to choke you out." Breandán tightened the vise around Tait's neck, and Tait struggled violently to pull his head from Breandán's clutches.

Breandán increased the leverage under Tait's jaw and cut off the blood supply to his brain. He wasn't about to give the man leniency anymore, especially since the idiot had pulled a knife on him. He advised Tait once more, "Give up, Northman, lest I put you to sleep."

Tait continued to jerk and writhe, leaving Breandán with no other choice but to apply the last bit of pressure to his throat. It took a few seconds more, but eventually, Tait's body wilted and collapsed across Breandán's legs.

He sighed and released the Northman, collapsing on the floor himself in exhaustion.

Mara ran to Breandán and slid to her knees, her voice and hands both trembling as she saw that his left brow was split and bleeding. "Are you all right?" She lifted the corner of her tunic to his wound.

He nodded, breathless as he watched her gaze fall across Tait.

"Did you kill him?"

Breandán sat up, though his weakened body was not quite ready to do so. The muscles in his arms ached and burned from ratcheting Tait's neck. He ignored the pain and looked her in the eye. "He's only sleeping, Mara. I swear to you. He's not dead."

Blood trickled from his brow and streamed down his face. She gathered more of her tunic and pressed the wad of cloth above his eye. He wanted to comfort her, to tell her he barely felt the sting of the gash. But in came Ottarr, Nevan, and a third Northman, shocked as they laid eyes upon Tait's motionless body.

A streak of anger flashed on Ottarr's face, and Breandán knew he had only moments to explain before he'd have another angry Northman to wrestle. "I've not killed him. He's merely sleeping."

"Sleeping?" Ottarr snarled between his teeth. The idea sounded even more preposterous as he repeated it.

"I tried to get Tait to calm down, but he drew his dagger. And with Mara in here—"

"Well done," Nevan interrupted. "How long will he be…" There was a sense of hilarity in the king's voice as he cocked his head. "Asleep?"

"Not long, I'm afraid. When he does wake, rest assured he'll have a splitting headache."

"And you?" Nevan asked, eyeing Mara curiously. "Are you all right?"

"I am."

"Good," Nevan declared emotionless. He glanced at the Northmen at his side. "We've all seen the furious side of Tait. Let's not wait around any longer to see his enraged side. Ottarr, Gunnar. Carry him to the mead hall. And tie him up too."

Ottarr and Gunnar did as they were told, though neither looked pleased as they lifted Tait's body. Breandán knew he walked on eggshells when it came to the Norse on the isle, and now with this little incident, he'd crushed all hope of earning their favor.

"My apologies to you, Nevan, for the trouble I've caused you."

"Nonsense," Nevan replied, crossing his arms. "We all expected Tait's abhorrence with your presence—though no one would've predicted this outcome. My apologies to you for not getting here sooner. I'm merely grateful no one was hurt, especially Mara." He smiled at her for a long moment before addressing Breandán again. "We have much to discuss now that Tait is here. I shall send for you when he awakens."

As Breandán watched the king leave, he wasn't exactly looking forward to facing everyone in the mead hall. He was glad for the king's support, but a bit nervous as to how little the Northmen would care for his opinions after their chieftain had been rendered unconscious and defeated.

Defeated.

The notion of bringing the Norse chieftain to his knees should've brought a smile to his face, but frankly, he wished there could've been some other way. At least for

Tait to have kept his dignity in the process.

He recalled the heated struggle. The repeated warnings he'd given the Northman in hopes he'd come to his senses. The fool proved to be too stubborn and too blinded by his own rage to foresee his own defeat.

Mara stood to gather water from a ewer and some clean cloths from the storage, fixed on tending his wound. Breandán made an attempt to follow her, but she came rushing back to him on the floor.

"Stay," Mara said, falling to her knees. "Let me help you."

He looked at her and sensed her reluctance. He didn't think it was the sight of blood that caused her to be shaken. She'd seen enough of it in her day. "I'm well. Don't fret over me."

She ignored him and soaked the cloths in the cool water, seemingly deep in thought as she wrung them out.

"Is it that bad?" he asked.

His words brought her back to reality, and she forced a half smile, shaking her head. She didn't reply, but she took great pains to be careful as she cleaned his laceration.

"I'm sorry I caused you so much distress. I hope you understand Tait gave me no choice once he pulled his dagger."

Mara met his gaze for a split second and went back to her task, wiping the damp linen down his jaw and neck. "You did what you had to."

Breandán battled with an impulse to embrace her, to comfort her. As an alternative, he let the moments tick by, hoping to give her time to recuperate. He recalled this morning's archery lesson and how wonderful it was to interact with her and see her smile. He wanted her to get back to that moment, back to when she felt secure with him. Comfortable. As he focused on the way her hand trembled and the unsteadiness of her breathing, he knew she wasn't comfortable anymore. He couldn't begin to imagine the things she mulled over.

"What are you afraid of?" he asked.

Mara's gaze jumped to his. She pressed the wadded-up linen upon his brow, trying to stop the bleeding with pressure. She held it for some time before she spoke. "I was afraid Tait was going to kill you."

He smiled, appreciative of her concern, but she didn't understand his question. He reached up and covered her hand, helping her to press the linens more firmly against his brow. "I mean…what are you afraid of now?"

Chapter Twenty-one

Mara stared at Breandán's hand clutching hers, her mind caught in a whirlwind. The whole time Tait and Breandán were fighting, she was beside herself with worry, especially after seeing the look in Tait's eyes when he drew his dagger. He had every intention of killing Breandán on the spot, and she knew it. But she had no idea she'd feel this much when it came to Breandán's safety.

If not for Tait lying motionless on her longhouse floor, she would've embraced Breandán like she'd never hugged him before. And probably even kissed him. She closed her eyes, trying to sort out her scrambling emotions and an answer to Breandán's question.

"What are you afraid of now?"

"You can tell me," Breandán encouraged.

She opened her eyes as she felt his tender touch across her cheekbone while together they still held pressure to his brow.

"I'm afraid..." The words she wanted to say didn't sound right in her head. She tried another way. "I think I want to kiss you. I think. But...I'm afraid. I'm afraid when I close my eyes, all I'll see is Dægan. And that's not fair to you. I don't want to hurt you."

She watched that thought tumble around in his head as he tucked a strand of loose hair behind her ear. She assumed he might take his hands from her and slip back into the reserved gentleman he'd always been. Strangely, he didn't seem interested in letting her go and still held tight to her hand upon his wound.

"Is that all you're afraid of?"

His stare captured her as he gazed deep into her eyes. He was such a beautiful man, patient and thoughtful. She could only nod.

Breandán released his left hand from hers and cradled her face, though she remained holding pressure above his eye. He caressed her cheek ever so lightly. "If you fear you'll only see Dægan when you close your eyes, then leave them open."

Her heart stopped as he drew near. Her breath caught as his eyes fell on her lips. He was going to kiss her. He was actually going to kiss her, and she hadn't the will to stop him.

She wanted this.

Wanted it more now than ever.

Chills shivered up her spine, and heat pooled at her core. It had been so long since she'd felt the anticipation of a man's kiss, she barely remembered how those sensations felt. As his lips hovered over hers, he spoke in a heated whisper.

"Open your eyes, Mara. Open them and know 'tis I who kisses you."

She dragged them open, his voice like a subtle touch, soothing and erotic. He held her spellbound with his gaze and softly pressed his lips to hers. All she could see and feel was him. All she could think about was how wonderful his mouth felt on hers, how sensual and passionate his kiss was.

"Breathe, *a thaisce*."

Until he spoke, she hadn't realized she was holding her

breath and was doubly amazed he was perceptive enough to notice.

He slowly pulled away, his gaze still captivating her. "Tell me," he whispered. "Who did you see?"

A smile graced her lips. "Only you."

He smiled with her and returned his grasp upon her hand clutching the blood-stained linen at his brow. "I know you love Dægan. And I know he still occupies a significant place in your heart. But I'm not here to replace him. Nor will I ever try. I only wish to fill the space that's left, if you'll let me."

His kind, heartfelt words flowed like a cool river through her heated soul. But she was still unconvinced she needed this. Needed him.

Oh, I want him. Her body told her that. But needing him was quite a different matter. She was a mother now, whose main concern was her son. And what would Lochlann think of this? What would he think about Breandán being in her life?

She didn't want to make Lochlann feel second best, or make him think she didn't love his own father anymore. Lochlann, being six, only had the mind of a six-year-old, and those thoughts would no doubt run through his brain. Having been without a father for so long, he might not take well to someone else in his life.

Then she remembered this morning, when Breandán had carried her son on his shoulders and the sound of his laughter filled her ears. Lochlann had warmed up to Breandán, so much so that she began to think he might be open to the idea of Breandán as a father.

She blinked back the sound of those words. *A father? Where did that come from?*

She'd never given thought to anyone being a father to

Lochlann. She could barely bring herself to think it when Tait had suggested Gunnar as a suitable husband. But with Breandán, the idea seemed to come naturally. And it didn't scare her to imagine it. If anything, it brought her a sense of peace. A sense of knowing Lochlann would be better for it. That having Breandán in his life would be what was best for him.

And if her son was happy, she was too.

If only she could stop feeling guilty for feeling happiness. If only she could kiss Breandán without thinking how it would affect everyone else and, though it hardly mattered, how it would make Dægan feel. That was the hardest of all. She felt she needed his permission.

"Are you all right?" Breandán asked. "Did I say something wrong?"

She inhaled deeply and met his eyes. "Nay, you're correct. I do love Dægan, and I always will." Her gaze fell as she could no longer look him in the eye. "I'd like to think I have a place in my heart for you, considering all you've done for me in the past, and what you continue to do for me now. But I'm not certain I have any heart left. I gave all of mine to Dægan."

It broke her heart to hurt Breandán, but she felt she had to let him know. It pained her to want him so badly and to hold back for fear Dægan wouldn't approve.

A tear slipped from her eye and slowly trickled down her cheek. Breandán reached out with his free hand and caught it with his finger, lifting her chin in the process. "If you haven't a heart left, then take all of mine."

A smile flitted across her lips. "How can you be so witty at a time like this? How is it you know exactly what to say to me?"

Breandán slid his hand along her jaw and threaded his fingers in her hair. "I've never been good with words. But when I'm with you, they seem to emerge straight from my heart to my mouth." He leaned forward now, his eyes darker. "Love is not a choice, Mara. 'Tis what happens. Naturally."

She wanted to look away, to keep from glancing at his beautiful lips, especially his bottom one. It was fuller than his top, and she, despite her effort, was hopelessly drawn to it. She wanted to feel his kiss again. To kiss him more deeply and with her tongue. But she knew she shouldn't. She wasn't ready to feel that kind of passion from him. Not now, when her mind was still spinning.

"I need time," she whispered. She saw the subtle flinch of disappointment in his expression, and he squared his shoulders.

"Of course you do. I imagine Nevan will be sending for me soon anyway." As he drew back, he pulled her hand from his brow, removing the need for her closeness as well. "I don't mean to press anything upon you, but now would be a good time to let me know what you decided about your father. If you want to go to him, I'll not leave your side. It has become increasingly dangerous for you to travel across Connacht with him in such a vulnerable state. If you choose not to, then this meeting with Nevan and Tait will be rather unnecessary."

Mara's heart sank. "And what does that mean for you? Would you leave the isle?"

"I wouldn't want to, Mara, but the reasons that hold me here will not please Tait. And I've already caused enough trouble for you."

She knew this day would come, but between the joy Breandán had brought to her and the friendship he'd won with her son, she hadn't had much time to ponder her choice.

Breandán had admitted he'd stay because of her. But if she decided she didn't want to see her father, then she'd be taking away his only reputable excuse. She'd be forcing him to leave, and leave he would. She believed it because this was Breandán. He'd always put her first above his own desires. And even now, as they sat alone on her longhouse floor, when there was virtually nothing to stop him, he put aside his deep-rooted yearnings and remained honorable.

"Mara," he whispered, covering her knotted fist with his palm. "Don't let anything sway you—not me, not Tait, or even the dangers you may face. If you want to see your father, I shall take you. And not because Cathal Mac Conor has ordered me to, but because I want to. Your safety is all I care about, and I'll protect you with every breath I take."

Honorable indeed. "And what about the dangers you face, Breandán, if I choose not to go? The ones Angus mentioned. What has my father threatened you with?"

Breandán inhaled deeply. "I was hoping you'd forget Angus's words."

"Hardly. Especially when it involves putting you or your family in the path of my father's menace. I've learned a great deal about my father in these last seven years and what he's capable of. And if he's threatened you in any way, I want to know."

"That is all they are. Threats. Naught more."

"To you perhaps, but I've never known my father not to carry out the threats he makes."

Breandán drew near again, his eyes as honest as she'd ever seen them. "And I've never known him to forsake his daughter either, but he certainly did."

She swallowed, his proximity thwarting every ounce of restraint. Her body yearned to be closer to him, to feel the warmth of his arms and to smell the deep, rich scent of his skin. If she fell into his embrace now, she'd never want to leave.

"If I don't go to my father, I fear I'll regret it. At least if I go, I can find the answers I've been asking for so long. Am I wrong for wanting those things?"

He smiled kindly. "Of course not. You have a right to know. Though," he said, pausing, "I imagine his reason, if he tells you at all, may be hard to swallow."

Mara narrowed her eyes. "Why do you say that?"

Breandán rid the bloodied linen from her grasp and took hold of her hands. "Your father and Nevan have an unsettled feud between them, yet they both allow you to stay on this isle without question. Don't you find that odd?"

"I do," Mara agreed, watching his thumbs pass over the tops of her knuckles. "I've asked Nevan about it many times, but he won't discuss it. He says it was a long time ago and only time can rectify it." A thought suddenly came to her. "How did you know about their quarrels?"

"When I first came here and spoke of my purpose, the islanders drew their swords upon me as soon as I mentioned Cathal Mac Conor's name. After that, Nevan had admitted to their shared hostility but shrugged it off and insisted his men do the same. If I had to guess, Nevan seemed...almost pleased by the news of your father's failing health."

"Pleased?" Mara asked. "Or perhaps relieved their feud would soon be over?"

"Is there a difference?"

"Nay. Nor does it matter, I suppose."

Breandán squeezed her hands tenderly. "Are you sure this is what you want?"

She closed her eyes, hiding the burn of her long-repressed tears. "It is."

"Then I'll certainly convey your wishes when Tait awakens." Mara opened her mouth to speak, but he said, "Shh, *a thaisce.* Tait shouldn't be your concern. He's done his worst, and the most he can do now is berate me for what I've done to him."

"And what if he deems you unfit to escort me to my father?"

Breandán's eyes danced with delight. "Are you saying you'd want me to accompany you, then?"

"Yes, I am," Mara professed. "If I had to choose anyone to take me to my father, 'twould be you."

"Then it shall be done."

Chapter Twenty-two

"Untie me!" Tait bellowed.

He sat in a chair, adjacent to Nevan at the head of the assembly in the mead hall, tied to its arms and legs. Bound like a hostage, he glared at everyone in the hall, but no one budged to help him. No one had the gall, especially after Nevan had given strict orders.

Breandán gazed around the room at the many men gathered there. Some he recognized, while others he couldn't name. One thing was for certain: the tension in the room was thick, even more than when he was confronted by Ottarr and the other islanders upon his landing. Beyond the overall hostility, there were some men who seemed pleased that he'd taken down the bear, so to speak. Irishmen, he imagined. The others, who wore their displeasure like a crown, were presumably Northmen. Among those most aggrieved were Gunnar and Ottarr.

Breandán sat at one of the benches in the spacious room, with Marcas on his left. While some found seats near them, he still felt isolated amid the group. It was hard to feel comfortable when everyone stared and murmured behind their drinking horns.

He tried to ignore their judgmental looks and brushed the rain droplets from the soft surface of his dove-gray hare cloak. The storm had finally hit with full fury over the isle when they'd summoned him from Mara's longhouse, and he anticipated an even bigger storm would soon erupt within these sturdy walls.

"Shall we begin?" Nevan asked from his central throne, glancing around the room. "We have much to discuss and little time to come to a mutual decision."

"Mutual?" Tait growled. "How can anything be mutual when I'm held bound against my will! I'm a chieftain on this isle, and I refuse to be treated in this manner!"

Nevan glanced dispassionately at Tait. "And as your king, I refuse to let you treat our guests in such a manner. We were respectful enough to await your return before coming to a ruling, so I suggest you hold your tongue lest I be forced to remove you from this assembly and make the decree myself. Agreed?"

As a reply, Tait exhaled through flared nostrils and glared at Breandán for the degrading lecture he just received in front of his fellow men.

"Breandán Mac Liam," Nevan summoned, his voice carrying throughout the room. "Would you please deliver the message you were asked to bring forth by Mara's father, Cathal Mac Conor."

Breandán saw the sharp jerk of Tait's head in Nevan's direction and the bewilderment in his eyes. He wasn't sure what had made Tait react so strongly, but then again, he hadn't understood anyone's conduct on the isle when it came to the reference of the Connacht king.

Reluctantly, he stood and transferred the message, tracing his gaze around the room as he spoke. "Cathal Mac Conor is on his deathbed, and he has but one dying wish." He glanced at Tait now, wondering how he'd respond to the next part. "He asks to see his daughter."

Tait's eyes widened and fixed on Nevan again. "Am I to believe, since my mouth is not gagged, I have permission to address this so-called assembly?"

Nevan gave one deep nod. "As long as you can do so with a civil tongue."

Tait grimaced as he eyed Breandán. "If you're merely Cathal's messenger, then why are you still here? You could've conveyed your king's wishes to Nevan and been on your merry way."

Breandán heard the sarcasm in Tait's voice, hinting at the idea that Breandán could've avoided confrontation had he left before Tait returned. He wanted to smile but thought better of it. "With the dangers Mara would face in traveling across Connacht, I'm also here as her escort."

"And what dangers would those be?"

"Duncan Mac Flann. He is the High King of Ireland and has once fought with the Uí Briúin and failed. Since he's succeeded Nial Glundubh, he's made many threats upon us, and with Cathal in such ill condition, he knows the Connacht men are at their most vulnerable. 'Tis very likely he'll strike, especially if he knows the king's daughter is venturing through Connacht lands."

Tait scoffed. "And Cathal sends..." He glanced at Breandán and Marcas with derision, "a mere two men to see to his daughter's safety."

Breandán actually found humor in the Northmen's assessment. "That's where you come in. I assume since you care deeply for Mara, you'd not agree to such a thing without the insistence of your own men supplementing our efforts."

"You're correct in one assumption—that I'd be adamant about my own men protecting Mara. But you've gone amiss with the other...thinking I'd allow you to come with us."

"You'll need me," Breandán said plainly.

Tait chuckled. "Is that so?"

"The usual path you travel to Connacht will be the one Duncan expects us to take. If you want to keep Mara safe, you'll need me to show you the alternative routes. Some are a bit treacherous, but better than walking into an ambush."

"Your concerns have been noted, but we'll do fine without you."

"That is not good enough," Breandán declared. "Mara deserves your utmost protection, and I'll not slight her safety to accommodate your pride."

"I have to agree with Breandán on this," Nevan said.

"Have you lost your mind, Nevan? Do you not know who this man is?"

"Indeed I do." Nevan stood from his chair. "He is the very man who, seven summers ago, was determined to save Mara from the perils of Domaldr Ræliksen's ruthless ambitions. He was also the man who had saved Dægan from the fires of death ignited by his own brother, and then aided him in breaching Cathal Mac Conor's walls. While I know Breandán brought Domaldr to our shores, you know as well as I, Domaldr would've found his way here, with or without Breandán's aid. Furthermore, I believe Breandán's actions that terrible night gave all of us a forewarning of Domaldr's intent—yet we simply underestimated it. And I'll not make the same mistake again with Duncan Mac Flann."

Tait thrashed in the chair, furious. "Nevan, I beg you to reconsider."

The king looked over at the Northman to his right. "The decision has been made. Breandán will lead the best of both my men and yours through Connacht. This includes Ottarr and Gunnar. And you, Tait, will stay on the isle with me."

If not for the ropes confining Tait's limbs, Breandán swore he would've choked the life from the king. His eyes turned dark as he clenched his jaw.

"Give me one good reason why I'm not permitted to go along on this journey and protect the widow of my former chieftain?"

"I shall give you two," Nevan retorted, crossing his arms. "Thordia is due to have your child any day. She'll need you more than Mara will. And secondly, Breandán will have his hands full evading a possible ambush from Duncan Mac Flann. He needn't watch his back as well."

Tait's face turned a deep shade of red, but Nevan hardly gave it notice. "All right men, settle in for the night. Eat your fill. Enjoy your wives. Tomorrow morning, first light, you leave for Connacht under Breandán Mac Liam's command. Ottarr and Gunnar, when the storm subsides, prepare the ships."

Everyone rose slowly from their benches and straggled out the door, mumbling to each other about the trip ahead. Gunnar, however, came to his chieftain's aid, his dagger in his hand for cutting Tait's ropes.

"Leave him," Nevan said. "He and I still have to talk."

Gunnar gave Tait a pitying look but waited for his permission. When Tait gave it, Gunnar sheathed his dagger and plodded past Breandán, purposely running his shoulder into his.

****

Nevan waited until everyone had left the mead hall before standing and unsheathing his own dagger from his belt. He held the blade at the ropes at Tait's wrists and paused, eyeing Tait cautiously. "Surely you know what this means."

Tait glared at Nevan. "I do. It means you've willingly turned your back on me by siding with a traitor."

He rolled his eyes and sighed, giving up on the idea of cutting Tait free. Instead, he paced the room. "God's teeth, Tait, could you open your eyes for one moment and see beyond yourself?" He clenched the dagger in his hand and spoke as calmly as he could bear. "For years I've waited for this. Waited for that bastard Cathal Mac Conor to either spill his guts of the truth to Mara or die." He turned on his heel toward Tait. "Do you know how difficult it has been for me to stand by as Mara's true father and watch her suffer, watch her grieve for Dægan? Yes, I've comforted her as best I could, but being bound to this vile secret of a despicable man's doing has nearly brought me to my knees. Countless times, I've wanted to tell Mara the truth, only to be halted by my own honor. By my own vow to a man to whom I owe nothing!" Nevan felt his hands tremble with anger as he stared at the well-whetted blade of his knife. "Cathal took from me the only woman I've ever loved and then had the audacity to claim and raise *my daughter* as his own. The day has finally come when I'll get what is rightfully mine." His eyes burned with raging hot tears. "And you'll not deny me my redemption."

Tait held Nevan's glare. "Is that what you think I'd do? You really think me that selfish?"

"If we're speaking of the man who tried to take Breandán's life in Mara's own home, then aye. I think you that selfish."

"You don't know Breandán well enough to judge me. If Dægan were here, he would've done the same."

"If that is what you need to convince yourself, then so be it. But I know better. Dægan was a man who contemplated the consequences of his actions well before jumping into them. And you're nothing like him." Nevan knew his words incited Tait's temper again, but at this point, he hardly cared. He only hoped to strike a chord with the Northman and get him to see he was wrong for what he'd done.

He watched Tait breath heavily through his teeth, waiting for the Northman to counter. It took a while before he finally found a courteous tongue.

"Why do you favor this Breandán so much? Have I been gone so long that you've forgotten my loyalty toward you? Toward your people? Toward your daughter? I'd give my life to protect Mara and anyone else on this isle. You know this. What can Breandán possibly bring to her that I've not already given?"

Nevan closed his eyes and let his head fall back. "You're so blind, my friend." He let Tait ponder those words. But Tait's silence proved he had no idea what Nevan was talking about, or that he was too stubborn to admit it. "From the moment Mara caught sight of Breandán on this isle, she has been...content. Happy. He's brought her joy the likes of which no other man has been capable."

"Enough!" Tait barked, shaking his head.

"Mara has hardly found reason to smile since Dægan left her."

"I said that is enough, Nevan."

"And Breandán loves her. I can see it in his eyes. The way he looks at her, the way he embraced her when she ran to him. Yes, she was thrilled to see him, and he, her."

In the chair he was bound to, Tait scooted in little hops, as though to shield his sensitive ears from such blasphemy. When that was not enough, he began humming loudly, blocking out Nevan's steady discourse.

"...and Mara may not realize it yet, but she needs Breandán. Lochlann needs him."

Tait twisted his head around. "How dare you bring Dægan's son into this!"

"'Tis true, Tait. Lochlann needs a man in his life to teach him things only a father can—"

"I can teach him," Tait said fiercely. "I can teach him everything Dægan would have."

"When?" Nevan asked. "The boy is six years old, and you've yet to find the time to teach him anything. I'm no fool, Tait. Mara has begged it of you many times, and still the boy goes without your attention—at no fault of your own, mind you. You have your own son to raise. But Breandán has already taught Lochlann how to shoot a bow. And, I think, given time, he can break down the boy's walls and reach him where everyone else has failed. Including myself."

"Untie me, now," Tait said shakily.

Nevan looked down at the dagger in his hands, considering the idea. "You certainly are that selfish man. And it pains me to see you sink to such a level. Perhaps the only way for you to see above your haughty self is for you to crawl upon your knees as Dægan once did."

He walked around the chair and faced Tait, lending the impression he was going to cut him loose, but, instead, drove his dagger into the wood beam high above the Northman's reach. He then strolled casually down the length of the mead hall. From behind, he heard Tait curse and cause as much commotion as he could from his limited confines. Nevan opened the large wooden door and stepped into the pouring rain with no desire to look back.

Chapter Twenty-three

Tait knew he'd been sitting alone, trussed to his chair in the mead hall for no more than a few minutes. But it seemed like hours as he stewed in anger, and his only means of escaping was tauntingly four feet above his head.

He stared at Nevan's dagger as if willing it to fall to his lap. He swore when he was freed, he'd walk right up to Nevan and punch his teeth in. As soon as he thought it, he knew he'd never do such a thing. He and the king were too close friends, but he certainly wanted to.

He pulled harder at the twine around his wrists, trying to narrow his fists enough to squeeze out of the knots, but to no avail. The skin around his hands had now reddened to the point of bleeding, and his head pounded like a war drum. He changed his mind. He'd punch the man who tied these wretched knots. Finally, the door of the longhouse opened and in stepped Gunnar, the one man he longed to see.

"My lord," Gunnar breathed as he ran to the aid of his chieftain, unsheathing his dagger from his belt.

Tait didn't say a word as Gunnar cut his wrists free. He just rubbed the life back into them and waited as Gunnar worked at his leg restraints.

Gunnar glanced up warily before totally liberating him. "Why did Nevan leave you this way?"

Tait didn't have the stomach to discuss his indecorous treatment at the moment. He was too humiliated for conversation. He snatched the dagger from Gunnar's hand and cut his own ankles free.

Gunnar tried another approach. "You need not worry over the goods in our ships. We were able to unload everything from our merchant journey before the rain came."

Tait remained unemotional. "How long was I out?"

"Long enough to empty four ships."

Tait grimaced, his distaste for what Breandán had done to him gurgling up his throat like sour bile. "Did my son... Does he know?"

Gunnar nodded reluctantly.

Tait took a long deep breath, trying to accept the fact that Alfarinn had seen his own father lose to another man. It was utterly demeaning, and it only fed his desire to redeem himself.

"Are you truly not going with us to Connacht on the morrow?"

Tait pressed his palm into his eye. He loathed Nevan for overriding everything he'd said in council as if he were no longer capable of leading his people. Aye, Mara was Nevan's true daughter, and he had a right to voice his concerns when it came to her welfare. But she was also his late friend's widow and, in his loyal head, that made her as much his responsibility as Nevan's.

Tait looked at Gunnar long and hard. "Nevan is correct. If I go, I'll only end up wanting to kill Breandán. So I'm counting on you to be there in my stead." Tait noticed a fire burning in Gunnar now, and it pleased him.

"What is it you want me to do?"

"I want you to keep your eye on Breandán. I never trusted that man, especially after he'd told Dægan—to his face— that he was in love with Mara. I was barely able to hold Dægan back from killing him right then and there, and I know if Dægan were here now, no matter what Nevan thinks, he would've put a stop to this. He would not allow that Irishman to even think of gaining Mara's love. You," Tait added, pointing a stern finger at Gunnar, "need to make certain Mara comes back alive, safe and sound. I owe it to Dægan to see to her safety, and if you do this, I'll reward you. Tenfold."

"My lord?" Gunnar asked, not grasping the full picture.

Tait leaned forward for emphasis. "What is it you most desire?"

Gunnar drew his face backward. "You know what I've always wanted. Mara."

"Then I'll grant you her hand in marriage the day you bring her back from Connacht unscathed. I'll gladly reward your loyalty, since everyone else on this isle seems to have forgotten mine."

"What will Nevan say?" Gunnar asked in concern.

"He had no qualms about going over my head this day. And so I've no reservations about going over his." Tait put a hand on the man's shoulder. "Do not fail me, Gunnar."

****

Tait left the mead hall with his mind in shambles. Though he gave Gunnar specific instructions, he still had his doubts. If he were to go to Connacht himself, he'd feel much better about Mara's safety. But he knew the king was right, and he needed to stay close to his expectant wife. The birth of his child was very important to him, and he didn't want to miss it.

As he hurried to his own longhouse, he was glad of two things: the rain had finally ended, and Thordia would be there to greet him. She always was. Even when he'd be gone for only a short trip into Galway's port, she'd greet him with an embrace so tight, he thought she'd been given both his war god's name and strength.

He opened the door and stepped inside. His first sight was of his precious Thordia and her smile. She came to him and hugged him fiercely around his neck, her large round belly jutting into his pelvis. He relished the feel of her soft, swelled body and cradled in his arms two of the most precious things in his life. He drew back a bit so he could admire her better. She looked different—more beautiful, if that were possible. Her blue eyes sparkled as she smiled, her golden hair shone, and her breasts, now plump from the pregnancy, ballooned in the most enticing display of cleavage he'd ever seen.

He dared to cup them and find out just how wonderfully heavy they'd feel in his hands, but his son ran in and joined their embrace, hugging him around his legs.

"Hello, Father," Alfarinn said, regarding him with concern. "I was scared that man hurt you."

Tait's irritation returned. Not with his son, but because of the humiliation he'd suffered and the fear Breandán had put in Alfarinn's head. The only thing Tait could be thankful of right now was that Alfarinn didn't actually use Breandán's name.

Thordia tousled Alfarinn's hair. "As you can see, your father is well."

Tait eyed his wife and realized she too had been worried. "Your mother is right," he said, pretending to pass off his loss as a minor setback. "The Irishman did naught I cannot recover from."

Alfarinn looked up at him with utter confusion. "But he won the fight. I thought no man was stronger than you, Father."

Tait bypassed his family and reined in his temper as best he could. "He simply won a battle, Alfarinn, but he will not win the war."

Thordia cocked her head in concern, watching her husband shake with fury. "Alfarinn, why don't you run along and play now that the rain has ceased? Your father has had a trying day."

Disappointed, Alfarinn padded out the door, and his wife planted her hands on her hips. "He'll not win the war? What is that supposed to mean, Tait?"

Tait slumped onto the nearest boxbed, releasing a heavy sigh. "Don't be naïve, Thordia. You know well what it means. I've been disgraced in front of my men, my family, this entire isle. Even my own son thinks less of me. I'll regain my dignity before this is all said and done."

Thordia approached him and dropped to her knees between his legs. "I don't favor this side of you. 'Tis not the man I know and love. Ottarr told me what you did. That you pulled a knife on Breandán and aimed to kill him. Do you not know how difficult it was for me to see you carried out of Mara's longhouse like that? I thought you dead. My heart broke in two seeing you lifeless and…"

Her voice cracked as her lower lip trembled. Tait reached up and touched her face, stroking her cheek. "I am well."

"Because Breandán allowed you to be," Thordia said scornfully. "He could've easily killed you but was the bigger man because he did not."

She could've kicked him in the groin and it would've

hurt less. His heart bled. "Is that what you think?"

Thordia took his hand in hers. "You had no good reason for turning on Breandán as you did."

Tait jerked his hand away from her tender grasp. He never would've believed Thordia to do or say anything to such a degree. "Is my own wife against me too?"

She climbed up his bent legs, grasping the kirtle at his chest to pull herself astride him. Her hands twisted tightly in the fabric, and the weight of her body settled comfortably across his lap. If she wasn't delicate with child, he might have tossed her aside on the far length of the boxbed and stormed out the door.

Though his mind opposed his wife's unfair tactics, his body found solace in her closeness. Against his will, his hands came up around her full bottom and steadied her across his thighs as he waited for her to speak.

She laid her forehead against his. "Do you recall the day we met?"

Tait had no idea where she was going with this. "Of course."

"And all you wanted was to get me away from my father."

His lips twitched at the thought of their first romantic encounter more than eight years ago. "I wanted to get you away from everyone. Including that foolish knave who followed you around like a sniveling dog in Hlymrekr's harbor." Tait shifted her bottom and nestled it right over his groin, reminding his wife what she'd craved from him that day.

Thordia giggled at his sudden fervor. "You were a persistent man."

"I knew what I wanted," Tait said. "And kissing Ottarr's arse was not enough for me to gain it. I had to go into his house and steal his daughter in the night."

She brushed her lips across his. "Nothing could've kept you from me. And I was helpless against your charm."

Tait's lips curved into a wry smile as he remembered the evening they spent rolling in the hay. "You hardly looked helpless when you hiked your skirts for me."

Thordia slipped her hands beneath the fabric at the keyhole neckline of his kirtle and fanned them against his bare chest. "Is that all you remember?"

Tait realized she was coyly gentling him so he'd forget all about his burdens. For the moment, it seemed to work. In one speedy motion, he lifted her body from his and rolled, careful of her belly as he hovered above her on all fours. "What I remember is you calling my name over and over again."

Thordia smiled brazenly. "My father would've killed you had he ever found out."

"He'd still kill me if he knew I deflowered his daughter before her wedding night."

"And yet it never stopped you."

Tait reached down and hiked her skirt just as he'd done back then. "Do you dare stop me now?"

"Never."

Though he knew he'd been snared, enticed, and fooled by her feminine wiles, he didn't care. He nudged her nose with his and captured her lips in a long, heated kiss, unleashing his desire that had been pent up for days. When he pulled away breathless, she took up the conversation exactly where they'd left it.

"What if my father did stop you?" What if he'd married me to the *knave* you despised so much?"

He drew back and looked into her eyes. "I would've

rather died than know another man was going to have what was mine."

He tried to kiss her again, but she avoided it by saying, "Then why would you want to do that to Breandán and Mara?"

Tait froze as he took another kick in the balls. "Did you…" He couldn't believe she actually had the nerve to say that bastard's name at the moment he aimed to make sweet love to her. His voice quivered. "Tell me I heard you wrong, Thordia."

"Mara has been so happy since Breandán's return to the isle," Thordia explained. "He's brought a smile to her face and she—" Tait scrambled to leave her embrace, but she seized his kirtle in her fists. "Tait, listen to me. Mara enjoys his company. He appeals to her in ways no one else has since Dægan died."

"Thordia," Tait warned, his jaw clenching.

"I'm not saying she's in love with him, but if it happens, would it not be grand?"

"Grand?" Tait repeated. He punched his fist at the bedding beside her head. "There is nothing grand about Mara, my best friend's wife, falling in—"

"Widow," Thordia corrected, stroking his tortured face. "She's been a widow for more than seven years. She deserves to find love again."

"Not with that man," Tait snapped. Thordia caressed his chest and shoulders, weakening him with her touch. "Stop it," Tait said, closing his eyes. He was well aware of her trickery now and swore he'd not succumb.

"Look at me and say that," Thordia prompted.

He couldn't. In all honesty, he never wanted her to stop touching him. He heaved a long sigh and shifted to sit beside her, crossing his arms as he stewed.

Thordia sat up and untucked his arm, wrapping it around her as she cuddled against him. "Do you love me?"

Tait stared distantly. "Of course, I do."

"Then listen when I tell you that you have no idea what you're talking about where Mara is concerned. I know you want the best for her," she continued. "And you want her to one day find happiness with a man so her heart can heal. So, why not let Breandán be that man? Let Mara feel whole again with Breandán."

There was no way he'd let that happen. Gunnar, Tait thought to himself. *She'll find happiness with Gunnar.*

Chapter Twenty-four

Gustaf awoke before Æsa and watched her sleep. Her dark lashes feathered against high cheekbones, and her long auburn hair splayed over her pillow as she lay curled in the nook of his sidelong embrace. She looked innocent as she slept, but as he'd recently found out, she was anything but.

They'd made love more times in the past fortnight than he could ever remember in all his years as an adult. She was free with her body, and he gave her no reason to change. In fact, he had encouraged her to tell him all her fantasies so he could fulfill every single one, and oh, how grand it had been to satisfy every imaginative desire she'd thought of.

As he reminisced about their days spent in rapturous bliss, he brushed his fingertips along her arm. She moaned and stirred, then opened her eyes resplendent with icy flecks of frost and aqua.

"Good morning," Gustaf murmured.

Æsa smiled and rolled to her back, stretching like a nimble cat, when a knock at the door drew both their attentions.

Gustaf stared at her. He wasn't expecting anyone, and for a split second, he wondered if she was. Though it killed him to think she hadn't given up her old ways completely, he asked her, "Who would that be?"

Her expression told him she had no clue, followed by a slight twinge of fear as though he were about to turn on her. He imagined she'd endured many accusations, from both deceitful, scheming husbands and furious wives, and felt instantly guilty for being one of them.

He stroked her cheek in apology, then brought his finger to his lips.

She nodded in understanding and kept silent, though the fear in her eyes spoke volumes as the knock at the door became a series of impatient pounds.

Gustaf found his breeches, slipped them on, and reached for his belt. He slid his sword from the scabbard with the utmost care so those at the door wouldn't hear, and tiptoed toward the door. He glanced once at Æsa, readied his weapon, and ripped the door open.

The familiar faces of his hirdmen stared back at him, and he lowered the blade with an audible sigh. "Have you all lost your minds?" Gustaf exclaimed as his heart pounded from the surge of tension racing through him. "I could've run you through."

Jørgen hardly seemed to care, jumping headlong into the matter at hand. "My lord, we've come with great news."

"Oh?" Gustaf mumbled, still waiting for his heart to settle. "What news would that be?"

"I'd rather discuss this in private," Jørgen said, stressing his point with a severe expression. "May we come in?"

Gustaf glanced at Æsa clutching a blanket at her bare breasts and realized she wasn't exactly properly dressed to receive company. "Give me a moment," he said, closing the door. He sheathed his sword and looked at her. "We have visitors. My men…"

A seductive smile curved her lips. "Is it spring already? Have we been so consumed with each other that we're oblivious to anything outside our naked embrace?"

He came to her, wishing he could appreciate her jest the way it was meant. But with his men returning only weeks after they'd parted, he feared that the much-needed respite he'd taken from his vengeful mission was about to end.

He sat beside her and leaned down to kiss her one more time. As determined as he was to find and kill the last of his father's murderers, he had come to enjoy and appreciate a life without violence and bloodshed. A life that involved going to bed in the arms of a woman and waking up to her sweet smile in the morning. It felt incredibly strange to want these things, as he'd never wanted anything outside of avenging his father. Either he'd gone soft after all these years, or Æsa's love was a full-bodied concoction of ecstasy and arousal too potent to resist.

****

Gustaf looked at his men gathered around his fire pit, all seven of them, their faces beset with urgency. "Out with it, any one of ya."

Jørgen spoke tentatively. "My lord, 'tis with great satisfaction we bring you the name of the last man who killed your father."

Gustaf cocked his brow. "You're certain?"

"Indeed," he said with confidence. "But the rest of what we found out, I fear, will not please you."

"Let me guess. Someone else has already killed him."

"On the contrary. He's alive and well."

Gustaf couldn't understand why Jørgen was being obscure, but he anticipated there must be a catch involving the details of their last fugitive. "What complications do we face?"

Jørgen's face turned white. "He lives with your family."

Those words echoed inside Gustaf's head, and he didn't know whether to be angry or overjoyed. So much time had passed since he'd seen his family, and through his mission, he'd never heard word of their whereabouts. In truth, he'd convinced himself they were gone so he wouldn't feel the need to search for them and possibly put them in harm's way. But to find out after all this time that the last cowardly man had hidden himself away within the safety of his loved ones was infuriating.

Gustaf's blood boiled as he struggled with this turn of events. He tried to put his emotions aside and think rationally. He'd never been rash in the past, and he never wanted to kill an innocent man because of it. He wouldn't start now. "What makes you certain this man is our last target?"

"We met a man who—"

"You what?" Gustaf leapt to his feet, towering over his sitting friend. No one was to know anything about their activities, and it was crucial to their mission that no one even knew Gustaf existed. "You brought someone else into this?"

"Not anyone, m'lord, but a friend of your father's. He says he knows you."

"And that is even worse, Jørgen! You've jeopardized this mission and the safety of my family. What is there to keep this friend of my father from running to them and squealing?"

Jørgen stammered as he spoke. "M-m'lord, he cannot exactly squeal to them when he is here...with us."

"You brought him here?"

"Aye, he is here. Along with his mercenaries, all two hundred."

Gustaf thought the top of his skull would blow off. "And why would I need two hundred strangers when I'm perfectly able to kill one man with my bare hands?" His hands, without his realization, had formed a ring in front of him as if he were choking the life from someone. Jørgen's neck would easily substitute.

Jørgen grew more nervous. "He insisted, m'lord."

Gustaf raked his hands through his hair, then balled them into fists. "Am I to assume you take orders from him now?"

The door opened suddenly, and in walked a large man, bearded and burly, with shoulders like an ox. "Don't get your breeches in a bunch, Gustaf. He still follows your orders. I, however, follow any son of Rælik, especially if it means righting his wrongful death."

Gustaf couldn't believe his eyes. He remembered the resolute Northman from when he was a child, and how he had strived to be like Havelok, fearless and commanding. *Stalwart.*

Havelok was, as Jørgen mentioned, a great friend of his father's, but he still had reservations about Havelok's involvement. With more outsiders in the mix, the risk of things going wrong was too great, and he hated to make mistakes, especially when victory was this close.

Gustaf approached Havelok, amazed that age hadn't changed him much except for the deep wrinkles at the corner of his eyes and the gray discoloring his blond hair. As he embraced him soundly, he also found the man's strength was exceptional, hard to believe as he knew the man was coming on sixty. "'Tis good to see you, Havelok."

The older man gripped his shoulders and took one

hard look at Gustaf. "Ah, your father would be proud if he could see you now."

"Then you know I have a duty to him. I cannot permit you to join in on my vengeance. 'Tis mine. And I'll not be thwarted of it."

"Words of a good son," Havelok praised. "I'm not here to hinder your plan. I only wish to aid you."

"As you can see," Gustaf gestured over his loyal men, "I have more than enough support already. They've been with me through this long search, and I don't wish to replace their passion with anyone else's. They deserve to feel the satisfaction of triumph, and I will give them that."

"I don't doubt it. You've always been an honorable man, much like your father. But if you want to get to the last man, you'll need me."

"With all due respect, Havelok, I've found each of the nine bastards without your help, and I think I can handle the last one myself. In truth, I've barely enough silver left to compensate my own men, much less all of yours."

"Neither I nor my men expect payment."

"Then why so much fervor?"

"Because one of my own mercenaries had a hand in Rælik's death, and I cannot stand by and let him get away with it. Your family, unaware of this man's past, is in grave danger. And I owe it to your father to protect them."

Gustaf felt a sick feeling in the pit of his stomach. He had to sit. "Where *is* my family, Havelok?"

"On an isle off the west coast of Ireland. Inishmore. They've lived there for many years now, allied with the Irish. Your brother, Dægan, took them to the island a few years after you left."

"And how do you know all this?" Gustaf asked.

Havelok sat beside him. "I had the privilege of fighting alongside Dægan seven years ago."

"Against whom?"

Havelok paused through the span of a few breaths. "Your other brother, Domaldr."

A fire inflamed his soul. He knew all too well the kind of man Domaldr was, and it didn't surprise him that he had returned to inflict his evils on the family he betrayed so long ago. "What did Domaldr do this time?"

"It seems Dægan had taken an Irish wife, the daughter of the Connacht king. But your brother, Domaldr—"

"Do not call him that. He's no brother of mine."

Havelok took back his back words immediately. "Forgive me. Domaldr had wanted to take Connacht so he could gain status with Sigtrygg Gale during their fight for control over Dubh-Linn, but he knew he'd have a better chance if he had leverage."

"Dægan's wife…" Gustaf presumed.

"Aye. And Domaldr succeeded. He took the princess right out from under Dægan, killing Vegard, Sveir, and many more of your father's people in the process. He burned everything to the ground as he left, and he even aimed to kill Dægan, but he failed."

"And Dægan called upon you to help him get her back?"

"As I once told Dægan, when I heard I had the chance to fight alongside a son of Rælik, I nearly fell over myself to get there."

"So what happened?" Gustaf asked, dreading the rest of the story, as his family didn't often secure many happy endings.

"Dægan was able to retrieve his wife and slaughter Domaldr's men, but not before acquiring his own share of wounds. We were able to take him back to his home on the isle, but eventually his injuries proved fatal."

Hot tears burned Gustaf's eyes. "And Domaldr?"

"The king of Connacht hanged him for the crimes against his daughter."

"You're sure?"

Havelok put his hand on Gustaf's shoulder and gave a reassuring squeeze. "I saw him myself."

Gustaf took a deep breath, trying to cool his rising anger. "And you're telling me one of your mercenaries...who fought side by side with you and Dægan...is the man who killed my father."

"I know it sounds preposterous—"

"Indeed, it does!" Gustaf barked. "It makes absolutely no sense."

"What if I told you that man was my son? Would you believe me then?" Gustaf pursed his brow and slowly turned his head in Havelok's direction, and Havelok explained further. "It sickens me to know my son was capable of doing such a thing. Of stabbing me in the back and twisting it deeper with his lies. He and I never had a good relationship, but when he came to me years ago— begging for protection against King Harald Fairhair—I took him in, not realizing what he'd done. I assumed Harald was after him just as Harald was with so many of our people from Hladir, and my son assumed the same. He said he feared for his life, and what was I to do? I was his father. Neither of us knew it was you and your men who were after him."

Gustaf listened intently, pitying the man as he spoke.

"I only found out what he'd truly done a few moons ago. And even now, it sits in my gut like a stone."

Gustaf pinched the bridge of his nose. "You put me in a very difficult situation, Havelok. I have every intention of following through with my vengeance. I have a duty to my father. And I'll not fail him. But knowing 'tis your son who looks death in the eye…" Gustaf hung his head. "It tears at my heart."

Havelok sat up straighter. "Don't let my relationship cloud your senses, Gustaf. He may have my blood coursing through his veins, but he is no son of mine. Not anymore."

Gustaf eyed the Northman carefully, confusion still harping at his mind. "And so I ask you again. Why such fervor? Why such vehemence when you know your son will die?"

Havelok gathered his thoughts. "Your father never wanted to admit his son, Domaldr, was foul blood. No father ever wants to admit that. But because he closed his eyes to it, Domaldr hurt many people. Your people. If I can learn anything from your father, 'twould be not to look away from your enemies. Especially if they're family."

Gustaf grew antsy. He knew his men looked to him for guidance and were anxious for their orders, but with Havelok in the picture, it seemed nigh on impossible to come to a decision. A choice he'd have to live with for the rest of his life.

He thought ahead, imagining himself, dagger in hand, looking eye to eye with Havelok's son. Could he do it? Could he actually find it in himself to take this man's life knowing what he knew now?

As he mulled over the situation, another question popped into his weary mind. "How would we do this without endangering my family?"

"Because he thinks 'tis Harald Fairhair who's after him, he won't suspect a thing when you show up on the isle to celebrate."

"Celebrate? Celebrate what?"

"Your resurrection, of course. Your people think you died at the hands of those men who killed your father. Rest assured, when they lay eyes on you, there'll be a feast fit for Odin himself."

Chapter Twenty-five

Breandán admired the fluency of the Northmen who prepared the swift longships and the sizeable *knarrs* for the journey ahead. They'd worked all the previous evening and into the morning hours loading goods, weapons, extra linens, and stockpiles of food, while checking the rigging, support masts, and strakes with a thorough eye. He was glad to see nothing slighted because of haste. Everyone seemed to understand the gravity of this voyage, with only Mara's safety at the forefront.

He also noted Tait was especially cautious, verifying that no wear or fraying had damaged the woolen sails, and that the ship's oak sides were sound and well caulked, even after Hansen, their master shipbuilder, affirmed their superior condition.

Though Breandán knew Tait didn't fuss over the vessels' reliability for Breandán's own satisfaction, it still pleased him to know the Northman cared enough about Mara to put his larger-than-life pride aside. He would take every bit of scorn from Tait, and even the occasional shove from the others when he'd accidentally get in the way, if it meant heightening the chieftain's diligence toward Mara's welfare.

Breandán and Marcas had helped where they could. They'd never done anything of this nature before and found that furling the huge sails, loading heavy pine masts, and carrying crates and chests of supplies to the ships was rather exhausting. Nevan and the islanders were also present to lighten the workload, and perhaps discourage another heated brawl.

Tait took every chance he got to insult Breandán throughout the day, or take something from his hands as though he wasn't capable of carrying it. Childish behavior, really, but Breandán didn't let it get to him. He knew Tait was trying to torment him enough to spark a rematch.

He smiled inwardly, finding it humorous that the Northman went to such extreme lengths to goad him. Even Gunnar tried his hand at it on more than one occasion. And Breandán refused to give them the satisfaction of thinking they'd gotten under his skin.

Truthfully, they didn't. He was a grown man with big enough shoulders to tolerate their ridicule. Marcas, however, grew weary of it.

"How much more can one man take of this?"

Breandán patted his friend's back. "'Twill soon end once we're aboard."

"You mean once you're aboard with Mara."

****

Marcas was right. When they'd boarded the deep hull of the large *knarr*, he was as content as he could be in Mara's presence. He was doubly glad to be separated from Gunnar, who was better fit to operate the steer board of the longship, and had found relief from his long, hard stares.

They stood near the mast in the central hold at the lower level of the *knarr*, where the horses were stalled. Above them, at the stem and stern, higher platforms housed the men who sat at benches built for rowing the impressive sea-going craft. Although the rowers were vulnerable to the elements, the weather this day proved to be welcoming. To Breandán, the sky could've been filled with dark steely clouds and torrential rain, and it still would have been bright and sunny in his world.

He looked at Mara, taking notice of her long face. "Are you comfortable?"

Mara smiled, though it seemed forced. "As comfortable as one can be upon a ship." She stroked her horse's soft muzzle. "I only wish Lochlann could've come. I've never been away from him."

The ship rocked and unsteadied her. Breandán immediately side-stepped and stopped her from falling backward. He reached around and placed her hands on the horizontal tie-off beams for support. "Hold here while I find something for you to sit on."

Mara attempted to dissuade him, insisting she was fine standing, but he was already lugging a sack of cargo large enough for the both of them to sit on. He gestured with a long sweep of his hand over the wide canvas-covered rucksack as if it were a gift, and relished her smile—an honest one this time—as she took a seat.

She intentionally left room for him, and he obliged himself. "You understand why 'twas not in our best interest to bring Lochlann with us. 'Tis not safe for such a young boy. If not for Cathal's failing health, I wouldn't have allowed you to make this journey either. Believe me, it doesn't sit well with my heart to have to disappoint you so."

She glanced at him. "I may be disappointed, but I too wouldn't want to put my son in harm's way. Besides," she said, releasing her grip on the beam and folding her hands in her lap, "'tis better for him never to meet the man who's forsaken him."

Breandán heard the pain in her voice. "'Twill soon be over, Mara. And then you can return to your life." She studied him carefully. Probably poring over his words. He didn't mean for them to come out that way. To sound so dismissive, as though her life were ordinary at best. As he thought about it, his words also seemed to insinuate that her life would soon be without him when he'd fulfilled his end of the bargain. "What I mean is, you can put this all behind you and move on."

She nodded. "I do wish for that. Though my heart will still bear the scars."

Before he could console her, another wave rammed the ship's side and propelled Mara into his arms. He couldn't help but smile at his good fortune.

Though it practically killed him to release her, he took her hands and placed them back on the beam in front of her. "Perhaps you should hold on," he recommended. His hands lingered upon hers, at least until he felt her grip tighten around the truss.

"*Go raibh maith agat, a chara,*" she uttered in Gaelic.

The endearment she closed her thank-you with made his heart skip. He tried to keep his composure in such tight quarters, thrilled that she'd considered him a friend. But he wanted to be more than the platonic companion his avowal had promised. He longed to feel her lips and dwell in the pleasures of her kiss as he held her close.

Breandán briefly looked away and caught sight of Marcas eyeing him. He was a homely fellow with coarse red hair, a beard—which had grown wild and unsightly these past days—and small beady eyes. His shoulders and arms, like Breandán's, were fit and strong, but his stomach had begun to protrude over his belt, largely from the steady consumption of mead. He'd acquired habits quite unbecoming, Breandán noted, which were enough to turn anyone's stomach. Of the worst was his constant slurping of droplets that settled above his lip and in his mustache. It was utterly disgusting to hear, but the Irish islanders that gathered around his friend and laughed at God knows what didn't seem to mind.

Aye, the sight of Marcas was tolerated only by a broad-minded lot of hardy fellows. His only hope for finding female companionship, Breandán imagined, would be a woman who sampled the drink as often as his friend did.

****

Once they had reached Galway's bay, the Northmen docked their ships at the wharf and dispensed the cargo through an efficient assembly line of crew members and warriors alike. One after another, the horses were unloaded, and supplies and weapons were tied down to their saddles. Breandán and Marcas slipped away to gain their own steeds from a friend who had agreed to stable them until their return.

"Ye brought quite a cavalry with ye," Turlough remarked as he cautiously eyed the throng of foreigners accumulating in the port. "Why ye be needin' so many?"

Breandán patted his horse's neck, satisfied that Turlough had cared for it properly in his absence. "They've come along to protect the princess."

Turlough jabbed his elbow into Marcas's ribs. "From yerself, no doubt."

The two laughed at Breandán, knowing well his

fondness for Mara. But he paid no heed to their jest, or the next few that followed. He mounted his horse and looked out amongst the Northmen, confirming Mara's safety. She was also mounting her steed with Ottarr's help.

"If you keep two stalls open for me, I shall pay you twice what I gave you last time."

Turlough nodded humbly. "The wife loves the brown hare cloak ye gave her. As do I. Ye never thieve me family of what's due, and I'm grateful. If I had me pick, I'd rather turn away ten horses than lose a trade with ye. Now, be not a stranger anymore, ye hear? We've been a missin' ye round these parts, we have." Turlough glanced over his shoulder at Mara. "With things looking up as they are, perhaps ye can see to tradin' here yerself again," he suggested, gesturing toward Marcus, "instead of sending this ill-reputed sod in yer stead."

Breandán gave a jolly chuckle after seeing Marcas's distain for being the butt of Turlough's joke. "I'll keep it in mind." And as they rode away, he thought of the other opportunities he'd been hopeful for now that Mara was in his life, and wondered if any were likely to happen. God willing, when all this was done, she'd remember the kiss they shared and the connection they'd made as two lost souls eager for a chance at happiness.

****

Breandán led the excursion through the rocky terrain of Ireland's west coast, which eventually turned densely wooded. As he'd warned, they were not following the normal trail. They blazed through near impenetrable brush, steep inclines, and dodgy streams, avoiding a run-in with

Duncan Mac Flann's crooked army at all cost.

In the past, Mac Flann's entourage had consisted of stragglers—bands of rogues with no more than thirty men to each group. He'd dispersed them amongst Connacht's roadways, thieving and breeding fear amongst the Uí Briúin. But with the news of Cathal's deteriorating health, Breandán suspected Mac Flann was smart enough to rally the scoundrels into one organized group, using both their numbers and a commandeering strategy to his advantage. If he wanted to gain Connacht with barely any effort, all he'd have to do was abduct the king's daughter and hold her for ransom.

Breandán was not about to let that happen.

He'd ordered that Mara be placed in the very center of the group, offering her ample protection from both ends, and be disguised as a man. She wore a kirtle and breeches—the garments of a Northman. If she were dressed as her countrymen in only a leine and cloak, her slim feminine legs would be spotted a mile away. He also stuffed her long silky tresses into the shroud of a mail curtain hanging from a helmet, and strapped an armored chest plate to her torso in order to conceal her curves.

This is ridiculous, he recalled her saying. But he didn't care. All that mattered was she was relatively hidden from suspicious eyes and safe in his care. If he had more time, he would've smeared the dark sludge of the peat bogs across the creamy skin of her face to resemble a beard. But he knew she wouldn't yield to such a measure. She was already put out by her attire.

At least Ottarr seemed impressed with his meticulousness. He'd nodded his approval after seeing her in the guise of a Norse warrior, then laughed under his breath as he reined his horse away and resumed his spot in line.

They traveled for many hours without stopping. Once they reached the quarter mark of their journey, Breandán decided it was best to stop and make camp before it became too dark to see. His choice was a secluded area of dense forest along a much-needed stream for satiating their horses' thirsts.

He dismounted with ease and led his horse toward Mara, who was now trotting up through the brush. Her body showed signs of fatigue as she no longer sat high and proud in the saddle. Her face was pained and devoid of any smile as she caught sight of him. She halted her mount in front of him and practically threw herself from the saddle. He caught and steadied her on the way down. "Are you all right?"

She mumbled something akin to yes and swayed in his arms as she adjusted to the solid ground beneath her feet. Breandán removed the conical helmet from her head and the plated armor from her chest, alleviating her of the strains from their heavy weight. He threw her armor over his shoulder and tucked the helm under his arm. "There. Is that better?"

She nodded, wiping the beads of perspiration from her forehead. "I'd feel better if I could lie down and sleep."

"You should eat first," he advised, taking her reins. "There's a spot beyond, in yonder clearing where you can rest yourself. We'll make a fire there soon, and you can eat. Will you be all right while I tend to the horses?"

She nodded sleepily, and he wondered if she'd truly heard what he asked.

"Don't wander off on your own. If you must relieve yourself, come to me first."

Again she only nodded, but this time Breandán noticed a restlessness in her legs beneath her breeches. He laughed at her in spite of himself. "You have to go now, do you not?"

She bit her lip and gazed around at all the menfolk swarming the place. "I've never had to do so in front of…and how do I do so in these breeches? 'Tis not as if I can do what I must standing up."

Breandán laughed harder as she locked her knees together, and motioned for Marcus.

"I'm serious," she said, dancing. "Where can I go?"

Marcas took the reins and armor from Breandán and quirked a grin at her unusual jig. "You may want to take her farther upstream if she'd like to wash up as well," he suggested. "Some of the men have already relieved themselves while watering their horses."

"Thanks for the warning. And keep a sharp eye while I'm gone."

Marcas grabbed Breandán's sleeve and whispered in his ear, "For Mac Flann? Or for that Gunnar fellow? Between the two of us, I don't much care for him."

Breandán glanced around at the remaining men unpacking their belongings. Gunnar was nowhere to be seen. "Both," he whispered back. "And I feel the same, just so you know."

Chapter Twenty-six

Breandán kept his eyes on the surrounding terrain, though he was barely able to ignore the princess who crouched behind him in the bushes. He'd instructed Mara to simply pull the breeches to her knees and sit on her heels to do her private business, but she wasn't convinced she could. So there he stood, with her trousers in his hands and the image of her naked bum in his head.

"So, tell me more about Gunnar," he said, trying to redirect his mind.

"What is it you want to know?"

Breandán looked around, making sure no one was within earshot before he spoke. "Why did he decide to stay on the isle after Dægan died? Wasn't he one of Havelok's mercenaries?"

"Actually, he's his son. But yes, he was one of his mercenaries."

"So why did he stay?"

"I don't know. And I never asked."

Breandán heard a rustling and turned for a flinching second, only to find her standing with her hand out, her lower half still concealed by the shrubbery. Painfully aware of her unclothed state, he politely turned back around and handed her pants from over his shoulder.

"I heard from the talk that he was tired of the mercenary life," she added while dressing. "I know he's been very loyal and trustworthy since he's been with us.

And Tait is pleased to have his company."

"Do you trust him?" Breandán asked.

There was a pause, as if she'd stopped dressing. "Why do you ask?"

"I have a duty to protect you whilst we're visiting your father. And I've always believed it wise to keep friends close and enemies closer."

Mara appeared from behind the greenery, her face puckered with confusion. "You consider Gunnar an enemy?"

Breandán crossed his arms. "I consider him a potential threat, the same as I would Tait if he were here."

"You mean a threat to *you*?"

Breandán bit his tongue and ushered her through the woods toward camp. "You may think that, but as far as I'm concerned, any person on this journey who hasn't your best interest at heart is a threat. And by the way, you didn't answer my question."

Mara stopped briefly and furrowed her brow. "I thought I did."

"You countered me with three questions of your own, but you never answered mine. I asked if you trusted Gunnar."

Mara thought long on the issue. Far too long for Breandán's taste. He grabbed her by the arm and pulled her back before she could enter the clearing where the others gathered. He looked her deep in the eyes. "Mara, this is important." He enunciated each word for her. "Do you trust him?"

She held his gaze. "Gunnar has given me no reason not to trust him. He's always been there for us. He's even been there for Brondolf, Lillemor's son."

Breandán's attention was piqued. "Go on," he

encouraged.

"Brondolf was one of the first to come upon Svanhild, Dægan's mother, on the morning she died. He and Gunnar had found her in her bed. For a four-year old boy, that was very difficult. He was quite distraught. And since then, he hasn't spoken a word."

"Not a word? At all?"

"Not even to his own mother. But Gunnar has taken it upon himself to help the boy. He's always there with him, shadowing him, more or less like a protective father."

Breandán noticed a glimmer of suspicion in her eyes. "But..." he prompted.

"But...from my perspective, it seems Brondolf doesn't welcome Gunnar's company as much as the boy lets on. He seems uncomfortable with Gunnar's presence. Even Lochlann stands clear of him when he can."

"Has Lochlann ever told you anything suspicious about Gunnar?"

"Nay."

"But you think Gunnar had a hand in Svanhild's death."

Mara drew back. "I never said that."

"'Tis me you're talking to, Mara. Whatever you say to me, whatever you suspect, will not leave my lips."

She closed her eyes and breathed deep. "I've never openly accused Gunnar of anything. Nor would I have any evidence to back it up if I did. But my heart feels something is amiss."

He was glad Mara trusted him enough to express her reservations. He had his own from the moment he saw Gunnar, but had no grounds for feeling it except for intuition. In any case, he'd watch him more closely now.

He tipped her chin up. "You're safe with me, Mara. You know this, right?"

She swallowed. "I do."

At the instant he thought about kissing her, a rustling behind them caused her to flinch and turn away. Breandán frowned as he saw Marcas approaching. If his friend was anything, he was always rather untimely.

"Is everything well?" he asked, pushing his thoughts of Mara's kiss elsewhere in his frazzled brain.

"If by 'well' you mean Gunnar is taking charge of things, ordering us all around, aye. Things are more than well."

"If it keeps him occupied, let him. In the meantime, I'll be scouting the area. Take Mara back for me and make sure she eats before she sleeps."

Mara seized his arm with an urgent look upon her face. "Please be careful, Breandán."

He smiled for her, her well-wishes like a harp's strum on his heart.

****

The next morning, Mara awoke to the low dulcet sound of her name. She opened her eyes and found Breandán squatting beside her, his handsome face smiling warmly.

"We're all saddled and ready to go," he said, holding out his hand to her.

She took it and sat up, seeing all the men were as he said, mounted and in lines, waiting for her. She must have fallen into a sound sleep soon after her meal. The last things she remembered were the men meandering around the fire, chatting about their day, drinking to the days to come, and guffawing every now and again over who knew what. She stretched her back from lying on the hard ground, amazed she hadn't heard a sound after she'd closed her eyes.

"You must have been exhausted."

She stood up and brushed off her clothes, disappointed when she realized she was still dressed in men's breeches. She understood why Breandán was overzealous, and for his sake, never made a peep of complaint, even when he secured the armor around her chest and handed her the heavy helmet.

As she tucked her hair into the mail armor hood, Breandán reached up to help her, his knuckles grazing her cheek. She faltered a bit, glad that he'd steadied her, and blamed the weight of her accessories.

"Two more days of this and we should reach your father," he consoled her. "Think you can make it?"

"Of course she can make it," Gunnar announced as he walked up, his strides arrogant. "She's a strong woman."

The tension between the two men rose on the spot.

"I make no arguments against it, Gunnar. But if our course is too swift for her or the route too treacherous, we should certainly adjust to accommodate. Would you not agree?"

Gunnar crossed his arms over his barrel chest. "If anything needs adjusting, 'tis Mara's placement in line. She'd be better protected if she were near me. Instead, you have her in the center where I couldn't see her if I wanted. You leave her vulnerable."

Breandán's eyes darkened. "If an attack were to be made, 'tis more likely they'd ambush the front and flank the rear, using confusion and fear to their advantage. Having been a warrior for hire, Gunnar, I'd think you'd know this."

Mara wanted to smile as he stormed away and rejoined Ottarr at the rear of the group. She'd never seen anything like it. No one dared stand up against Gunnar and Tait, and yet Breandán withstood both of them in less than a few days. And lived to tell about it.

The rest of the journey was relatively calm when it came to the two men butting heads. As long as Gunner kept his mouth shut and his complaints to himself, Breandán hardly gave the Northman his attention. At least that was what it looked like to everyone else. Mara knew better. While Breandán scouted the countryside, checked broken twigs on the paths, analyzed footprints in the soil, or studied things that looked out of place, he also had his eyes inconspicuously on Gunnar. There wasn't much that got past Breandán. He was conscious of everything going on around him, and that included her and her comfort over the course of the trip.

Each night when they stopped to make camp, Breandán performed his usual task of holding her breeches while she ducked behind the bushes. He seemed to have gotten used to the idea of being her servant while she tended to her ablutions, and he carried on conversations as though she weren't behind him half-naked, until the night she asked him if he'd stand guard while she washed up in the nearby stream.

She remembered his reaction to such a request. His lips thinned and his nostrils flared. He was a fidgeting mess, but never peeked from his post. When she finished, he escorted her back to the camp as silently as he'd stood guard. Then, under his watchful eye, she fell asleep at the warm fire.

The next morning, they rode out early, and, within a

few hours, they finally came upon the Lough Ree. Her father's keep towered in the distance, and she never felt so relieved and anxious at the same time. She had hoped she'd be ready for this moment, but as the motte-and-bailey stronghold stared back at her, she knew nothing could've prepared her.

Her mouth went dry. There was a catch in her throat she couldn't clear, and her emotions bubbled inside her. She wanted to turn her horse around and race back home—to Inishmore. To her son. To a place safe and familiar.

Dún na hAbhann should've seemed familiar as she'd spent her entire childhood there. But seven years felt like an eternity and thus eroded all connection she'd felt for the predominant dwelling on the hill. It even looked different. Prepared or not, she'd see her father again and hopefully find answers to all her nagging questions.

Breandán rode up to her, a discreet sense of empathy on his face. "Are you ready?"

She wasn't, but nodded anyway.

"This is as far as we go," Ultan announced, speaking for the Irish islanders of the group. "We'll wait here."

Mara understood why, and Breandán didn't argue. He bowed slightly to Nevan's brother, then led the way. Mara and the other Northmen followed him across the valley where Dún na hAbhann awaited, and as she gazed over its solid palisade walls and impermeable stone gatehouse, they looked higher than she remembered. The fortress taunted her. She heard voices whispering in her ears to turn back. Chills ran down her spine when they rode through the barbican and beneath the sharp metal grates of two portcullises raised high above them. They looked as if any moment they would fall back into place, trapping her inside.

Get a hold of yourself, she scolded.

This had been her home, her safe harbor. Thinking her own father would do her harm was utterly absurd. She was his daughter, and blood was thicker than water.

Then why did he turn her away in the first place? Without explanation. Without cause. Without so much as a farewell. She wanted to know why so she could put all this needless wondering and worrying aside.

If she could get through Dægan's death, then she certainly could get through this. The worst her father could say was, *I wish to cut all ties from you and never see you again.* It would be no more appalling than what she'd heard from him before. If anything, she could admit she'd grown numb and indifferent to his words, and decided to approach this occasion emotionally uninvolved. Even as Fergus, her father's advisor and lifelong friend, greeted her and Breandán with a respectful bow and invited the Northmen to drink and eat their fill, she remained dispassionate. She refused to expose her vulnerable heart.

Mara was the last to dismount. She glanced around the spacious courtyard at places she used to frequent, like the flowery garden in front of the chapel or the servants' quarters where she'd eavesdrop on local entertaining gossip. She even recognized familiar faces in the bailey, some of whom would have once run to her and embraced her. Now, as she stood there among them, they addressed her with saddened eyes. She couldn't tell whether they were despondent over the deteriorating health of their king or the fact she'd become a stranger to them.

Despite her efforts to shield her heart, she wanted to cry. Things had changed, and time was a cruel enemy.

Breandán circled her horse and wrapped a comforting arm around her shoulders, gripping her upper arm with a strong hand. "You're not alone." He ushered her toward the keep, where Fergus had already begun to walk.

"I want you to come with me," Mara said in panic to Breandán before they reached the stairs leading to her father's chamber.

He smiled warmly. "I'll not leave your side."

Mara took in a breath and started up the stairs behind Fergus. She might have been gone for seven years, but she certainly didn't need his guidance. Many years she'd spent in this keep. Many days she'd spent going up and down this wooden staircase. She could do it with her eyes closed.

At the top was an open room where sentries stood in pairs at three corresponding doors. To the right was her bedchamber—was. And to the left was her father's. The middle door had been her mother's, though, since her passing, no one had been permitted entrance. For a moment, she wondered if either chamber was occupied by someone else now.

Mara stared at her father's double doors. They were guarded as she expected, but no less comforting to know he was just beyond them. She swallowed, trying to rid the dryness from her mouth.

Fergus cleared his throat. "We were beginning to think you would not come."

Mara looked up at him sharply. "Would you have blamed me if I hadn't?"

He bowed humbly, unable to look her in the eye. "Indeed not."

Mara stared a bit longer, feeling Breandán's presence behind her. In no way was he standing close enough for their bodies to touch, but she could feel him as profoundly as if he were pressed against her. Though he probably didn't know it, his company gave her strength. It put confidence in her weary heart and solid legs beneath her trembling body.

"Does he know I'm here?"

"Aye," Fergus said.

No chance of retreating now. "Breandán will come in with me."

Fergus glanced over her shoulder at her companion. His expression showed reluctance, but for whatever reason, he yielded to her demand. "'Tis not as if Breandán won't find out sooner or later."

"Find out what?" Breandán asked for her.

Fergus ignored him and stepped between the guards, opening the door. It was dark in the room. Gloomy, with only a few lit torches on the far wall.

Again, she swallowed. Took a deep breath. Told herself this was not going to affect her. That seeing her father one last time was not going to rattle her. But no amount of coaxing could've readied her for the moment she walked into the room and saw her brash, bold-lipped, cantankerous father lying there, sunken into the mattress, a pale, fragile, elderly man.

Her heart sank, and pity overwhelmed her as she slowly approached his bed.

"Father?" Her voice was barely audible, but he opened his eyes, looking as if the exertion of lifting his lids was all but impossible.

His eyes glazed over as he stared at the ceiling, unable to turn his head in the direction of her voice. His dry, cracked lips came together for a moment, as if he were trying to say her name.

She knelt beside him. "I'm here, Father."

His pallid face was stoic and sagging, though she thought she saw him try to smile. His voice finally emerged, but in a wheeze. "You still look...as beautiful as ever...like your mother."

Mara smiled, grateful he remembered her.

His chin trembled as he spoke his next words. "How...is Lochlann?"

Her breath escaped her. A feeling of exuberance took hold of her as her father remembered her son's name and asked about him. "Lochlann is well." She searched the room for Breandán, verifying his presence within, and smiled. "I wanted to bring him—for you to meet him, but..." She hesitated, her emotions climbing. "'Twas not safe."

Cathal closed his eyes as if to say he understood. "I would not...want to...put him in...danger."

Mara lifted the blankets and sought his hand. It felt frail in her own, cold to the touch. She rubbed it soothingly, trying to bring warmth to his bony fingers.

Cathal obviously felt her kindness and smiled. "I'm glad you're here."

"As am I, Father." Before she could say much more, Cathal coughed violently, and his face puckered in pain. "Shh..." she consoled. "You need not speak anymore. I'm here. I'll not leave you."

Cathal endured a long episode of coughing and gasping before he was able to settle down again. He grimaced as he gathered his breath. "There is...something I must...tell you."

"Please," she begged. "There is no need to talk. You will only encourage the cough."

"I have to tell…you this," he said breathlessly. "My heart…aches…for hurting you…but I…was only…trying to protect you."

Assuming her father was apologizing for shunning her, she shook her head, interrupting him. "It matters little now, Father. Please, try to rest."

Fergus stepped around the foot of the bed and gained Mara's attention. "Let him speak. This is all he's wanted since he grew sick. He hasn't much time."

Mara had no idea what could be so important to risk her father's well-being for the sake of getting out a few last words. She knew he loved her and didn't have to hear it from his dying lips to believe him. Aye, she doubted it seven years ago when he'd turned her away, but as she watched her father struggle to breathe, none of that mattered anymore.

"Go on, sire," Fergus urged.

Mara stared at her father, hoping he wouldn't exhaust himself coughing. His Adam's apple bob as he swallowed, and his eyes fluttered through his struggle.

"I love…you," he finally said.

"I love you too, Father."

"And I…have always…loved you."

"I know this," she crooned, squeezing his hand between hers.

"But you're…not…mine."

Mara's first instinct was to scoff. Was he starting to lose his mind? Would he only talk nonsense now? She faked a smile, detaching herself from the pain of that statement. "Why would you say something like that, Father? You know I'm yours."

Cathal tried to shake his head, but it hardly moved against the thick, propped pillows. "Your mother…and

I…never…"

"Father, enough," she said as calmly as she could.

"She loved…another before me. You're not my daughter."

Suddenly, Cathal coughed again, and the violence of the fit increased as he thrashed about, trying to gain his breath. Mara grew fearful. His words balanced on the brink of her thoughts while she witnessed him huffing and panting.

Fergus came to him now, his one hand resting kindly upon Cathal's shoulder. "Settle, sire. 'Twill soon pass, but you must settle. Relax…"

His fight worsened, and his eyes widened in panic. He could no longer draw a breath, as if his lungs had closed. His coughing subsided, but his chest caved deeply with each desperate inhalation. His dire need for air mounted.

Mara panicked. "What is happening?"

"He cannot breathe."

Mara stood up, having a difficult time watching her father die. She'd watched Dægan die in her arms, and seeing Cathal's struggles to breathe only reminded her of her husband's last moments.

She backed up, not knowing what to do, barely able to speak. She grew hot and felt the room close in. And spin. Her stomach turned over, but she couldn't leave the room to vomit. She felt as though her feet were nailed to the floor.

This was not what she'd imagined. She was supposed to be unattached and impassive. Instead, somehow, she'd gotten sucked into caring again. Into baring her heart wide open.

At last, she pried a foot from the floor and took a step

backward, but the solid wall of Breandán's body stopped her abruptly. She spun around and buried her face in his chest.

Breandán held her close, and the warmth of his embrace sheltered her from the dreadful images swarming in her brain. The pleasant smell of his heady scent brought about new things to reflect upon, like the steady sound of his breathing and the peaceful, rhythmic thrum of his heartbeat in her ears.

She concentrated on those things and tried to count the beats, tried to slow her respiration to match his, tried to squeeze out the sting of her hot, burning tears.

She barely knew she was crying until the sound of her father's struggle ceased, and her whimpering broke the stillness of the room. She held her breath now. The silence was deafening. The thought that he'd finally succumbed to his death pounded in her head.

Confounded by impulse alone, Mara turned ever so slowly in Breandán's arms and looked at her father, now deceased. Her legs buckled, and she felt two strong arms lift her limp body off her feet before she lost consciousness.

Chapter Twenty-seven

Breandán descended the narrow staircase of the keep with Mara in his arms, his heart aching. She'd already endured so much and had come so far to see her dying father, only to find out he was not her father at all.

Bastard!

How could Cathal do such a thing? What purpose did it serve to reveal such defamation when he knew it would only hurt her? And then to leave this world without telling her who her real father was.

If not for Mara draped within his arms, he would've asked Fergus those very questions. But all he cared about was getting Mara the fresh air she needed and whisking her as far away as possible from this heartache. He wished they were somewhere other than her childhood home, abundant with people who'd no doubt concern themselves with her condition and swarm in. As he took his first steps into the open courtyard, a collective gasp of bystanders greeted him, followed by a concerned pair of Northmen.

"What happened?" Ottarr asked.

Breandán glanced around at the many who stared upon them, and decided it was best to take this discussion elsewhere. "We're leaving. Gather the men."

Ottarr caught on rather quickly and didn't waste time amassing their group. Even Gunnar appeared eager to leave as he helped to bring the horses around.

Breandán barely walked a few steps across the bailey

when a man he'd never seen before stepped in front of him. The man was young and wore an unmistakable scowl upon his face. When he made no attempt to help Breandán or the woman in his arms, Breandán made an attempt to go around the rude fellow, but the man blocked his path.

"So, this is the woman to whom my father gave all his love and respect...instead of his legitimate heir."

Breandán glanced down at Mara, thankful she wasn't aware of what the lad proclaimed. "Who are you?"

A callous twitch pulled on the one side of the stranger's lips. "The *legitimate* heir."

It was bad enough Cathal had stooped so low to raise Mara as his own and keep her real father a secret. But now he'd gone even lower by siring a son, from a mistress no doubt, and concealing him until it proved beneficial—like now, when a new king was direly needed. Cathal Mac Conor truly disgusted him.

By the look on the lad's face, Breandán suspected he didn't care much for the man either. What bothered him most was the contempt the young man had for Mara. She'd done nothing wrong and, like this bitter legitimate heir, was caught in the same web of lies.

"I hope she and her whore mother rot in hell."

"Teague. That will be enough." Fergus's voice resonated through the courtyard, and Breandán watched the lad turn around, his face devoid of emotion.

"Is it over?"

Fergus looked at Breandán first, then nodded at Teague.

"Then your services are no longer needed," Teague declared. "And neither are yours," he sneered, now looking at Breandán. "I know the alliances my father kept with the Uí Briúin Bréifne and your Northmen friends. And with his death comes a severing of those treaties. You'll never be welcome here again. Know this well as you ride off."

Breandán happily concurred with the disdainful new Connacht king. "You needn't tell me twice." He shook with fury, his grasp on Mara tightening as he turned his back on Dún na hAbhann. He couldn't quite blame Teague for the resentment he held in his heart. It was not his fault he'd grown up without the love and respect of a proud father. He was only redressing the wrongs in his life, and by being both the victim and heir, he had every right. Breandán only wished he could gain some sort of vindication on Mara's behalf. She at least deserved that.

He stopped midstep as he reached the gate and remembered the promise he'd made to Angus. *Inform Fergus I'll be coming for him, with or without Mara, and he'd better have answers for me.* He called for Ottarr and gently passed Mara's limp body into the Northman's arms. Ottarr didn't ask why, but waited as Breandán strolled back through the courtyard.

He approached the yet-to-be-coronated king and took pleasure in the young man's surprise. "Permission to speak with Fergus."

Teague nearly scoffed. "Speak all you like as he is no longer an advisor of the crown."

Fergus slowly stepped forward, oblivious to what Breandán wanted.

Breandán stood tall as he eyed Cathal's friend. "I assume Angus brought you my message."

With hesitance, Fergus nodded. "He told me you would have questions."

"All were answered but one. Who turned Mara away after her husband's death? And a second time after her son's birth?"

Fergus's eyes dropped guiltily. "'Twould be me, but I was only following orders."

Breandán had never been so glad to hear those words. He threw one hefty punch and watched with great delight as Fergus fell on his less-than-noble backside. He half expected Teague to order his guards and have him thrown out of the bailey. But no one moved a muscle. The only thing he saw was the proud grin on Ottarr's face as he turned around.

"Now we leave," he stated to the Northman.

****

Mara opened her eyes, and her first conscious thought was of her father—or the man she'd believed to be such. She assessed her surroundings and realized she no longer stood at his bedside but lay on the ground, in the dark of night, near a campfire. A private one, it seemed, as the only person in her company was Breandán. He sat alongside her, and a look of sincere protectiveness overcame his face as he noticed her awakening.

"Where am I? Where is everyone?"

He brushed back her hair and glanced toward a distant area to his right. "Everyone is over there. I thought you'd need some time alone."

He was correct. She really didn't want to face anyone right now. It was difficult enough to accept what Cathal had told her. In truth, she wanted to crawl into a hole and disappear. All her life, she'd believed she was the daughter of a king. A princess. Even Dægan thought he'd married a princess. Everyone had. But who was she now? Whose daughter was she? And how could her mother never tell her? How could her loving mother hide this secret from her and take it to her grave?

A painful lump hardened in her throat, and tears burned in her eyes. Unable to stop herself, she wept once, then suppressed it.

"Shh…" Breandán soothed, stroking her cheek with the back of his fingers. "You need to forget all about Cathal Mac Conor. He's not worthy of your tears and sadness. If anything, you should be pleased you no longer have a blood tie. You're better off without him."

Breandán's words were true, but her broken, scar-ridden heart had difficulty accepting them.

"Are you hungry?" he asked.

She shook her head.

"The best thing for you to do now is rest. We have a long journey ahead of us."

Mara watched Breandán leave, and a deep sense of longing pulled at her aching heart. She'd no idea where he was going, but all she knew was she didn't want him to go. Her lips fell open to call him back, but her voice failed her. Even the muscles of her own body failed her as she lay on the ground. She squeezed her eyes shut and blocked out the world around her.

It felt better to close her eyes. This way she could imagine being home again on Inishmore, surrounded by those who loved her. Immersed in the tiny arms of her son. Welcomed by the people who had long accepted her as their own.

No matter how hard she tried to envision herself with those she called family, her thoughts always seemed to wander back to her father—*Cathal*, she corrected—who'd forsaken her. She wanted more than anything to forget him, but she couldn't overlook the fact that he'd once lovingly raised her as his own. He'd unselfishly given of himself when her mother was ill and dying, and had devotedly cared for her thereafter. Cathal had loved her as his own blood. There was no doubt about it. But why? Why would he allow himself to love another man's child?

Perhaps he cared that much for her mother. Perhaps he loved her so much he was unwilling to tarnish her mother's reputation by letting others find out about her pregnancy from another man. She hardly thought Cathal capable of such a sacrifice, especially after all the grief he'd caused her in the past seven years. But it seemed to be the only viable reason. She'd never heard him say one ill word about her mother and could only recall the way he'd smile when she'd walked into the room. Though he'd always been a self-righteous, hard-bitten old king, his feelings for her mother must have been stronger than his own superior self.

For a slight instance, a smile curved her lips.

It had been a long time since she'd smiled over that man, and it felt good to think of him in a better light. To think of him not as the man who denied her his love for seven years, but a man who generously loved her and her mother until the day he took his last breath.

She felt better remembering Cathal that way. She refused to let her heart harden over things in the past. She'd move forward with strong determination, if not for her own sanity, then for the son who waited for her back home. She'd hold on to the things in life that mattered.

Mara opened her eyes and brought to mind something else that mattered: the one man who had stood by her without fail: *Breandán*.

She thought back to the last moments she'd spent in Cathal's chamber, remembering her sudden impulse to flee and remove herself from his familiar struggle with death. She recalled the helplessness she felt, the crushing weight of watching him suffer, and the solid, warm wall of Breandán's body behind her as she stepped back. She recollected the way he'd held her when she turned to bury her face in his chest. The way he'd wrapped his arms around her as she cried, and the way he scooped her in his arms when she hadn't the strength to stand anymore.

Aye, she remembered that. She might have blacked out, but she couldn't forget the feel of those mighty, protective arms around her back and knees. Breandán had been there for her, and she hadn't even told him how much it meant to her. How grateful she was for his faithful companionship despite the risks he took in this journey.

She wanted to see him. She wanted to be in his arms again and feel the comfort of his embrace as she relished the sound of his heartbeat in her ears. She needed that peace. She needed his remarkable kindness to make all her grief disappear.

She needed *him*.

****

Breandán removed his clothes and draped them over a tree branch, then sank low in the cold water of the nearby stream in hopes of washing away his troubles. Never before had he felt so helpless. So useless.

Mara had been told she was not Cathal's daughter, and he couldn't do a thing to console her. Initially, her pain had come from losing a husband. But now her sorrow came from not knowing who her father was or from where she came. Unless she could discover who she was, she'd never find true happiness.

For a man, having a name—a surname—meant everything. It gave a son a sense of pride to carry the name of his father or grandfather. Without it, a man was just a man, indistinguishable from the rest.

For a woman, he doubted it had similar meaning. But having no name at all was quite a different matter. Knowing Mara faced this dilemma, he felt discouraged and incapable of truly consoling her. He exhaled and felt the cold line of the water's surface rise above his chest, and his neck, then over the tips of his ears, until he was completely submerged.

****

Mara crept aimlessly through the dark. The fractured light of the pale moon through the forest limbs barely helped to light the way. She knew Breandán would probably scold her for wandering alone in the forest without the aid of an escort, but she'd been searching for too long to give up now.

As she ambled through the labyrinth of trees and brush, she never strayed too far from the distant red-orange glow of the men's campfire light. And she certainly hadn't expected Breandán to wander too far either. He always seemed to be near, even when he was out scouting the area.

The farther she meandered, the more she believed she might not find him. Perhaps he'd fallen into trouble. Just as she dared to call out for him, she caught sight of something gleaming in the moonlight. She cautiously drew near until the object materialized into Breandán's beautiful white-gray hare cloak hanging over a tree limb. His belt and kirtle were also draped beside it, while his quiver of arrows and bow lay on the ground.

Realization sank in. Breandán was bathing.

She glanced to her left. The shimmer of moonlight reflected in the quiet stream nestled within the hardwoods. She wrung her hands, distraught to know that somewhere in this deep pool, Breandán was without clothing.

Water sloshed behind her, followed by the trickling of droplets. For a moment, she held her breath. Wild thoughts of Breandán's bare torso, slick with water, swept across her mind. She envisioned his abdominal muscles surrounding his small, attractive navel, and his lower half concealed in the depths of the stream.

She wondered if he'd seen her standing there, or if he'd immersed himself beneath the water again. This would be the perfect time to bolt and save face. She drew in a few unsteady breaths and whirled on her heel, but froze after the first step. Breandán stood in waist-high water with the glimmer of moonlight on his broad shoulders. She gasped and turned back around, an apology hanging on the tip of her tongue.

"You shouldn't be out here alone, Mara. 'Tis not safe."

She squeezed her eyes shut, knowing he was absolutely right, but found herself challenging that fact. "I'm not alone, Breandán. I'm with you." She gathered her bravado and faced him once again.

He glanced around the area with a careful shift of his eyes. "You do realize there are others among us who guard this forest."

"I'm a grown woman. If anyone grows suspicious of what I'm doing here, 'tis not my concern."

"Why *are* you here?"

Her lips clamped shut, keeping her from saying what

she'd long held inside her. Even as she said it in her head, it sounded absurd. She'd already been cast aside by someone who'd meant a great deal to her, and to be shunned by Breandán as well, the one person she needed the most, would devastate her.

Her knees shook fiercely. "Perhaps I spoke too boldly. I shouldn't be here." As she scrambled to leave, she heard an enormous splash and the footfalls of his dogged approach. He blocked her path with the advance of his dripping wet body, trapped her between himself and the tree limb that held his clothes.

She purposely cast her eyes at anything other than Breandán in his wet, naked splendor.

"Look at me," he whispered.

She swallowed hard and closed her eyes, trying to find the strength to do as he ordered. It was quite unbecoming for a princess—

Her thoughts rammed her square in the stomach. She wasn't a princess. Not anymore.

"I said look at me." This time he reached up and turned her face. His eyes pierced her soul. "What is it?"

She averted her eyes, but he caught her chin.

"You came to me for a reason."

"Aye, well," she stammered. "You're making it rather difficult for me to think clearly."

"You went through much to find me. Talk to me, Mara. What is it?"

She had no idea how to express her emotions except to just blurt them out. "My heart has always beat for the love of Dægan, and for it to…ache like it does for you…it's all new to me." She closed her eyes. "I feel alive when I'm with you. And when you left me alone by the fire, I felt empty. As if a hole had been carved in my heart. All I could think about was being in your arms, being close to you. But..."

She hadn't realized her chin had dropped until Breandán raised it again.

"But..." he repeated.

She swallowed the hard, dry lump in her throat. "But after what Cathal had said...after knowing I'm not his rightful heir...I can only imagine the disappointment you must feel. The regrets you must have in leaving your family behind and risking your life for a woman who's not even a princess. For all you know, I could be an unfree man's daughter." The thought settled deep and jagged in her chest. "Perhaps that's why you left me at the fire and hid yourself away in this forest."

Breandán drew back slightly, and his gaze washed over her face. "Mara, my love for you has never depended upon who you are. But who you are to me."

Tears welled in her eyes. "And who am I to you?"

"Mara, you're my next breath. You're the reason I breathe at all."

His profound words stole her own breath from her lungs. Then his hands clasped her face and pulled her into a kiss so passionate, she nearly collapsed to the ground. As his tongue swept into her mouth, his arms came to her rescue and drew her close. His skin was cool and slippery, but the solid wall of muscle beneath her palms made her fingers clench. She slid her hands up his chest and over his shoulders until she could wrap her arms around his neck.

She'd never yearned so strongly for any man save Dægan that she almost believed these recent desires were nothing more than straight lust and desperation. She pulled back from his kiss and pushed herself from his arms.

He stood motionless and disenchanted. "You're scared," he reasoned. "I respect that. And I'm sorry I—"

The sound of a whistling songbird cut off Breandán's apology. He scanned the dark woods, throwing on his leine and cloak. "Someone is coming. You have to go."

Mara watched him dress with fluid dexterity and peered into the grim maze of trees and shadows all around her. As disoriented as she was, the lingering sensation of his wet, hard-muscled body made it worse. "H-how do you know this?"

Breandán made quick work of his belt and quiver, then ushered her forward. "Trust me, Mara. Go!" His voice was hasty and tense as he picked up his bow and sent her back on her way to the safety of the group.

Chapter Twenty-eight

Mara ran back to the fire, her heart pounding so hard she thought it might escape her chest. The urgency in Breandán's voice contributed to her rapid heartbeat, but so did the thoughts of their incredible kiss.

She could still feel the thrill, heat, and strength of his arms holding her to him. Her brain refused to let her forget how handsome and virile he looked. And try as she might, she couldn't stop thinking about his words: *"Mara, you're my next breath. You're the reason I breathe at all."*

Were his feelings for her that intense? His strong words seemed more akin to what a husband would say or feel about his wife of many years. No sooner had that thought crossed her mind than another sprang into existence: what it would be like to wed Breandán. Aye, she'd contemplated him being a father to Lochlann, but she never really thought about what it would take to make him one.

Marriage.

Marriage to Breandán.

Was it really that farfetched? Was it so difficult to envision, especially after a kiss like the one they'd shared? She looked around, embarrassed, her cheeks flushing. She was glad the men congregated around another campfire so she could think in privacy. She needed to sort out her feelings and understand where these emotions came from.

Lillemor had said a woman had needs, things only a

man could fulfill. Was Breandán the man who could give her what she needed? Could he give her son what he needed?

Brooding over these questions gave her a headache. She threw a log into the fire and sat down to watch it burn. Like the heat of the flames, Breandán's kiss smoldered on her lips. His touch set ablaze her skin.

Excitement.

There it was again. That simple little word that encompassed everything ever since Breandán had come back into her life. Her spirits soon plummeted as she realized he wouldn't be around much longer. He'd return to his home in Connacht once their journey here had ended.

She hung her head, not ready to say good-bye. She had a hard time picturing him rowing away in the distant ocean toward Galway's bay.

"Are you all right, Mara?"

She turned her head and saw Ottarr standing in the light of her fire. She hadn't heard his approach until he spoke and wasn't prepared to bare her soul with her late husband's advisor. She opted for a little white lie instead. "Aye. I'm well."

"I was worried about you," the old Northman admitted. "I came to check on you, and you weren't here. So I went searching in the woods and came upon you and Breandán."

Her breath caught. She wondered what he'd seen.

"You ran from him. Did he say something to upset you?"

She breathed easier. "Breandán would never say anything to upset me. If anything, he was comforting me."

Ottarr sat down beside her. "I'm very sorry for what Cathal has said to you. It must be very difficult not knowing who your real father is. But I hope you never forget the family you still have."

Mara looked at the Northman. His kind words astonished her as he'd never been the sort to show sympathy. He was a brash old man who often spoke his mind, not caring for the feelings of others. She almost had to remind herself who was speaking so compassionately.

"Dægan brought you into our family, and you'll always be welcome among us. You never have to fear that, Mara."

She felt compelled to touch his hand, but she didn't. "I'm grateful."

Ottarr shifted, looking as though he was uncomfortable with the conversation. "Dægan once told me true happiness is found in the arms of a woman."

She looked at Ottarr oddly. He seemed to sense her wariness and backtracked.

"We often talked about things…affairs most men wouldn't regularly admit to discussing. Nonetheless, I believe Breandán has found happiness with you."

Mara sat, awed. She tried hard not to look so shocked, but it proved to be a bit more complicated given the rarity of this situation.

"What I'm trying to say is," Ottarr amended, "no one should go through life alone. And if you can find happiness with Breandán, then so be it. I'll not harbor any resentment toward you…or him. There. That's all I'm going say on the matter." He rose to his feet, then said, "You should try to sleep, Mara. Tomorrow's journey home will be long."

****

Breandán was wrought with the intensity of his desires

ever since he'd kissed Mara in a moment of passion. No woman had ever stirred a fire this great within him, and he feared he'd not be able to extinguish it. He walked a slow pace from the stream to where Mara lay beside her campfire, giving him ample time to collect himself. He flirted with the idea of joining the men at theirs and having a drink of something more potent than the water in his pouch. But this heavy burden of not being able to say to Mara all that he'd wanted before they were interrupted weighed on his mind.

He approached her with mindful steps, wary that she might have fallen asleep. If she had, he'd leave her to rest. Her sleep was more important than resolving his issues. As his shadow swept in front of him, she bolted upright, giving him the impression she was eager for his return.

"There you are," she said. "I was beginning to worry."

"There's no need to worry," he said as he sat beside her, conscious of the distance between them. "I've scouted the area myself and have assigned watchmen for the night." He noticed she was shivering now. "Are you cold? I could throw more wood on the fire."

"Or..." she intimated, raising her fur cloak to accommodate him if he so wished.

He stole a glance in the direction of the other fire. "I suppose I could lie with you" he said first, then corrected himself. "For the sake of warmth, of course. 'Tis much colder this night than it has been."

She smiled. "You wouldn't want me to freeze to death out here, would you?"

"Nay, I would not." All this time, he'd worried that he'd been too forward with Mara, especially after she broke away from their kiss in the forest. But it seemed he was wrong.

With his apology still resting on the tip of his tongue, he climbed his way behind her and drew his fur cloak over them as well. Lying on his side, he hesitantly wrapped his arms around her and pulled her body close. She tucked her legs in and nestled her back against his front, sighing as she melted into him. Forever was a long spell, but he swore he could hold her until the end of time.

"Better now?" he asked. Another long breath escaped her, and her eyelids drifted closed. He'd dreamt of this moment for so many years that for a split second, he wondered if she were another figment of his imagination. "Mara?" he whispered. But she barely stirred, suggesting she was deep in peaceful sleep.

He hugged her closer and decided he didn't care to know. He closed his eyes, drew in her scent that enveloped him like a satin cloud, and snuggled in for the night.

Chapter Twenty-nine

Tait had spent a week pacing the shores of Inishmore waiting for Mara to return. From the moment they'd sailed away, he'd had a bad feeling. The days had crept by at a snail's pace, and all the wondering and worrying took a serious toll on him.

"It should be any day now," Nevan said to pacify the distraught Northman. "I have every faith in Breandán that he'll bring her home."

Tait gave the king a sideways glance. "Easy for you to say."

Nevan strolled closer, looking out across the sea as Tait was. "'Twould be easier on yourself if you didn't have so much pride."

"Did you come here to nag?" Tait asked scornfully. "I'm a man of little patience this day."

Nevan laughed. "I can't recall a day when you had any."

Tait ignored the king's jest and continued to watch the ocean for ships.

"I suppose that wasn't very considerate of me," Nevan said after a few quiet moments. "I didn't come to nag. I came to express my apologies. I don't particularly care for this wedge between us."

"'Twas not me who put it there."

"Fair enough. I'll admit I'm guilty of positioning said wedge, but you continue to drive it deeper. How far will you hammer it in before it divides us entirely?"

Tait abhorred the metaphoric speeches Nevan often resorted to. "I'm not Dægan. Your figurative chatter doesn't amount to much in my brain. If you wish to talk to me, do so plainly."

"All right, then," Nevan said, clasping his hands behind his back. "When are you going to stop acting like a spoiled child and realize there're others beside your haughty self in this world? You've always behaved as if the only feelings worth expressing are your own. And until you realize you're not the only one with principles, emotions, and legitimate perspectives, you will always be a horse's arse. Is that direct enough for you?"

Tait was just about to give Nevan a piece of his mind when a voice from behind them stole his opportunity.

"Father, look!"

His son pointed toward the ocean at many dark objects shifting and bending in the expanse of the sea like a mirage. It was impossible to make out what littered the horizon, but the magnitude of their breadth occupied most of the ocean's surface. Gradually, the distorted images emerged from the haze, and Tait's heart plunged into his stomach.

"God in heaven," Nevan exclaimed. "Are you seeing what I'm seeing? That's a great number of longships."

"That is a fleet, sire." Tait had seen marauding raiders before, but never of this multitude. With their own forces absent from the isle and engaged in a task far away, it wasn't hard to imagine a massacre.

Panic set in, and Tait felt his blood drain from his body. "Alfarinn, get your mother. Get everyone to the fort. Now!"

Nevan backed up slowly, unable to tear his gaze from

the hoard of sinister vessels advancing in their direction. "I'll alert the few men we have."

"Wait," Tait said, motioning for the king to halt. He fixed on the foremost ships of the approaching army. "I've seen those warships before."

"Are you certain?"

Tait double-checked to be sure, then shouted in exultation. "Aye, I'm certain! 'Tis Havelok!"

Nevan hardly believed him. "Now is not the time to be mistaken, Northman."

"I'm not mistaken. I'd recognize those ships anywhere. Trust me." Tait slapped Nevan's back and laughed in relief. He took a second glance at the king and realized the man didn't share the same emotion. "Why the long face? 'Tis Havelok. An ally."

"Oh, I recall the man," Nevan said. "But I'm concerned with the man's objective in bringing all Scandinavia with him."

Nevan's sarcasm wasn't missed, but there *was* a greater number of men in Havelok's army. Tait reassessed the numbers. "Something must be amiss."

"What's going on?" Thordia called. "Alfarinn said we must get to the fort?"

Tait whirled around, forgetting he'd sent his son on a mission. He ran to his wife, whose face was white with fear. "I'm so sorry. The urgency has passed. 'Tis only Havelok who comes. See?" He enveloped her delicate pregnant body in his arms and pointed out toward the sea.

An hour later, the entire shoreline was littered with longships, each one as impressive as the next. The grand assembly brought back many memories for the islanders when seven years prior, Dægan had rescued Mara and returned only to die in her arms. As then, emotions ran high as the warriors leapt from the sides into knee-high water and trudged through the breaking surf.

The villagers accumulated in a gaggle of curiosity. Lillemor threw her protective arms around Brondolf. Thordia drew Alfarinn near, clinging to her husband's reassurance, and Nevan stood amongst his people, both apprehensive and hopeful.

Havelok was the first to climb the shore with determined steps. Tait met him at the embankment and extended his arm in an open welcome. "Havelok, my friend. 'Tis good to see you."

The two embraced in a hardy hug, thumping their fists on each other's backs. "Been far too long for friends to go without visiting."

Together they walked ashore, Havelok's scores of hirdmen following behind.

"Nevan," Tait said, gesturing in the king's direction. "You remember Havelok. The great warrior from the Hebrides."

Havelok let out a guffaw. "Ah, you flatter me well, Tait." He held out his hand, and Nevan graciously gripped his arm with both hands, awarding a firm shake.

"Any ally of Dægan's is always welcome here," Nevan announced.

"So what brings you to Inishmore?" Tait asked.

Havelok threw an arm around his shoulder. "I have a surprise for you." He glanced around the islanders and indicated their inclusion. "All of you." He pointed toward the nearest ship, and a single man bounded over the gunwale into the crashing waves. He stood ramrod straight with his chin held high. His dark blond hair blew in the wind, and his wolfskin cloak flapped like a gray flag at his back. There was pride in each stride, and the closer he came, the quieter the islanders became.

"How can it be?" Tait mumbled. He took slow, precise steps toward the stranger, and when he finally reached him, he stood stock-still. His eyes pored over every inch of the warrior's face, clothes, and weaponry, hardly believing who stood in front of him. "Is it really you, Gustaf?"

"Aye, Tait. 'Tis I."

Tait let out a cry of joy that all of Ireland could've heard. "It is you! Where have you been? We thought you dead!" The two men exchanged abrasive hugs, and their joyous laughter echoed above the ocean's clamor.

"Believe me, Tait. If I could've returned to my family, I would have a long time ago—"

Tait cut Gustaf's explanation short by embracing him again, not caring what his reasons were. All that mattered was he was alive and well. "I cannot believe you're here! Come. I want you to meet my family."

Tait hauled him ashore and led him into the group. An uncommon hush fell over everyone as the man's familiar face took them by surprise, especially Nevan. The king's color blanched, and his eyes widened.

"Dægan?" Nevan stammered out.

Tait laughed. "Nay, this is Dægan's older brother, Gustaf." The king expelled his breath in utter astonishment and staggered, but Tait caught and steadied him. "Are you all right?"

Nevan gave a nervous chuckle. "Of course I'm all right." He took another long look at the handsome Northman, still unconvinced he wasn't seeing an aged version of his departed friend. "Forgive me, Gustaf, for mistaking you for Dægan. The resemblance is quite uncanny. Though I don't place much confidence in apparitions, I could've sworn you were his ghost."

Gustaf lent a helping hand to the king and grasped his elbow. "I take no offense to it. I'm honored you would think of me in Dægan's greatness, even if 'tis only in appearance."

Nevan continued to stare, a smile on his lips. "You bear a likeness to his humble generosity as well. It gives me great pleasure to stand in the presence of another valiant son of Rælik." He patted the brawny hand upon his arm. "I welcome you and your men to our shores."

"And this, Gustaf," Tait said, pulling his pregnant spouse into his arms, "is my wife, Thordia."

"Ah, Thordia," Gustaf said, taking her hand and looking her over. "I remember when you were a young girl, ogling Tait when he was barely twelve years old. Either your father, Ottarr, finally gave in, or Tait didn't give him much of a choice in the matter."

Laughter erupted amongst everyone. Even Thordia took pleasure in it, clasping her hands to Tait's face and kissing him. He accepted her kiss, and dipped her over his forearm to finish it.

Cheers went up around them. It was a special moment to have Gustaf on the isle, and Tait continued to introduce those around him. He laid his hands on his son's shoulders. "And this is Alfarinn."

Gustaf knelt in front of the lad, exuding pride. "You're your father made over. I'd wager," he claimed as he tapped the weapon at the boy's belt, "you're quite the skilled swordsman."

Tait tousled the boy's hair. "Indeed, he is."

Gustaf arose, taking notice of another boy nearby. "And this must be Dægan's son."

Lochlann stepped forward, his bright blue eyes gleaming. "How did you know?"

Gustaf winked. "Anyone who's ever known Dægan couldn't fail to recognize his offspring." He sent a look toward Nevan. "Now that is what I call uncanny."

"Then I'm certain you can determine whose son this is," Tait replied, pulling a shy Brondolf forward.

Gustaf shook his head. "He's got to be Eirik's."

"And this is Eirik's wife, Lillemor," Tait said.

The shapely woman walked up to Gustaf and embraced him. "My heart is overjoyed to see you again. Eirik would be so happy to know his eldest brother is alive."

Gustaf closed his eyes and held her tight, as though his heart ached for the loss of his brothers. Tait assumed Havelok had been the one to divulge the tragic story of their deaths before arriving. It was pitiful to watch the eldest son of Rælik contend with all his emotions at once. His head hung wearily as Lillemor stepped back from his arms.

Gustaf glanced up at everyone, taking in all the numerous faces focused on him. "I cannot express my joy in finally being reunited with my family. I've long yearned for this day. What would make it most ideal is if I could see my mother." He turned to Tait now. "Where is she? Has she aged so much that she cannot greet me on this shore? Please, Tait, take me to her."

A haunting silence descended upon the diverse congregation, and all eyes shifted toward Tait. Perspiration prickled under his scalp as he tried to imagine breaking the tragic news of Svanhild's death to her oldest son. Being the bearer unnerved him to the point of pain.

"Gustaf, your mother..."

His might foundered. He wasn't strong enough for this. He'd seen so many suffer, so many broken hearts in his lifetime. He looked to Nevan for encouragement, but he too was at a loss.

Gustaf gazed off toward the sky. His jaw trembled. "When?" was all he could ask.

Tait took in an extensive breath. "Not long after Dægan died. She held on for a few years, but..." Was it really necessary to go into the details? Tait hoped he'd not ask. "Her passing was peaceful. In her sleep. Gunnar found her one morning—"

"Who?" Gustaf mutated from a grief-stricken son to seething madman.

"'Tis all right. Gunnar is a friend," Tait explained. "Havelok's son. He used to be a mercenary but decided to give up that life and—"

"I know who he is," Gustaf growled.

Tait stepped back, noticing the storm raging in Gustaf's eyes. "I know you didn't expect to come here and learn of your mother's death. 'Tis not something any loyal son is ready to hear."

Gustaf lunged forward and gripped Tait's kirtle with both hands. "Where is he? Where is Gunnar?"

Tait threw his hands up and broke away from Gustaf's grasp. "Settle yourself, my friend. You have every right to be saddened, but not angered with a man who's been naught but loyal to your family since he came here. Why such hatred for a man you've never met?"

Gustaf backed away from the crowd. "Havelok, you best speak up now lest I tear this place apart looking for him."

Tait looked to Havelok for answers. "What is he

talking about?"

Havelok rubbed the gray stubble across his jaw. "Where is my son, Tait?"

Tait narrowed his eyes in confusion. "He's not here at the moment. He's with Mara journeying across Connacht—"

"Is he alone with her?"

Tait drew back, baffled by the line of questioning. "He's with Ottarr and our men. Mara was in need of a protective escort to see her father. He's on his deathbed. Why?"

Havelok glanced at Gustaf before confessing. "My son is not the man you think he is."

A slow grin eased across Tait's lips. He couldn't help but think the two men were joking. "What do you mean Gunnar is not the man I think he is?"

"He was one of the ten men who killed Rælik, and if you say he was the first to come upon Svanhild, then we have every reason to believe he may have killed her too. If he had any suspicions that she recognized him, he may have done so to silence her."

Tait looked between Gustaf and Havelok, not knowing who was the craziest. He thought at any moment one of them would give in and admit it was all a tasteless joke. But they didn't. "You two have lost your minds. And you…" He looked down his nose at Havelok. "He's your son. How can you even think—"

"We haven't the time for this, Tait," Gustaf interrupted. "Mara is in grave danger. We have to get to her."

Tait took Gustaf's allegations toward Gunnar personally and snapped back. "What makes you so certain he did anything to Rælik? You left right after your father died, with not a word or a good-bye to anyone. You deserted your family. And yet you stand here, accusing my friend of something so monstrous, so…" His words and good sense disappeared. "At least Gunnar was here. Where were you when your family needed you most?"

Before Tait had finished his last word, Gustaf punched him in the jaw, and he fell to the ground. He scrambled to his feet and lunged at Gustaf, spitting mad, but those around him held him back. "The truth hurts, doesn't it? You may have walloped my chin straight into next summer, but I'd wager you hurt more than I. Guilt is a crushing weight, my friend."

Gustaf surged toward him. "The only guilt I have is not getting to Gunnar sooner. I've been avenging my father for nearly half my life, hunting down every last cowardly bastard who took his. And Gunnar is the last man. I'll carry out what I aimed to do so many years ago, and if I have to go through you, so be it."

Tait shook his arms free, then looked at Nevan, whose grip he couldn't shake. "Release me."

Nevan slowly relinquished his hold. "Perhaps we need to hear Gustaf out. He seems very certain of himself."

Havelok intervened now. "Tait, I know you feel betrayed."

"Betrayed? Only by you. Not Gunnar." He pointed his finger at both men. "He's been a steadfast friend to me since the day you left him here, Havelok. And I'll not let you—either of you—accuse him of treachery. You all have sunk to a level deeper than I care to go."

"Tait," Havelok tried again, but Tait waved him off.

"I'll not hear any more of it. Be off with you."

"'Tis true." A tiny voice emerged from the crowd. A

voice so familiar yet so strange to Tait's ears. Tait whirled around and saw Brondolf standing in the forefront, his body trembling. A wet stain darkened his breeches just below his belt as he urinated uncontrollably.

Lillemor fell to her knees in front of her son and embraced him, her tears of both happiness and sorrow spilling from her eyes.

Tait came to the lad, kneeling down as well. "Did you say something?" The boy clamped his mouth shut as though he'd said too much, but Tait took hold of his frail arms and pled with him. "Brondolf, you have to talk to me. You have to tell me what you know."

Brondolf shook his head fanatically.

Tait tried again. "I know you're scared. But if Gunnar did something to your grandmother, I need to know. Please. For the love of God, please speak again."

Brondolf looked at his mother now, his eyes begging for help.

"Son," Lillemor encouraged. "'Tis all right. Gunnar is not here. He won't know what you say. Please, my son. Tell us what you know."

Everyone was held riveted with overwhelming anticipation, eager to hear what Brondolf had to say about Svanhild's death. Filtering through the adults, Alfarinn and Lochlann joined him on either side, standing together and giving him the strength and courage he needed.

"You can do it," Lochlann said. "I know you can."

Brondolf swiveled his head to his other side, looking at Alfarinn, who also encouraged him with a deep nod. He squared his little shoulders as though he were ready to face his demon.

Tait noticed a difference in the boy with having his two best friends beside him. He remembered his own two friends, Dægan and Eirik, who'd stood by him through thick and thin. Even when they were children, and he'd stolen his own father's prize horse when seeking Thordia's attention only to fall off and break his arm, they never let him bear his burdens alone. For months until he was able to use his limb, Dægan and Eirik did his chores for him so his father wouldn't find out. And now, as he regarded this trio of boys, he knew they'd be just as loyal from this day forth.

"I saw Gunnar," Brondolf began, his lips quivering. "He was standing over Grandmother…"

"Aye, go on…"

"He put a pillow over her face. And he held it there for a long time. He didn't know I was watching." A tear streamed down Brondolf's cheek, then he panicked. "I wanted to stop him. But I was afraid. I couldn't move. And then he saw me."

Tait stared at the boy, his story grueling to hear and so very hard to accept. Taking into account the hardships the boy had gone through to tell it, he knew the lad didn't have it in him to make up such lies. Not this grand. Not this horrendous.

"Why did you not tell anyone?" Tait asked. "Why did you keep this within you for so long?"

Brondolf lost his self-control and sobbed. "Gunnar said if I spoke one word, he'd kill me and my mother both."

…if I spoke one word. One word.

Tait hung his head in mournful realization. The boy had interpreted Gunnar's threat literally, and how could he blame him? He'd been but a four-year-old child, scared and hardly old enough to differentiate between an exaggerative statement and a heinous threat. He'd been frightened for his life and his mother's. What child wouldn't take it literally?

Tait's heart split in two for the boy. All this time, all these years, Brondolf had kept his mouth shut, never speaking to anyone about anything. He'd missed so much in his life. His innocence had been stolen from him. His childhood scarred and maimed. And this innocent boy was his best friend's son—Eirik's helpless child—whom he should've protected. Should've taken better care of. He should've seen through Gunnar's deceit and, more importantly, should've noticed the boy's desperate cry for help.

Tait threw his arms around Brondolf and gave him the love and affection he'd not given him in the past. With his embrace, he tried to make up for the lost time and all the things he'd failed to do.

He was their chieftain. And he'd failed them all.

Suddenly, a long moan of pain reverberated from behind him. His wife was bent at the waist and holding the swell of her belly from the bottom.

Tait ran to her, his heart jumping in his throat. "What is it, Thordia?"

She looked up at him, eyes wide and her mouth puckered as she tried to breathe through the pain. "I think the babe is coming."

Chapter Thirty

Tait paced the mead hall floor, his mind scattered between thoughts of his wife screaming in labor and Gunnar's blatant duplicity. Nevan, Havelok, and Gustaf accompanied him, though they kept their distance and strategized a plan for the search and seizure of Gunnar.

As Tait marched back and forth, he kept one ear on the discussion and the other on Thordia's painful delivery. Another long, shrill cry broke through the thick wood walls of the mead hall, and Tait growled. "If this child does not come soon, I swear I'm going to pull him out myself."

"Well, I imagine the source of the problem is that she has your stubbornness," Nevan said. "We could be here for days waiting on her arrival."

Tait halted his in his steps. "She?"

"Aye. Only a daughter could make a father pace until his mind is gone. 'Tis what they do best."

Tait shook his head and carried on with his mindless to-ing and fro-ing. It wasn't that he opposed the idea of a daughter. He just didn't care for Nevan's humor at a time like this.

Gustaf rose from his chair and wrapped an arm around Tait's shoulder. "Sit with us, and let's plot."

"I cannot even think of plotting against Gunnar without—" He drilled his fist into his eye socket. "How could he do this? Why would he do this?" He charged toward Havelok. "He's your son. How could he be capable of killing Rælik and Svanhild, and then befriend me? Is his heart made of stone?"

"When you arrive at that answer for Domaldr after what he did," Havelok stated coolly, "I hope you'll enlighten me as well."

Havelok was right. If Domaldr—Dægan's own twin—betrayed his father and tried to kill every one of his people thereafter without thinking twice, then why couldn't Gunnar?

Because Gunnar has been so loyal to me, that's why.

It was hard to admit he'd been fooled for seven long years. Never once had it occurred to him that he'd been glibly deceived or lulled into a false sense of security. He felt like such a fool, as though he'd let everyone down, including Dægan.

That was the hardest of all. He was left to protect and lead Dægan's people, and all he'd done was harbor and assist an enemy.

"I know you feel guilty for what Gunnar did," Havelok said. "But 'tis more my fault than yours. I brought him here. I delivered him to Rælik's family. You couldn't have known any more than I. The only thing we can do now is stop him from carrying out his plan."

"And what is his plan?"

Havelok sighed. "To get rid of everyone who might know of his past evils. I wouldn't doubt that Svanhild knew who killed her husband, and he made sure she couldn't tell."

Tait remembered his last words to Gunnar, his promise: *"I'll grant you her hand in marriage…"*

How could he do such a thing? How could he blindly offer the world to him when Mara's hand was not his to grant in the first place? He glanced at the king. "Nevan, I fear Mara is in more danger than you realize." He paused and swallowed what remained of his pride. "I promised her hand in marriage to Gunnar."

Nevan's eyes widened. "You what?"

"I was angry with you, Nevan. I'm sorry...I overstepped my bounds."

Nevan came to his feet in a flash and stuck his finger in Tait's face. "You stabbed me in the back. You had no right." He left the mead hall and slammed the door behind him.

Tait squeezed his temples between his hands and tried to expunge the remaining pain in his head. "All right, Havelok, Mara is now our greatest concern. How do we get to her without Gunnar suspecting anything?"

"To my knowledge, Gunnar has no idea who's been avenging Rælik all these years. If he knew, he would've gathered his own army long before this and hunted Gustaf down. As far as he knows, our arrival in Connacht, with such a grand number of men, will be due to your interest in Mara's safety. We'll tell him you called upon me to aid you. I'm certain, knowing the kind of chieftain you are, 'twould not be beyond you to do so."

It was rather unfathomable to hear Havelok conspire against his own son, even if it were for righting a wrong against his old friend Rælik. He looked at Gustaf now. "Are you going to be able to do this? Knowing the relationship between Gunnar and the man next to you."

A scary determination flared in Gustaf's eyes. "'Tis not a question of whether I'm going to. I have to. My father and my dear mother deserve justice. I didn't spend my entire adult life hunting down those ten spineless men to walk away now. I will avenge my father's death."

The mead hall door burst open, and Alfarinn's frantic voice pierced the silence. "Father! Mother needs you!"

His son's command was urgent, and Tait didn't hesitate to tear out of the hall and dash to his longhouse. He burst through his door, and the sight of his servants rolling up the bloodied linens unsettled him. It was horrific to see the copious amount of blood left behind from the birth, but not as haunting as seeing his Thordia, drenched with sweat and seemingly lifeless.

He staggered toward the boxbed, his heart laboring to beat. The notion of her ruin after she'd suffered to bring his child into the world broke him down to nothing. He barely heard Lillemor's voice.

He slowly turned his head and saw her wrapping the baby in warm linens. He could hardly rejoice at the sight of his newly birthed child, the tiny wonders of its clenched hands reaching out from beneath the swaddling cloth. All he could feel was the devastating hole his wife's death had left in his soul.

Lillemor smiled warmly as she cradled the babe. "Tait. Thordia is all right. She's only sleeping."

He fell to his knees in relief and threw himself at her. "Thordia," he whispered as he brushed away the wet strands of hair from her face.

She stirred at his touch and dragged her eyelids open, a smile creeping across her reddened face. She murmured his name.

"Shh..." He pressed his lips to her forehead. "Sleep. I'll be here when you awaken."

He watched her brows furrow. "What about Mara?" she asked under her breath.

"Worry not. We'll leave in the morning and bring her home safe. You just sleep. I'll not leave your side."

Thordia fell back into a deep slumber, and Tait was content to watch her. To revel quietly in the fact she was still with him. To praise the Christian god of his new faith for allowing him this one small gift.

Small blessings...he remembered Dægan saying once, and he smiled.

"Tait, would you like to hold your daughter?" Lillemor asked, carrying the little bundle toward him.

"A daughter?"

"Aye, and you'll be a good father to her," Lillemor said. "I know it."

Tait held his arms the way he thought he should, trying to remember how he'd placed them around Alfarinn many years ago. He felt nervous holding such a delicate thing as a fragile babe, but once Lillemor positioned her in his arms, it all came back to him. He cradled her tightly and gazed upon her petite round face. He wanted to cry. And eventually, he did. He wept as he held his precious daughter close.

****

Tait had remained with Thordia all through the night, and helped her care for the baby who awoke every few hours to eat. In the beginning, Thordia had been too tired to hold her head up, and he took it upon himself to prop the infant at her breast. He found nursing to be a difficult task as he was more adept at drawing a bow than drawing nourishing milk from his wife's engorged bosom. Nonetheless, it was an interesting experience to assist in activities suited for a wet nurse, and quite gratifying as well.

Now the light of a new day dawned, and Tait looked

up into the cloud-covered sky from the doorway of his longhouse, assessing the weather for his upcoming journey. He'd have to say good-bye to the woman who made him so proud, and leave her in Lillemor's capable hands so he could make things right with Nevan. The only way to do that was to find Mara and bring her home safe.

From behind him, a hardly there whimper mewled from the boxbed and roused Thordia from her sleep. He looked over his shoulder. Thordia had already scooped the infant in her arms. Tait was hard put to hide his smile as he came and sat beside her. He traced her veiny, hard-swelled breast with a gingerly touch, and called to mind that they hadn't been so distended last night. "It looks like it hurts."

"A little."

He adored the cute rosy lips suckling at her nipple. "She's a hungry little one." He then looked up and found his wife staring at him. Although drained and haggard, she was the most beautiful woman he'd ever seen. "Have you given thought to her name?"

Thordia gazed down upon the feeding child in the crook of her arm. "I was thinking…Arnóra."

He tested the name on his lips. "Aye, I think that name suits her well. Arnóra it is, then." He reached out and cupped her face in his palm. "You've made me so proud this day. I love you, Thordia."

"And I you, m'lord."

After a time, Lillemor entered the longhouse with Alfarinn running past her excitedly. The boy cheered as he leapt into his lap. "I was afraid you'd left already, Father."

Tait hugged him tight as the other two boys straggled in. "You know I'd not leave without saying my farewell to you, son. And how do you fare this morning, Brondolf?"

Alfarinn looked up from his father's hold. "He never

keeps his mouth closed."

Tait laughed. "Not a thing wrong with that. I think he's entitled, wouldn't you say?" Brondolf smiled, but Tait detected a hint of worry on the lad's face. Lochlann's as well. "Come here you two." He took all three of the boys and sat them across his lap. "Everything is going to be all right. Half of Havelok's men are staying here to protect the isle whilst we're gone. But I still need you three to keep a sharp eye. Lillemor and Thordia are going to need you too. Think you're up for the task?"

All three nodded simultaneously.

Tait turned to Lochlann. "And don't you fret. Your mother is with Breandán." He stole a glance toward his wife to see her delight in the way he finally spoke respectfully of the Irishman. "And if I know him, he's not taken his eyes off her. We'll bring your mother safely back to you. Together we will. This I swear, Lochlann."

****

Tait waded through the wake of the Atlantic and jumped over the gunwale of his longship. With his sword at his belt and his bow and quiver at his shoulder, he was ready to take on the world. Everyone was aboard the streamlined vessels, their oars in hand, waiting on his command.

He took his place at the steer board and searched for Nevan. The king had never spoken openly about his decision to come along, but Tait would've bet his right arm that he was somewhere in tow. Oath or not—the one Nevan had made with Cathal Mac Conor not to step foot in Connacht—Nevan was not about to stay behind when his daughter's life was in danger. He caught a glimpse of the king sitting in Havelok's ship. He didn't look happy, nor did he cast his eyes in Tait's direction. Nevan was too stubborn for that.

Gustaf took command of the steer board two ships over, just as Dægan used to do. Tait still found it hard to look upon the man's face, as Gustaf resembled his brother in so many ways. He had a proud stance, a determined look in his eyes, and an overall similarity in build and hair color. Then it occurred to him: if he took a second glance every time he looked at the man, what would Mara do? How would she react? This worried him. Not for Breandán's sake, but for hers. She'd gotten along well after the loss of her husband. Would this make it all come back? Would the very likeness of Gustaf open the wound in her heart so deep, she'd never recover?

There was no time to worry about it now. His only thoughts needed to be on protecting her from a calculating mercenary warrior. He gave the signal, and the longships lunged backward. His son waved to him from the door of his longhouse, and within moments, Thordia joined him with a bundled babe in her arms. The sight of his family pulled at his heartstrings, and he prayed to the Christian god that he might return on a swift and mighty wind before he had a chance to miss them.

Chapter Thirty-one

Breandán was the first to arise the next morning. As Mara lay tucked in the pocket of his shoulder, he couldn't recall a time when he'd been this happy, nor could he remember a night when he'd slept so well. If he hadn't had to relieve himself or ensure that Mac Flann's men weren't waiting to strike at dawn, he would've burrowed beneath their cloaks and caught another hour of sleep.

Reluctant to leave Mara's warmth, he slipped out and headed into the forest. The brisk morning air seeped through his clothes, necessitating that he take to his tasks quickly. He blew warm air into his hands and chose a spot suitable for emptying his full bladder.

By the time he finished, the men began to stir, stretch, and make slow efforts to pack their belongings and tack up their horses. Some lingered by the smoking fires in hopes of soaking up the last traces of warmth, while they stuffed their mouths with stale biscuits and hard cured meat.

Breandán felt his stomach rumble and wished he had time to hunt for fresh venison in the thriving forest of Ireland's lush terrain. It was the perfect morning for such a thing. The air was crisp, and a thick layer of dew covered the promising juicy leaves, berries, and grasses that the red stags loved to graze upon. Instead, he made a quick reconnaissance of the camp's perimeter and then headed for the picket line where their horses were tied.

As he saddled his mount, heavy footfalls caused him to

look up. Gunnar descended the hill where he'd been assigned as guard and came toward him on a direct path. Breandán noticed he looked exceptionally calm and couldn't help but wonder what schemes the Northman had cooked up in those long, solitary hours.

Gunnar circled the equine's hind and leaned against its flank. Breandán fastened his girth strap without missing a beat and spoke to alleviate the silence of the Northman's evil glare. "I'm grateful you kept watch through the night. I'll have someone else take your turn for you this evening."

"How kind of you," Gunnar muttered through his teeth.

Breandán disregarded the snide comment and secured the girth with a solid tug.

"You think you're cunning, don't you?"

Breandán never gave Gunnar a second glance as he collected his bridle and fastened it on the horse. Gunnar lost his composure and shoved him backward.

"I'm talking to you, *Éireannach*."

Breandán found his footing and stared the Northman down. "And I'm listening. I've heard your every word."

Gunnar took a step forward, emphasizing his own taller height. "You can pretend all you want that you stand above me. That you're smarter than me. But I know what you're doing. And you can continue to put me as far away from Mara as you think will suit you. 'Twill not benefit you when we return. Nor will it serve any purpose for her." After his threat, Gunnar plowed past and purposely ran his shoulder into Breandán's.

"What was that all about?" Ottarr murmured as he moved in and tended the antsy horses.

Breandán studied Ottarr, unsure if he should even confide in him. As he decided on whether or not to put his trust in him, the older man confessed.

"Between you and me, I never cared for Gunnar. I know Tait holds him in high regard, but his favor means naught to me. There's something peculiar about him. Always has been. Does that help you?"

Breandán would've never believed that Ottarr would speak ill of his own brother-in-arms. Then again, he never believed that a man who'd once threatened to kill him would take actions to befriend him. Through the course of this journey, Ottarr seemed to be changing his attitude, outlook, and loyalty. And Breandán hoped he read him right.

"What did Tait promise Gunnar when we return?" he asked discreetly.

"To my knowledge, nothing. Why?"

Breandán glanced around for eavesdroppers. "I believe Gunnar may have threatened Mara."

Ottarr's gaze hardened as he pondered Breandán's statement. "Threatened her? How so?"

"He didn't offer specifics. But his warning presaged disaster."

Ottarr finished securing his tie-downs and turned to look Breandán in the eye. "I think 'twould be best if you stayed near Mara in the line. Marcas can lead, can he not?"

"Aye."

"Good. Then I'll stay near Gunnar at the end. Keep everything else as it is." Ottarr didn't wait for Breandán to dispute it, and led his horse to where Gunnar congregated with the others.

Breandán tried not to stare at the old Northman as he left. It wasn't every day that he'd ally himself with a *Fionnghaill.* To say the least, the concept was a bit unsettling.

Dægan Ræliksen had been the first Norse ally he'd joined forces with, and although it had proven advantageous, it had come with its share of complications.

While he was confident in his choice then, he wasn't so much now. If Ottarr and Gunnar were deceiving him into believing they weren't amicable cohorts, it only meant Mara would suffer in the end and he'd be to blame. He threw a glance her way and verified that Gunnar was nowhere near as she tended to her bedroll at her campfire, and his heart constricted at the thought of something bad happening to her.

****

Mara didn't have much time to recollect her night wrapped in Breandán's arms after she'd awakened. The men who were there to protect her saddled quickly, eager to make their way back to Inishmore. They had several days of backtracking ahead of them, and getting an early start was their best bet for covering as much ground as possible.

The only person with patience was Breandán. He'd allowed her the time she needed to see to her ablutions and wash up in the stream without rushing her. He even assisted with suiting her up in her armored disguise. The only difference was that he did it all with the absence of a smile.

She loved his boyish grin and the way his chiseled face softened with the presence of his laugh lines and dimples. She wondered what had happened to make it disappear. What's more, she was curious if it had anything to do with why he rode beside her in formation instead of his usual position at the head of the line.

After much contemplation and coming up short on

answers, she decided to ask him point blank. "Are you going to speak to me about what's wrong, or must I guess?"

Breandán kept his gaze forward, his face straight as an arrow. "Naught is wrong. I'm simply protecting you as best I can."

She did feel safer with him trotting beside her, but she was still unsatisfied with his response. "By lying? How will that protect me at all?"

From the corner of her eye, she saw him glance her way. "I didn't lie to you, Mara."

"All right, then. You're not telling me the whole truth."

"Now we're splitting hairs."

"Breandán, it doesn't take an extraordinary intellect to know you're troubled by something. And if it pertains to my safety, would it not be wise to inform me of such dangers?" She tossed him a shrewd look in hopes he'd see her side of things.

"You could be correct," he admitted. "Though I fear 'twill merely upset you. If you're distressed, you'll be distracted from staying alert for possible danger."

"So I *am* in danger, then?"

Breandán rolled his head to face her with a look of resignation. "Fine. If you must know, Gunnar said something to me this morning that I didn't care for."

She went from complacent to concerned in a matter of seconds. "Did he threaten you?"

"Nay."

Her eyes widened. "Did he threaten me?"

"I believe so, but he spoke about it in such vague terms that I can't be too certain. Rest assured he's being watched closely by most everyone, including Ottarr and

Ultan."

Inexplicable or not, Mara didn't trust Gunnar any farther than she could spit, and being a respectable lady, she was neither practiced nor comfortable in hurling saliva at great distances. She huffed aloud in frustration. "I wish you'd tell me what he said to create such suspicions."

"It matters not what he said but how he said it. As if you or I would have no control over it anyway." He paused but spared her a glance. "Mara, is it possible Tait could've promised you to him?"

She was first surprised, then aghast. "Surely Tait wouldn't do that. I know I've disappointed him on many occasions when I've refused Gunnar as a husband, but he's never given me the impression he'd ever marry me off without my consent. I'd like to believe he cares enough for me not to do such a thing." She paused for a minute and gathered her thoughts. "Did Gunnar actually say something to that effect?"

Breandán shook his head. "All I know is whatever he has planned, 'tis for a purpose of getting even with me."

She huffed. "I'll never marry Gunnar. Never." She fixed her gaze on the wonders of the surrounding forest and tried to divert her mind to something other than marrying a man she could never love. A man she could never trust to be a good father to Lochlann.

Her vision blurred as her eyes glazed over the numerous vines and tall trees. When she absently followed their great lengths down into the ravine, she saw something move between the distant trunks. She leaned over her horse to peer farther, and just as she caught sight of armed men on the path below, an unexpected arrow struck her helmet and spooked her horse. The animal swung its hind end and sent Breandán's mount lunging. Before she realized what had happened or how to regain command of her panicked horse, Breandán yanked her from her saddle and pulled her onto his lap. His grasp around her waist pinched her ribs and crushed her stomach as they galloped away in search of cover.

She heard him call her name, and it echoed in her ears. He sounded terrified, but she couldn't find her own voice to let him know she was unharmed.

"Mara, for God's sake, speak to me! Are you hit?"

She heard the chaos of men shouting, the pandemonium of horses stamping, rearing, and shrieking in distress, and the infamous name of Duncan Mac Flann on everyone's lips.

Breandán's wide-eyed expression scared her. She'd never seen him this frantic before, or this fearsome. He drew her tighter against him and shouted a round of orders from a voice strong and commanding. She clung to him, frightened for her life.

And for his.

After dodging between trees and dense rhododendron, Breandán skirted around a huge boulder and leapt from his horse with her in his arms. He carried her behind a cluster of scraggly bushes and laid her down. There was no tenderness in his hands as he gave her head a hard shake. "Don't move from this spot. You hear me?"

Mara could only nod. All around her, men armed themselves and took cover behind trees and rocks as they retaliated with spears and arrows. She felt Breandán grope her hips in a frenzied search amid her oversized trousers. He jerked out a dagger at her belt and slapped it in her hand.

"If anyone tries to take you, use it!" In the next breath,

he relinquished his reins as well. "If they get to you, ride off! I'll find you!"

She watched him bolt to his feet and dash through the forest as he nocked an arrow to his bowstring. Only then did she find her voice. She screamed "No!" at the top of her lungs, but it was too late. He'd already plunged headlong into battle against Mac Flann's forces.

****

"Don't let them gain higher ground!" Breandán shouted as he fired arrows from atop a steep hillside into enemy territory. He and a few other skilled archers held off as many as they could, but it wasn't enough to stop them.

Marcas joined him in the assault, killing two men upon his arrival with two flawless arrows through the heart before delivering his awful message. "Breandán, Mac Flann has your family. Look, down there."

His friend's words caught him by surprise, but he took aim again and shot his target dead. He then darted for cover behind a massive tree trunk and peered into the valley below. Several sentries stood guard around three horse-drawn carts that caged an undeterminable number of hostages. Arms flailed from behind a lattice of wooden bars, and cries rang out to anyone who might hear them.

The first face he recognized was Sorcha's as her unmistakable ebony hair distinguished her from the others. Her clothes were tattered and torn as though she'd suffered a great deal before her capture. His anger escalated even more when he saw his mother and two sisters crouched in the corner, holding on to each other in sheer terror.

Breandán's first thought was of his father. Was he all right? Or had Mac Flann's men killed those whose health and age would've held them back?

An onslaught of arrows forced him to duck back behind the tree. He reached over his shoulder and nocked his own, listening for footfalls. Timing his attack, he stepped out from behind the tree and landed the shot. The others, however, were too close to affix another arrow to his bowstring in time. Their arrows were already marked for him.

He spun to avoid the first released missile, and threw himself down the hill feetfirst. Sliding on his bottom, he tripped one of the men, then unsheathed his dagger and stabbed the other. Before he could spring to his feet, a familiar voice called his name.

Grania.

He swiveled his head just in time to see one of the guards reaching through the bars and pulling her up by her hair. He was oblivious to the enemy closing in on him. All that mattered was saving his sister from the cowardly bastard who chose to brutalize a helpless child. He slashed and punched every man who tried to subdue him, and just as the guard drew his sword to run her through, he plowed into him with no regard for his own safety.

They tumbled to the ground like two feral cats, but Breandán rolled on top, struck him in the face, and drove his dagger into his chest. He barely had a chance to breathe when he felt the presence of others surrounding him.

Stealing the dead guard's sword, he came up hacking at anything that moved. Ottarr led the charge of Northmen down the hill, severing bodies and limbs as they passed, while Marcas and the archers eliminated the enemy forces by sniping from a vantage point.

As each of Mac Flann's men came after Breandán, he

fought them to the death and gave their weapons to those trapped inside the cages. Not only did he give his people a fighting desire to save themselves, but a means to do it. They rallied and used whatever they had available—their fists, their nails, their belts—until their captors' weapons could be taken and used against them.

Breandán climbed atop the cage, nocked his arrows, and took out any men who came near his family. At times, he even kicked a few who tried the same.

His mother called for him, and he knelt down, reaching his hand through to touch her momentarily. "Mother, where is Father?"

"I don't know what they've done with him. There were too many…"

His mother's words cut him straight to the heart. He couldn't make himself believe his father was dead. He wouldn't. "Father will be here." He glanced toward the towering ledge above them. "I'm certain of it."

Sorcha reached up as well and grabbed his arm. "Breandán, I'm so scared."

He looked into her tearful blue eyes. "I'll keep you safe," he promised, and he meant it. As long as there was breath in him, he'd do everything he could, but he knew he and the Northmen couldn't keep this up for long, especially when Mac Flann's army seemed to multiply as the battle wore on. They were outnumbered two-to-one, and, with their forces divided, it was only a matter of time.

Additionally, he feared for Mara as he couldn't be in two places at once. He had no idea what was transpiring on her end while he was defending his helpless family.

"Breandán, watch out!" Sorcha shouted.

A man with a battle-ax hurled himself at Breandán and missed, bringing the bloodied blade down with such force that it broke through the cage and jarred Breandán to the ground. He rolled beneath the cart to the other side, stood up, and drew his bow. The arrow darted straight through the man's shoulder and jolted him backward.

The man took hold of the shaft with one hand and broke off the fletching with the other. Breandán drew his bow again and aimed for a kill shot. As soon as that man dropped, a frenzied swordsman came running with his blade high above his head. Breandán had no shield and no time to nock and release an arrow. He bounced on the balls of his feet and gripped his dagger. At a clear disadvantage, he hoped he could at least evade the swing. Dying was not what he wanted to do today.

Then a lone mysterious horseman sprinted down the other side of the ravine and leapt from his horse onto the unaware enemy. Astonished, Breandán watched the helmeted warrior haul the foe to his knees and slit his throat in one swift motion. Breandán met his gaze and realized his savior was Tait.

A roar of robust excitement erupted from the Northmen. They brandished their swords high in the sky as a huge army of mounted reinforcements galloped full speed into the valley. A weary smile creased Breandán's lips as Tait unsheathed his sword and scythed his way through the cluster of brawling men, aiding those who needed it most. He was never more glad to see Tait than he was right now.

A second wind blew through him, reenergizing him for the battle that ensued and for freeing his people. He picked up the battle-ax left on the ground and severed the thick ropes that barred their escape. The door fell open, and his father's clan poured out. He did the same to each of the cages until all were free.

As Sorcha and his mother tried to exit the barricade, Breandán stopped them. "Get the women and children back inside. There's nowhere for you to go. You're safer inside. Stay."

"I don't want to," Sorcha begged, grasping his bloody tunic. "Please, we have to get out of here!"

Breandán seized her shoulders and shook her once. "I cannot protect you if you scatter about." He tipped his face closer to hers. "Please, Sorcha. Do as I command."

Sorcha's gaze flicked toward something behind him, and she gasped. Breandán reeled around and threw her body behind him, protecting her from an archer ten yards away who'd drawn his bow and taken aim.

A million thoughts ran through his mind. If he moved, Sorcha would die. But if he didn't move, he risked death himself. Even if he attempted to let it sink into a nonfatal area of his body, the injury would impair his ability to keep fighting and protect his loved ones from further danger.

No decision was a good one.

His world suddenly moved in slow motion. He watched the arrow launch from its home position, entranced by its trajectory, and neglected to keep hold of Sorcha behind him. She stepped in front of its path and fell into his arms with the projectile buried deep in her back.

"No!" he cried, thinking she'd unknowingly walked into the line of fire. But after seeing the quiet serenity of her sweet, satisfied smile, he knew she'd unselfishly and willingly given her life to save his.

His eyes coursed a red-hot path toward her killer, who trembled in nocking his next arrow, but a mounted Northman rode past and decapitated him with a momentous swing of his sword. The impressive helmeted warrior reined his horse around and locked eyes with

Breandán as though he were looking for someone in particular. When Breandán's face didn't seem to meet the Northman's criteria, he rode off and continued his crusade against Mac Flann's men.

"Breandán," Sorcha breathed, drawing his attention.

He lowered her limp body carefully to the ground and cradled her. "'Tis all right, Sorcha. I'm here."

Her falling tears left pale streaks on her dirt-ridden cheeks. "You're safe now," she said proudly.

He wanted to scold her for what she'd done. This wasn't supposed to happen. She wasn't supposed to give her life for him; he was supposed to protect her. And he could have if she'd listened to him.

Foolish girl. You selfless, foolish girl!

"Why…" was all he could muster as he held her.

"Because I love you."

What was he to say in response to that? He'd known she fancied him, but never had he given thought to her actually loving him. Perhaps he should've taken the opportunity a fortnight ago to tell her he loved only Mara. Maybe if he'd hurt her then, she wouldn't have sacrificed herself now.

"I'm cold," she said as her eyes glazed over. "I cannot feel you anymore."

He held her closer, giving her the solace she needed. "I'm here. I'll not leave you." How cruel he felt to hold the woman who'd given her life when he never gave her the time of day. Guilt, regret, and pain consumed him as he watched her fade away, and she no doubt thought he too truly loved her. He'd let her believe whatever she wanted. He'd not be so cold as to taint her last precious seconds on earth with the hard, bitter truth.

"This is all I ever wanted, Breandán. To be in your arms…"

He stroked her face with the back of his hand, soothing her with his touch until death rendered her motionless. Her eyes stared harrowingly at him with large, unresponsive pupils, and he reached up to close them. He embraced his friend one last time and said his silent farewell in her ear.

Chapter Thirty-two

Breandán jerked his head up the moment he heard his name called in the distance. To his joy, his father, along with a few men from his village, rode down into the ravine on slow, sure-footed horses. They were as bedraggled as he was, wearing the evidence of their own fight for survival against Mac Flann's attack on their faces and clothes.

With reverent care, he carried Sorcha to the cart and placed her body inside with his mother and sisters. He felt his mother's hand brush across his face in sympathy. It was difficult to look anyone in the eye after he'd failed to keep her safe.

His mother took his hand in hers. "Where is the princess you were to look after?"

Breandán's blood ran cold as he glanced upward toward the ridge. He had no idea if Mara was still crouched behind the bushes in hiding, or if she was even alive.

"Go to her, son."

Liam dismounted as quickly as a man half his age and limped to the cart to embrace his wife and children. Breandán laid a hand on his father's shoulder as he walked by, a quick gesture to let him know he was relieved and thankful he'd survived, then mounted the closest horse. Digging his heels into its flanks, he blazed a path up the steep embankment toward Mara and prayed she'd remained out of harm's way. If something happened to her as well, he'd never forgive himself.

As he passed Ultan and his group protecting the plateau above, he scanned the woods. It appeared they'd kept Mac Flann's men contained in the ravine, but there was no way to know for sure until he saw Mara safe and sound.

The woods were thick—thicker than he remembered—and quiet. He called her name, racing to where he thought he'd hidden her. But when he circled the area, she wasn't there.

He searched the ground, taking in the bunched-up leaves in haphazard piles and broken sapling branches. A struggle had taken place. He swallowed hard, and an icy chill settled in his bones. He called her name, then peered as distantly into the lush woods as his vision would allow. But there was no reply.

He made his way deeper into the wild grove, following the telltale tracks leading farther into the thicket. In desperation, he called for her at the top of his lungs, over and over again. His voice cracked from the misery strangling him.

Then he heard it. Mara's voice.

He jolted his horse forward and urged the animal to run as fast as it could, taking the slap of low-lying tree limbs in his face. As he raced through the wilderness, his only thought was her. His beautiful sweet *a thaisce.*

"Mara, where are you?"

She appeared like a heavenly angel, if angels wore armor and breeches, on the horse he'd given her to avoid danger. Her hair cascaded from beneath her helmet in long tangled tresses, and her smile beamed like the sun.

He hiked his foot over the horse's neck and leapt to the ground running. His feet felt heavy and uncoordinated as he tried to gain speed. She dismounted as well and tore off her helmet as she dashed to meet him. He stretched out his arms and crashed into her, lifting her off her feet in a joyous swing. He couldn't get close enough no matter how tightly he squeezed her, no matter how far he buried his face in the crook of her neck.

"Forgive me for not being here to protect you."

She smiled at him as if she understood the conflicts he'd gone through, and clasped his face between her hands. "Your family needed you. There's nothing to forgive."

"I had to make a choice between you and my family. And it nearly tore my heart out to have to choose." He set her on her feet and dropped immediately to his knees, holding her hands. "I never want to do that again. I want you to be a part of my family. And I want to be a part of yours."

Mara knelt with him, her eyes more intense and twice as green as he ever recalled before. "I know not who I am or from whom I came. The father I've always known is not even of my blood. How can you wish to be a part of my family when it doesn't exist?"

"You do have a family. You have Lochlann. You have Tait and all of Dægan's family. You even have Nevan and his people. Look around you, Mara. Every man here has protected you as though you were his own flesh and blood. And all I'm asking is for you to allow me to be a part of it." She opened her mouth to speak, but he cut her off. "Mara, I know you don't know who you are. But I know who I am. And I'm the man who should be with you at this very moment of your life. You once belonged to Dægan, a man who was twice the man I could ever be. I cannot fill the void he left in your heart. I'd be a fool to try. But I vow, with every breath I take, to love you and keep you safe until the one day you're reunited with him."

A single tear trickled down Mara's cheek. Consumed with an impulse to hold her, Breandán cupped her face and tenderly pressed her wet cheek to his mouth. "Marry me, Mara. And let me kiss away all your tears from this day forth. Let me make you happy again. Let me love you like—"

Her lips crushed his, stealing his words, his breath, and his wits. She'd never kissed him this way before. This was different. Her kiss contained as much fervor and passion as his own soul had felt for so many years, consuming him— so much so that he didn't notice the presence of another in the woods.

Thunderous hooves brought their kiss to an end, but the threat of being trampled split them apart. Breandán pushed Mara away and took the brunt of the man's shield. He toppled to the ground, a splitting pain reverberating through his skull. He squeezed his eyes closed and fought the blackness that threatened to overtake him. Every muscle in his body wanted to succumb to the flat ground beneath him. He had to stay conscious. Mara depended on him.

He heard the panic in her voice, the sound of her desperate pleas as she called his name. His body wouldn't budge. No amount of willing it to move could restore his muscles to working order.

"Breandán!" Her voice was closer now, as if she were right beside him. Aye, she was close. He could feel her hands touching him, urgently shaking him. And then they were gone—ripped from him as though she were seized and jerked away.

"Unhand me, Gunnar!"

Gunnar.

Panic ricocheted through his body. Fear jolted him awake. The brightness of the sky tore into his brain, and the forest spun.

He grabbed his head, trying to get his bearings. Through his struggle, he saw Gunnar haul Mara away and slap her across the face. The hairs on the back of Breandán's neck stood straight up, and his blood churned.

He dragged his sluggish self to his feet and charged forward. Gunnar shoved Mara aside and unsheathed his dagger a second too late. Breandán drove his shoulder into Gunnar's breastbone and tackled him to the ground, sending the knife skittering across the forest floor.

Mara caught herself on a tree and clung to its trunk for support as she watched the men roll around, punching and flailing. Every part of her wanted to help Breandán, but she knew better than to jump between two full-grown men. It was the most helpless feeling to stand aside and watch the man who loved her fight for his very life.

Her stomach turned. She felt powerless as Breandán rolled atop and straddled Gunnar, raining down solid fists upon him. Just when she thought he might have a chance, Gunnar bucked him off and stood quickly, scouring the ground for his lost dagger.

"Looking for this?" Breandán asked, maneuvering to his feet with the weapon.

Gunnar gave an evil grin and reached across his waist, unsheathing his sword in a slow, calculating manner. "Keep it. 'Tis my gift to you for what your death will soon be for me. Tait will reward me tenfold for doing what he wanted to do from the start." He lunged forward, taking huge steps to close the distance. Breandán darted to the ground and snatched Gunnar's shield, successfully blocking the first hard blow of the Northman's sword.

Gunnar swung his weapon repeatedly in a roundhouse fashion that kept Breandán on the defensive, backing him up with every strike.

Mara looked around her, hoping someone would see the predicament she and Breandán were in and put a stop to it. She feared no one knew where they were, as Ultan had demanded she hide deeper into the forest when Mac Flann's men had begun to encroach upon the area they struggled to secure. All efforts had been concentrated on holding the enemy in the valley. No one would imagine a traitorous battle had broken out amongst their own.

Grunts, growls, and iron hammering wood rang out as the men battled. Little by little, Breandán's strength waned. He barely had a chance with only a dagger and shield.

Gunnar took one last hard swing and split the shield in pieces, then backed Breandán against a tree, with the sharp edge of his sword inches from Breandán's throat. The only thing keeping Gunnar from slicing him open was the knife blade in Breandán's right hand and Gunnar's wrist in his left. Both men shoved as hard as they could, their faces red from exertion. There was no escape for Breandán.

"Give up, *Éireannach*," Gunnar gritted through his teeth. "Mara is as good as mine."

"Over my dead body."

"At least we're all in agreement, then." Gunnar slashed his sword across Breandán's midline and caught an unprotected abdomen.

Breandán cried out and staggered away from the tree, holding pressure to the slice on his stomach. As he tried to catch his breath, his legs gave out, and he fell to his knees.

Gunnar hovered over him and sneered.

"And to think Tait was going to marry me to Mara for bringing her back safe. I wonder what my reward would be for bringing your head to him on a spit?"

Mara watched in horror as Gunnar lifted Breandán's chin with the point of his blade, forcing him to look into the eyes of his killer. Her fingernails dug into the bark, and black spots speckled her vision. She couldn't just stand there and watch Gunnar kill him.

On the verge of delirium, she made a mad dash for Gunnar and screamed at the top of her lungs. He whirled around, but before she could gouge out his eyes or kick him between the legs, an arrow cut across her path and sank deep in his chest. Mara gasped and stopped short, watching Gunnar fall to the ground. She jerked her head in the direction from which the arrow came and saw Tait standing thirty yards away in full battle gear. He lowered his bow, looking as relieved as she felt.

Nevan suddenly appeared as well, running to her aid. He wrapped her in his arms for a brief emotional hug, then cradled her face as he looked her over for signs of injury. "Are you all right?" he asked.

She let out a held breath and nodded, unable to speak. How was it possible that Tait and Nevan were there? And why were they there to begin with?

From behind the cover of random trees, an army of men stepped out. Most were those who had initially accompanied her on this journey, like Ottarr and Ultan. And some were those she recognized from Havelok's mercenaries seven years ago.

To add to her confusion, a man who resembled her late husband in so many ways forged past her with Havelok on his heels. Her heart practically stopped at seeing this strangely familiar Northman. *Is that...? Nay, it can't be...* His hair color, gait, and facial profile were almost identical to Dægan's, and she would've believed him to be her risen warrior husband had he bothered to look her way. This man never gave her a second glance.

He walked up to Gunnar, who seemed just as surprised as she was, and drew his sword. "I'm Gustaf, son of Rælik, son of the man you slaughtered in Hladir twenty-three winters ago...in his own home...his wife to watch. I've come to avenge my father."

Mara and Nevan circled Gustaf at a discreet distance to get to Breandán. They knelt on either side of him, listening intently to Gustaf's speech. Never knowing what Gustaf looked like and thinking he was dead, Mara could hardly believe she was in the presence of Dægan's older brother.

"There were ten of you sent by Harald Fairhair. I've traveled through rain, snow, and bone-chilling north winds in search of each one. You, Gunnar, son of Havelok, are the tenth. Added to your crimes is the death of my mother, Svanhild. You *will* die this day, Gunnar Haveloksen. But you can choose to die either honorably or with shame. You decide."

Gunnar glared at his father and inched backward on the ground to no avail. "Are you going to stand by and let him do this? I am your son!"

Havelok steadied his voice, despite the tremble of his lower lip. "The moment you allied yourself with Harald Fairhair and killed my friend Rælik was the day I lost a son."

Gunnar propped himself up on his elbow and eyed the arrow protruding from his chest. "What kind of father are you to condemn your own son to death?"

"The kind of father who would prefer to see his son in Valhalla's halls. Now get up and fight Gustaf so that you might know the joys of Odin's bounty. If you don't, Odin will turn his back on you, and Thor will curse you for your cowardice."

Gunnar sighed in resignation and dropped flat on his back. "I can't."

"For once in your life, do something of which you can be proud," Gustaf chided. "Restore your father's pride in the son he's always loved, and fight like a man."

Gunnar laughed cynically, then coughed, spurting blood from his mouth. Drawing as deep a breath as he could muster, he sat back up on his elbow and gripped the shaft of the arrow as he fixed his gaze on his father. "I should've killed you too when I had the chance." With that, he drove the arrow deeper and pierced his own heart.

Mara didn't mean to make a sound, but it came out as she heard the squelch of Gunnar's ruptured blood-filled organ. She turned from the grotesque scene and buried her face in Breandán's chest. He moved to shelter her, but let out a groan himself. The injury he sustained pained him more than he let on.

Tait also came to Breandán's side and carefully hauled him to his feet, an act that was both gracious and contrite. An unspoken exchange of apology and forgiveness transpired between the two men, and perhaps the making of a newfound friendship.

Mara never thought she'd live to see the day when Tait accepted Breandán as an ally. They'd been bullheaded enemies since they'd met years ago, too stubborn to realize they wanted the same thing: for her to be safe and happy. Maybe now she could express her feelings toward Breandán without inciting Tait.

Bolstered by his selflessness, she wrapped her arms around both men and hugged them tight. "Thank you. Both of you. For saving my life." She felt Breandán's right hand and Tait's left on her back, hesitant at first as they didn't seem to know what to do in the presence of the other. Eventually, they pulled her in close and embraced her together.

****

Havelok and his crew set to work on building a funeral pyre for his son in dire hope that Gunnar hadn't displeased their All Father with a coward's death. Mara was acquainted with some pagan rituals from the Norse family she'd married into, but it was limited at best. Dægan's conversion to her Christian religion inspired others to forsake their heathen ways, thus allaying her need to learn the customs that she often thought barbaric in nature.

While Havelok grieved, Nevan and Tait helped Breandán to a nearby brook, where they slaked their thirst and tended any wounds they'd suffered in the battle. Mara did her best to find relatively clean linens for Breandán's gash, resorting to the cloth layers of her bedroll tied to the saddle of her horse. It was in times like these when she was thankful that horses were herd animals and didn't stray far from the group once turned loose.

She cut them into strips and soaked them in the clear stream as Breandán pulled one arm out of his leine and slid the fabric to his waist. She mentally prepared herself for the scrutiny she knew she'd receive under Nevan's and Tait's watchful eyes, as well as Breandán's when she had full view of the left side of his body from shoulder to navel.

"This will hurt," she warned before squeezing the cold water onto his five-inch laceration above his hip. Breandán winced and drew in a long breath through his teeth. "I'm sorry," she said, stopping abruptly.

Breandán smiled through his pain. "It's not your fault. This must be done."

As she wiped away the blood and dirt from the surrounding tissues, his words resonated within her.

"This must be done."

For so long, she'd worried about what others thought of her when it came to the relationship she had with Breandán. She finally realized that what they thought didn't matter. It wouldn't change how she felt about him.

As rash as her behavior had been when she thought Gunnar would kill Breandán right before her eyes, she'd been willing to risk it all, even her own life, to save his. Her reaction hadn't been driven by the goodwill of a platonic, casual friendship. What they shared was so much more than that. In all honesty, she could feel herself falling in love with him.

And falling for someone like Breandán was a good thing. It was a logical match that she shouldn't feel guilty for wanting or feel it necessary to hide. She was tired of masking her emotions and downplaying them in order to spare the feelings of those closest to Dægan. While she'd always considered others before herself, she realized she'd never find true happiness looking through the eyes of their approval.

"You're right, Breandán," she stated matter-of-factly. "This must be done." She threw down the wadded-up cloth and took hold of his handsome face. "And so must this..."

Ignoring the frozen stares from Nevan and Tait, she

bravely planted a kiss on Breandán's mouth as if it was the last time she'd ever have the chance. She savored the warmth of his skin beneath her palms, the velvety softness of his lips, and the flutter of her heart for which she didn't feel a bit of shame. Breathless and overjoyed, she pulled away and smiled at his panic-stricken expression. She stroked her thumb over his full bottom lip, which tempted her to have another taste, then said, "Do you still want to marry me and make me happy from this day forth?"

Breandán's gaze bounced between Tait and herself. "Of course I do. I always have. And always will."

"Then, aye. I will marry you, Breandán Mac Liam."

Before she could kiss him again, Tait stuck out his hand and stopped her from doing so, his face expressionless and unreadable. "If Breandán wishes to make you his wife, then he must first acquire your father's blessing. 'Tis only fair, do you not think?"

"I know not who my real father is. Cathal Mac Conor no longer claims me as his blood heir, and he died before he could say who does."

"What if I told you I know who your father is?"

Mara narrowed her eyes. "You know the identity of my real father?" Saying it aloud sounded even more absurd. How could Tait know if she didn't?

Nevan stood from washing his hands in the stream, his eyes soft and kind. "And I know as well. I've known for many years."

"Both of you know this? How is that possible?"

In tandem, Tait and Nevan answered, "Dægan."

She drew back, bewildered. Dægan had never mentioned such a thing before, and if he had, she probably wouldn't have believed him any more than she believed Nevan and Tait at this moment. How could her Norse husband, to whom she was briefly married, know such personal details about her conception?

Nevan took her by the hand and brought her to her feet. "When Dægan first met you, he gave you a gift. Do you remember what that was?"

"Of course I do. 'Twas a chest filled with expensive silks, spices, and gems."

"Indeed. And what did he tell you about it?"

Mara thought back to the day when she sat with him in his longhouse in Limerick. "He said it was given to him by a king who had once filled it for his true love."

"Did he tell you why the king was unable to give his true love the chest?"

"He did. He said her father had married her to another, which turned out to be his sworn enemy. Years later, the woman grew sick and died, and so the king tried to gift her widowed husband the chest as a truce. Unfortunately, the husband stabbed the king and left him for dead."

Nevan squeezed her hands gently. "Mara...I am that king, and your mother was—"

"It can't be," she stated firmly. "My mother was not an adulteress."

"Nay, she was not," Nevan agreed. "Our intimate relationship took place well before she was married to Cathal Mac Conor. And when he found out she was with child, the alliance he'd made with her father was more important than the scandal she'd bring if anyone found out. So, he married her and raised you as his own. Now, had I known she was with child, conceived from my seed, I would never have allowed the marriage to Cathal to happen. I would've fought for her...and for you. Please say you believe me, Mara."

She shook her head and stepped back. "This is all so...I can't even...how did...and why would Dægan not tell me?"

"If you recall the night Dægan breached Mac Conor's walls to save you from the charge of treason on your head, he confronted Cathal about it and Cathal didn't deny it. Dægan then used that knowledge as means to acquire peace. He promised Cathal that I wouldn't step foot in Connacht ever again, as long as Cathal allowed you to go free. I can only suspect that the reason Dægan never told you was because he feared you'd hate Cathal for keeping the secret, and me for walking away from your mother. When all that mattered was you were in my life now."

Mara placed her hand on her heart, trying to steady the pounding in her chest. "I want to believe you, Nevan, but..."

"Perhaps this might help you." Nevan pushed aside the leine and brat at his shoulder and revealed a gruesome raised white scar, proof of a knife wound. From Cathal Mac Conor's blade.

A tear slipped from her eye. Overwhelmed with mixed emotions, she could hardly make sense of them all. She pitied Nevan for all the pain Cathal had caused him. She felt saddened by the thought of her mother spending all that time on the River Shannon in hopes Nevan would return to her, yet he never did. And angered by the notion that her real parents' happiness had been plucked before it ever had a chance to take root.

Nevan brushed away her tear with his thumb. "I hope you can forgive me, Mara. I never meant to hurt you."

Of that, she was certain. It was the only thing she knew to be true. Nevan was a man of his word and had always been steadfast to her and Lochlann. She often wondered how a man could commit himself so dutifully toward her health and welfare when it conceivably didn't benefit him either way. It all finally made sense. Fathers did what they must for their children without expecting anything in return.

She threw herself into Nevan's arms and relished a true father's love and devotion. Surrounded by his embrace, she no longer felt the pangs of resentment or the dolor of heartache. She was the daughter of a king, an imperious chieftain of whom she could be proud.

A series of high-pitched trills and warbles resembling a common woodland bird whistled on the breeze. It was a sound no one paid much attention to, but one Mara quickly recognized as Marcas.

Breandán struggled to his feet and called back in the same songlike manner, indicating that it was safe to come out. Marcas emerged from the brush, guiding a particularly frail woman by the hand, along with two young girls and a white-haired man Mara could only assume was Breandán's father.

Breandán quickly tied a strip of cloth around his waist to cover his wound and fed his arm back through the sleeve of his leine before he walked to meet his family. They all swarmed and hugged him, unaware of his injury.

Mara watched as he suffered through their hearty display of affection, hugging each one just as eagerly. He kissed the top of his mother's head, then gestured in Mara's direction with an open palm.

"Mother, there's someone I want you to meet." He guided his mother to the edge of the stream and smiled proudly when he stood before her. "This is Lady Mara."

Out of reflex, Mara attempted to gather her skirts and lower herself in a bow, but remembered she wasn't wearing women's attire. Her face flushed as she became overly aware of the tattered breeches and leather armor adorning her body. Embarrassed, she bowed anyway, silently wishing she could've met his mother under better terms.

"Breandán has talked so much about you," Aoife admitted kindly.

"Even in his dreams," a little girl professed as she clung to Breandán's leg.

Breandán shot her a playfully scornful look. "I thought we agreed not to reveal such things."

Mara bent down on one knee and pressed the little girl's belly with the tip of her finger. "And you must be Grania."

She tilted her head upward at her brother. "You were right. She is beautiful." A clatter of light laughter broke over the group, but it didn't deter Grania as she dug into her sleeve. "I have a gift for you, Lady Mara." She pulled out a strip of white embroidered linen, wrinkled beyond belief, but surprisingly unsoiled.

Mara accepted it, admiring the work of a four-year-old and the care she'd taken in each of the colorful stitches. "'Tis lovely, Grania. I'm so very grateful."

Grania looked up at Breandán again. "She likes it, Brother."

Breandán patted her little back, then continued to introduce the rest of his family. "This is Clodagh, my other sister, and my father, Liam."

Mara stood and greeted them warmly. Likewise, she introduced those in her company, starting with her father, Nevan, chieftain of the Uí Bhriain, followed by Tait, Ottarr, and Gustaf. With the lands secure from the tyrannous reign of Mac Flann for the time being, the mood between the Irish and the Northmen was pleasant and joyful. Both conversed in a manner reminiscent of when Dægan was still alive.

He'd be proud, Mara thought.

About the time she looked at Breandán, Grania tugged the hem of his leine. He bent at the waist and stifled a wince, lending an ear to his little sister. "What is it, Grania?"

"Are you going to marry Lady Mara?" Her tiny voice carried well over the volume of everyone else's. So much so, in fact, that it silenced the entire forest.

Breandán stood tall and confident, meeting Nevan's gaze. "If her father will allow me the honor of his daughter's hand, it would be my greatest pleasure to take Mara as my wife and raise her son as my own."

Nevan put his hand on Breandán's shoulder and smiled. "There are few men who deserve my daughter's hand. But if she consents to the marriage, you have my full blessing."

Breandán held out his hand, and Mara took hold, moving gracefully into his arms. Floating with euphoria, she gave her consent in a passionate, long-awaited kiss.

Chapter Thirty-three

A fortnight later
Inishmore

On the evening of her wedding, Mara stood at the cliff's edge and looked out at the golden celestial sun hovering amid a blanket of red and orange clouds above the horizon. The Atlantic glimmered with vivid sparkles of light and crashed against the rocks below. Tait stood beside her, reflecting upon the impressive sunset as Dægan had done many times before.

"I used to think that as a chieftain," Tait began, "'twas my duty to make decisions for my people, for my family, and to decide what is best for them. But I realize now I'm to lead them in a way which allows them to make sound decisions for themselves, so in the event of my absence, they'll be capable of continuing down a path toward righteousness. Having been blessed with a daughter has shown me that." He paused a moment, taking in a deep breath of the fresh island air, and shifted to face her. "I've made many mistakes since Dægan has left this earth, and 'twas not because he failed to demonstrate the makings of a great leader. I was blind to his guidance. I hope you'll forgive me for not being the leader and...friend I was supposed to be."

His sad jaded eyes reflected the days he'd spent berating himself for trusting in Gunnar. "You're a great and noble leader, Tait. There is no one on this island who can say you gave less than your all in safeguarding both Dægan's and Nevan's people. Putting full faith in Gunnar was not your fault. He deceived us all. That being said, a great chieftain dwells not upon the past as he leads, but channels a path so deep that no one can stray."

Tait closed his eyes and sighed, almost as if he thought himself incapable of such a task. But Mara knew that despite the guilt afflicting him, he'd soon find the fire within to be the formidable leader he was born to be. It would just take time, like all things.

"I miss him," he said as a tear escaped.

The pain in those words tore at Mara's heart. Tait often lost his composure in anger or frustration over the littlest thing, wearing his heart on his sleeve. But when it came to Dægan and his death, few heard him speak of it, and fewer still saw him cry. There was nothing she could say that would make him feel better as it was a loss too great to heal with words.

"I miss him too. But I can still feel him. Dægan is here with us, Tait. I know it."

"I suppose this colorful sunset attests to that, my lady."

He was right. It had been a long time since a sunset as spectacular as this one had splashed across the western sky, reminiscent of the evening they had laid Dægan to rest seven years ago. She took this twilight grandeur as a sign that Dægan was happy she found love again and would always be there in her heart.

When she thought about how lucky she was to have found two of the most gracious men, she realized that Tait couldn't be excluded from that list. Ever since the battle with Mac Flann, he had exhibited a kind and courteous temperament, quite different from the man she used to know. To her surprise, he had helped Breandán bury those who'd given their lives in the fight and assisted Liam Mac Rourke to restore the stronghold that had also faced destruction during the campaign. What's more, he'd invited Breandán's family to stay for the wedding, providing them transportation to and from Inishmore.

"Tait," she said, realizing she'd not thanked him for all that he'd done for her and for Breandán. "I want you to know how grateful I am. For the kindness you've showed Breandán, as well as his family. I know it wasn't an easy thing to do given the animosity between you two."

He laughed a little. "Well, I've learned a few things since then. First being that pride's only concern is for *who* is right, whereas humility is about *what* is right. And secondly, that Breandán's much stronger than he looks." Mara laughed at his joke and accepted the hand he offered her. "Come. We don't want to keep your betrothed waiting."

"Wait," she said, pulling back and smoothing the bodice of her embroidered gown. "H-how do I look?"

Tait regarded her from head to toe, then bowed slightly. "You look as beautiful as ever."

****

The ancient stone fort of the Uí Bhriain housed yet again an assembly of Irish and Norse peoples. But this time, no one was suspicious of the groom or his intentions. There was no impending alliance to be secured or wary islanders to appease. This wedding was a union that no one could oppose or deny.

Island flowers garlanded the inner bailey and wall walk

in colorful strands of purple and yellow. Torches lined a permanent stone platform where Mara and Breandán would stand before God and guests, and a starry sky added the perfect backdrop to this much-anticipated ceremony.

Tait entered the bailey from the large wooden gates and joined Nevan and Breandán at the front of the congregation. Whispers abounded as to his whereabouts, as well as the bride's.

Nevan inclined his face toward Tait's ear. "Where have you been?"

"At the cliff. With Mara."

"Is she all right?"

"She is."

Nevan straightened his spine and inhaled deeply. "It seems you're trying your hand at contemplating life and all its wondrous moments. How is that glove fitting you?"

"Exceptionally well, actually. Did you see the sunset this night?"

"I did. 'Twas the most beautiful one to date. A good omen, wouldn't you agree?"

"I would," Tait said, but he wasn't so sure Breandán believed it. He elbowed Nevan and gestured toward the nervous groom. "It's even better when I see that poor bastard suffering the way he is."

****

Breandán exhaled at length and had no idea how many times he'd done so until Marcas brought it to his attention. "Stop sighing, *a chara*. You've waited seven years for her. What's a few more moments?"

An eternity.

He took in all the faces around him, his father in particular. All seemed at ease in spite of the nerves twisting inside his gut. As he struggled to compose himself, his attention was drawn to the distant gates of the stone fort, where Mara entered the bailey in a white linen gown. Her dark silken hair cascaded down her shoulders, and a ring of island flowers crowned her head. She was the embodiment of perfection, and she would be his to have and to hold, from this day forth until death did them part.

He swallowed hard as she stepped upon the platform and joined him at the ceremonial altar. She smelled of lavender, saxifrage, and sweet, perfumed oils, all of which blended in a clean harmonious scent that took his breath away.

Her eyes of emerald glory pierced his soul when she took his hand. The simple act of linking her fingers with his made him realize his dreams were finally coming true. His days of longing for her touch and pining for her love were over.

The monk who'd marry them stepped forward and wrapped the embroidered strip of linen that Grania had made for Mara around their clasped hands in the customary method of handfasting. Though the fastened cloth only symbolized their permanent union, there was no better way to describe how he felt. He was bound to her.

"*Tá m'anam is mo chroí istigh ionat,*" he said to her in Gaeilge, a beautiful endearment that meant *my heart and soul are within you.*

****

Breandán drew in a deep, calming breath as he stoked the fire in Mara's longhouse. He stared at the lively flames but never saw them. A storm raged within him, a mixture of fear, elation, and tension. All he could think about was Mara—*his wife*—and the moment they were about to share in consummating their marriage.

He paced back and forth in front of the hearth, waiting for her to step out of her chamber. What was keeping her? Was she having second thoughts?

Her door opened, and he stopped abruptly. She entered the room in nothing but a sheer white shift that exposed her naked body beneath. His gaze trailed from the small round nipples of her breasts to the triangular patch of soft dark curls below her navel. She was an angelic sight to behold.

She was nervous, he could tell, and a bit self-conscious. He curved his lips upward in a smile, though he didn't mean to. What was a man to do? She stood there, allowing him the pleasure of viewing all that was going to be his, night after night. All that was rightfully his to touch, taste, memorize, and cherish.

Slowly, he approached her and eyed the subtle curves of her body his hands itched to hold. His legs faltered beneath him at the prospect of feeling her pressed against him. He reached for her with trembling hands, but then balled them into fists at his side.

"Forgive me, *a thaisce*," he whispered.

"For what?"

"For staring. For shaking. You're so beautiful..."

Mara stepped into him and laid her hand over his heart, splaying her delicate fingers across the bulge of muscle on his chest. "You're my husband now. There's no need to resist me any longer."

Breandán covered her hand with his own. "My love for

you was born long before I was. 'Tis as much a part of me as my own soul." With his other hand, he brushed her hair from her face and gingerly stroked his thumb over the delicate ridge of her cheekbone. Touching her—and being free to do so—was a pleasure he'd never take for granted.

She unbuckled the leather belt at his waist and tossed the weighty accessory onto the boxbed nearby. She then lifted his leine over his head, and he watched her eyes as they moved over every inch of him. He saw the concern in her face as she caught a glimpse of the wound above his left hip. Tenderly, she reached out and traced it.

"Does it hurt?"

He shook his head, hardly remembering the laceration at all.

Without pause, she stood on her tiptoes and kissed him, feathering her fingertips across his shoulders and down his arms. Her lips were like the inner petals of a summer rose, delicate and soft. She soothed him more than any healer's potion or magic spell.

He picked her up in his arms and carried her to the double wooden doors of her chamber. His next steps over the threshold where they would unite as husband and wife would be the most significant steps of his life. But as he took in the sight of the intricately carved boxbed, he noticed the crimson bedding he was familiar with was absent. In its place was an embroidered masterpiece of blue and violet, a stunning blanket of woven patterns. Standing out among the designs were three people, hand in hand. He could only assume they were meant to represent Lochlann, Mara, and himself.

"'Twas a gift from Thordia and Lillemor," she explained. "They thought it more suitable for us than the one Dægan had once given to me."

"You've no need to explain. I know Dægan's gifts mean a great deal to you, and they should. I'm also not so naïve to have forgotten the love you and he once shared. The last thing I expect is for you to rid this longhouse of his memory. Everything you and Dægan have shared is precious." Mara snuggled into his neck, and he kissed the top of her head. "May I ask you what you did with Dægan's blanket?"

"I stored it away," she confessed. "I thought perhaps one day Lochlann would favor it for his wedding night."

Breandán smiled at her sentimental idea. She was a thoughtful and caring mother, and he grew excited knowing she would one day be the mother of his many children. He could almost hear them running in and out of this longhouse and their tiny laughter echoing against the walls.

"Do you not like the gift?"

She misread his silence. "On the contrary, *a thaisce*. 'Tis beautiful indeed, but I was thinking that 'twill be even more beautiful when *our* children are added to it."

He entered the closet chamber and laid her upon the large boxbed, the firelight from the main room casting soft shadows across her smooth alabaster skin. He heeled off his ankle boots and lowered himself upon her, slowly, gently. He relished the feel of her body beneath his and pulled her shift up over her head.

Dipping his head, he opened his mouth to her breast and swept his tongue across the taut nipple that he couldn't help himself from tasting. He heard her moan, a feminine sound which nearly undid him, and sucked harder, laving it with firmer strokes. He breathed her in, and the scent of her oils sent his head spinning. He wanted to savor her, to wallow in the fragrance of her body in hopes he'd never rid himself of that sweet aroma.

Lazily, he nuzzled his way up to the crevice of her neck and trailed a path of kisses along her skin as he went. He claimed her mouth and curled his arms around her, his demand stronger than his will to be gentle. But there was no way he was going to rush through this night, this moment, this ever so heavenly dream come true.

"I love you," he whispered.

"I love you too, Breandán Mac Liam. I admit," Mara added timidly, "in the beginning, I fought against loving you. I felt I had to. God knows I tried. But I couldn't stop myself from falling."

Her words shot straight through his heart. It was the first time she'd ever professed anything akin to love, and it was like a bird's song on a warm summer's morn. He took her lips in a long passionate kiss, moved between her legs, and united their bodies as husband and wife.

Chapter Thirty-four

Festivities for the union between Mara and Breandán carried long into the week and extended to the first of August, which commemorated the feast of Lughnasadh. This was a special time for the Irish to celebrate the beginning of the harvest season where the first fruits of the land were consumed and enjoyed.

Gustaf was pleased he was able to partake in the feast with his family and his newfound Irish friends. During most of his adult life, he'd never had the opportunity to enjoy such leisures. But now, with his task of avenging his father complete, he could freely indulge upon delicious food, bottomless mead, and joyous celebrations with his kin.

If it were up to him, he'd not leave. But with Havelok's ships loaded and ready, he knew his men were anxious to return home to their own families, and he would not deny them.

He regarded his family and the joy on their faces. He was proud of them and the life they found in this otherwise wretched world. He had Dægan to thank for that, and Tait, who continued to lead in his brother's absence. It was a good feeling to know his family was safe and that he also had a place to come home to once he'd sailed his loyal hirdmen back home. A place where he too could settle down and raise a family.

He thought of Æsa and the way he'd left her behind in

the Faroes. He wondered if she still waited for him, or if she trusted him to come back to her. He felt an ache in his heart and the only thing he could hold on to was her words. *"I'll wait for you as long as it takes."*

Breathing in the fresh sea spray, he comforted himself with the notion of being in her arms within a few short days. Right now, he had to get through saying good-bye to his loved ones. Though it was only temporary, it was still painful.

He said his farewell first to Tait, embracing him with hearty fist beats on the back.

"I hate to see you leave, Gustaf," Tait said as he regarded him.

"I will return here as soon as I can. This I promise."

Mara stepped forward and hugged him around the neck. "We will keep an eye on the horizon for your return. Please stay safe."

"I will, my lady." He looked at Nevan now. "And to you, I give my deepest appreciation for allowing my family to live on this isle. My brother was very fortunate to find a man such as you. Your immeasurable generosity as king and friend warms my heart."

Nevan reached out and took his forearm. "You've proved yourself to be a man of honor. And I'm grateful for the sacrifices you've made on my daughter's behalf. I speak for the entire isle when I say we're indebted to you and your men for your bravery. You're always welcome here."

Gustaf nodded humbly and turned to face his other family members, his sisters-in-law, nephews, and Tait's tiny newborn daughter. He embraced each one and spoke his farewells, pausing lastly at Lochlann. He looked down at the boy, his face somber as he gazed over a weapon laid across his forearms. "What do you have there, lad?"

Lochlann looked up at him, his eyes wide and drawn like a sad puppy. "This is my father's sword. The one his father gave to him. And I know if my father were here, he'd want you to have it." He paused a moment. "I want you to have it. I don't want you to forget me, Uncle."

Gustaf knelt before him, deeply touched by the boy's generosity. "I could never forget you, Lochlann. You're my nephew. My brother's son. And I need not a sword by which to remember you." He glanced down at the polished weapon, its rubies sparkling under the beaming sun. "I remember the day my father brought this home. 'Tis a great sword, indeed, but I don't deserve a gift this grand."

Lochlann extended his arms, holding out the heavy weapon. "But I *want* you to have it."

Gustaf knew if he protested any further, he'd offend his nephew. "I'll accept your gift on one condition." He unsheathed his sword from the scabbard at his hip and held it before the boy. "Trade?"

Lochlann's face lit up as he eyed the fine piece of weaponry. Without waiting, he made the trade and hugged his uncle. "Don't stay away long, Uncle. Please."

"I promise I'll return. And perhaps then we can accompany Breandán on his hunting trip for hare on the mainland. I could use a new cloak," he said with a wink. "Much like the one you have, Lochlann."

Lochlann smiled proudly as he readjusted his father's bear cloak at his chin. "Tait could use a new cloak too," the boy added.

"I'm not certain Breandán would want me to come along," Tait said wryly. "Especially since I'll only best him in snaring more hare."

"Is that so?" Breandán replied.

Tait crossed his arms daringly. "Would you care to make it interesting?"

Everyone's attention turned toward the two competitive men. Though they'd clearly made amends for all the past animosities, there was still some residual rancor from when Breandán outfought Tait.

"If I snare more than you, Breandán…then you'll give me an opportunity to fight you again so I can make good on my lost dignity, if you will."

"That is quite a wager, Northman," Marcas chimed in. "Apparently, you've never seen Breandán hunt."

"I'm not afraid," Tait concluded.

Breandán crossed his arms as well, accepting Tait's challenge. "And if I snare more?"

Tait thought for a moment, scanning over the many people engrossed with his answer. "I shall give you my steed." Breandán's gaze fell on Mara. "Aye, she told me," Tait confessed. "How you fancied my Fjordhest and wanted a horse like that of your own. If you win, I'll give him to you."

Breandán pondered the bargain. "Agreed."

Gustaf leaned toward Mara. "I'm going to hate to miss this."

Cheerful laughter filled the beach, and Gustaf gave his last partings to the group, wading through the water to reach Havelok's ships. With brisk steps, he neared the side and leapt over the gunwale, waving to those on shore. No matter what his journey brought him, he would come back and make his home on Inishmore.

****

Breandán and Mara took a walk to the daunting cliffs

beside Nevan's fortress and gazed over the resplendent waters, the afternoon sun glistening on the surface. "Are you happy?" he asked her.

She nestled closer to him and rested her head on his chest. "Of course I am. How could I not be? I have a husband who loves me and a son who adores him. What more could I ask for?"

Moved by her words, he pulled her closer. She felt so good there. So perfect. So right. Holding her in this very spot, the place where they had had their first deep, meaningful conversation about love and Dægan and his memory, was very special to him. He knew they'd journey through life together, with Dægan's memory not far behind. In truth, Breandán welcomed the valiant Northman who lingered in Mara's heart. Their relationship and all that had transpired made Mara who she was today, and that was what Breandán had fallen in love with from the very beginning.

As they watched the sun set together, he felt a presence. The gentle breeze wafted past, and a warm reassurance blew through him. He might not have seen or heard anything, but he swore he felt Dægan there. Protecting them.

After a few quiet moments, the sound of footsteps broke the peaceful silence and their tender embrace. Nevan approached them with a leather satchel in his hands.

"I hope I'm not interrupting," Nevan said considerately.

"Not in the least," Breandán replied, taking notice of Mara's interest in the unknown item in the king's possession.

"Is that...?" Mara uttered, reaching out.

Nevan offered it to her. "I thought you would remember, Mara."

She took it in her hands reverently, staring at it with dismay, then hugged it against her chest. "How ever did you get it back?"

"I never traded it after Dægan died," Nevan admitted, watching her revel in its return. "I knew what this book meant to you. And to him. I didn't have the heart to give it away."

"But our homes were completely destroyed by fire and we had naught with which to trade in order to gain the supplies necessary for rebuilding. How did—"

"Through my own past travels, I had accumulated enough goods of value for such an event. Besides, my daughter needed a home. And though you didn't know it at the time, I would've given my sword arm to keep you here."

"I cannot believe you saved it."

Breandán watched Mara open the leather bag with extreme care and slip out an old book, still not fully comprehending the magnificence of the age-old volume. "What is it?" he asked.

"Forgive me, Breandán. This book," she said, holding it out for him, "is St. Ciarán's book of the Gospels."

Breandán was still confused. "Why would you have a holy man's book from many centuries ago?"

"I'm glad you asked. Did you know that this book has survived damage from both fire and water?"

Breandán found it hard to believe her. He glanced at the book, its condition relatively unmarred. "Fire and water?" He flicked his gaze between Nevan, Mara, and the book. "May I?" he asked, wanting to inspect it for himself.

"Of course. Please do."

Careful not to tear the thin vellum pages, he split the book in half and studied the beautiful calligraphy and colored images of its content. Though he was not able to read, he was enthralled by the meticulous work that went into making such an impressive tome. Not only that, but he smelled rain.

Automatically, he drew in a breath and cast his eyes toward the sky. Not a cloud in sight. Again he drew in a breath.

Nevan and Mara both laughed at him. "What do you smell?" she asked.

"Rain, but I cannot understand why."

Nevan put his arm around them both. "I shall leave you two alone." And he walked away toward his fort, a leisurely skip in his step.

"In all seriousness, Mara, why do I smell rain?" he asked again, baffled by the odor.

She pulled him to the ground to sit and smiled. "Everyone smells rain when they open the book. Dægan once did. I did. And now you."

Breandán flipped through the pages, his interest climbing with each turn. "So tell me more about this book. And how Dægan came to own it."

"I would love to," she said, gazing into his eyes. "But first…" She leaned in and pressed her lips to his.

He opened his eyes when she pulled away and asked, "What was that for?"

"I wanted to thank you for allowing me to stay here. Like this book, I belong here. With my father, and with Dægan's family."

Breandán reached up and stroked her cheek. "Where you are, Mara, is where I belong. There is no other place I'd rather be."

THE END

Author's Note

If you enjoyed *Emerald Glory*, I encourage you to continue reading as I bring you full circle from the first two books in a way that will utterly surprise and delight. The unforgettable, ultimate climactic ending you've highly anticipated is yours to enjoy in book 3, Souls Reborn.

Vikings of Honor Series
Sunset Fire, Book 1
Emerald Glory, Book 2
Souls Reborn, Book 3
Tempered Steel, Book 4

As a side note, if you'd like to find out what happens between Gustaf and Æsa in their spin-off story, don't forget to check out the fourth book of the Vikings of Honor series, *Tempered Steel*.

****

Are you intrigued enough to read on? For your reading pleasure, I've included the first two chapters of *Souls Reborn*. I hope you enjoy!

Sincerely yours,
Renee Vincent

Souls
Reborn

Vikings of Honor, Book Three

Chapter One

Ireland, Present Day

Leif Dæganssen was soaked to the skin. The cool June rain beat on his back and thunder rolled across the heavens as he staked his shovel into the saturated ground outside his quaint Inishmore cottage. Normally, he'd never think of digging in the ground on such a terrible night. But every bone in his body urged him onward. He had no idea what he was looking for. His gut told him that something grand and unique might very well be hidden beneath his porch.

Leif was not a superstitious man. In fact, his livelihood as an archeologist never allowed him to consider supernatural practices. After years of schooling and countless, tedious digs, he only believed in things explainable through science, carbon dating, and the naked eye.

This was different.

He dug on a hunch, an innate feeling coursing through his veins. By rights, the storm should have slowed his progress, or at least made him think twice on the idiocy of this escapade. But the dousing Erin rain fueled a fire so great that he ignored the aching muscles in his back and arms. The more it drenched his clothes, the more he was determined to scoop the dark, sopping mud away from his lattice-enclosed porch. Shovelful after careful shovelful, he dug away the soil, ignoring the long heavy sighs of his younger brother, Kristoff.

"How long are we going to be out here in this storm digging for worms, Leif?"

Leif paid him no attention. He concentrated on the depth of his ditch around the front of his house and the silent calculations he made in his head. The perimeter hole he had already dug was about two feet deep, and he knew the topsoil would eventually give way to rock-solid limestone beneath. A few more inches—at max maybe another foot—and he'd find something.

He could feel it.

As sure as the rain dripped from every strand of hair in his face, he could feel his adrenaline rising at the thought of his shovel hitting something solid.

"Leif!" Kristoff yelled, jerking him by the arm. A flash of lightning ripped across the midnight sky. Both flinched at the heart-stopping crack and peered above. Kristoff turned his attention back to his brother. "This is insane. We're going to get killed out here."

"Then go inside," Leif said. "I'm not quitting."

"And I'm not letting you get struck by lightning over some stupid gut feeling over an artifact that may or may not be here."

Leif squared his shoulders and leaned in close, the rain spitting like needles in his face. "I'm not stopping," he repeated, driving his shovel deep in the ground. A low, dull thump thudded back. "Did you hear that?"

Kristoff looked at Leif skeptically. "I did…"

Leif's face lit up brighter than the violent streak of lightning that passed overhead. "I told you I'd find something." He dropped to his knees, throwing his gloves aside as he dug beneath the last bit of mud. Against his training that called for careful excavation, he tore away handfuls of soil. Within seconds, his fingertips scraped against something solid.

"I feel it," Leif said breathlessly. "It's right here." Like a dog pawing for its buried bone, he dug until the top could be seen.

"Holy Halfdan Haroldsson," Kristoff mumbled as he saw a distinct pagan carving come into view. As the rain washed it clean, a whole slew of carvings took form before their eyes.

Leif glanced at Kristoff. "Now, do you believe me?"

"I do now. Come on, dig it out."

Leif didn't need his brother's encouragement. For years, he'd been trying to convince Kristoff that this Irish island was the home of their Norwegian ancestors. More importantly, that the house he had bought two years ago was likely sitting atop their settlement. He had no proof. Only a vibe he felt from the moment he stepped foot on the treeless island.

Until now.

Even in the dark of night, through the shroud of Ireland's merciless rainfall, there was no mistaking the Scandinavian carvings on the wooden artifact. They were telltale coils of a history forgotten—instantly recognizable designs spiraling and twisting into a complex weave of creatures, demigods, and beasts.

To a young archeologist, it was like striking gold.

"What do you think this is?" Kristoff asked as he helped to dig.

"I don't know. Perhaps a shield…or a weather vane from a longship."

"No," Kristoff said, peeling away hunks of mud from

the side. "I think it's thicker than that."

Their excitement vaulted in unearthing the sizeable object from its grave. Words escaped them for guessing what they thought it could be, but one thing rang true. It was a large find—literally.

In the archeological world, antiquities such as a small coin or a glass bead were significant discoveries. Most times, they were found purely by accident. Then, once the find was made public, archeologists from all walks of life would try to establish the site as historical and gather funding for a further, more intensive dig. Finding anything beyond the small artifact took months or even years of dedication and meticulous excavation with skillful hands. Leif had found something substantial within a matter of minutes, and it was certainly nothing short of impressive.

As he and Kristoff lifted the heavy wooden relic from the mire of his crude excavation and set it on the grass in silent awe. They stared at the highly decorated object, with its complex loops and spirals making up the elaborate, dated designs.

This was no accident. This coffer had called to Leif—had beckoned him to buy this property. Though it proved nothing about his ancestors specifically settling here on this very spot, it did confirm that someone of Scandinavian descent had visited the isle. He was determined to find out who and hopefully link them with his Norwegian ancestors.

Gazing at the stunning carved box through the pelting rain, Kristoff broke the silence. "We're going to be famous."

Leif shot his brother a grave look. "We're not telling a soul about this."

"Are you out of your mind? Do you not know what this is?"

Leif ignored him. All he wanted to do was take it inside and get it out of sight, but he lost his footing in the slippery mud hole and fell on his backside.

"Here," Kristoff said, thrusting out his hand. "Let me help you."

Leif accepted his brother's aid, then hurried up the steps of his front porch, carrying the heavy box. Kristoff navigated past him and opened the door wide so he could pass through with ease.

In the dark, he walked straight into the open space of his living room and into the adjoining kitchen, where he set the object on the table. His heart hammered at the excitement of finally seeing his find under overhead lighting.

Stepping back, he reached for the switch on the wall, unable to tear his eyes from the dark object displayed on the table. He heard Kristoff's heavy footsteps approaching, but he didn't have the strength to flip on the light.

"Turn it on already," Kristoff demanded.

"Not yet."

"What do you mean, not yet? Turn on the light."

Leif studied his brother in the dark. "Kristoff, you must promise that what we see stays between us. No one is to know what we've found. And I mean no one."

"Why?" Kristoff asked. "We found something highly prized, and we could—"

"We're not going to tell a soul," Leif said. "If we reveal what we've found here tonight, this place will be swarming with media, treasure seekers, and museum enthusiasts. My home will no longer be mine and my life's work will be ruined. I've spent countless hours tracing our ancestors to this isle. And this...*this*," he said, gesturing toward the table, "could very well be the missing link to finding our distant family. Please, Kristoff. Don't spoil this for me. Don't take away my one chance of uncovering our past."

Leif heard his brother heave a heavy sigh. The moments ticked away with each drop of water on the cheap linoleum floor as he waited for Kristoff's response.

"Fine. I give my word. I won't tell a soul. Now turn on the bloody light."

Leif flipped the switch, but nothing could have prepared him for what he saw. It wasn't just a carved artifact sitting on his table above a puddle of muddy water on his floor, but a chest—a coffer that quite possibly held more riches than one man could fathom in a lifetime.

Chapter Two

Kentucky, USA

A billow of dust trailed behind Lorraine O'Connor's midnight-blue 1975 Corvette as she sped down the winding gravel lane and parked in front of Patrick's garage. At the sound of her slamming door, he stood from his stooped position, letting his horse's hoof slide from his dusty chaps and onto the ground. He leaned against the animal's hindquarter and patted its rump.

He watched his childhood friend march up the steps to the back entrance of his Cape Cod home and disappear behind the sliding glass door. Though Lorraine never glanced toward the barn, he knew by the resolve of her feet hitting the pavement and the hard draw of the door, short of shattering his glass, that something terrible had gone wrong.

"Looks like you're only getting the front shoes on today, Mr. Pride," he muttered to the horse. A slight smile tugged at the corner of Patrick's mouth. He couldn't help it. If something had gone awry with Lorraine and Brad on their Sunday afternoon picnic, then that would mean she was free from Brad's control. At least until they got back together again.

Oh, how he hated that asshole.

Brad was Lorraine's fiancé, but he certainly hadn't earned that title as far as Patrick was concerned. On more occasions than he could count, Brad treated Lorraine like dirt, often bringing her to tears. Then, he'd turn it around and make her feel as if she were the one to blame. She'd apologize like she always did and do something grand to make up for it. Being an only child and spoiled by wealthy parents, Brad would take advantage of her generosity, never thinking twice about the amount of money she'd spend on him. Lord knows she couldn't afford it. But that was Lorraine.

Many times, Patrick tried to talk some sense into her, to make her realize that Brad could never give her what she truly deserved. Lorraine would shrug and defend Brad with excuses Patrick never bought.

What had really upset Patrick was when Lorraine's parents both died in a tragic car accident last year and Brad had the gall not to attend their funeral. He claimed funerals were too difficult for him.

That was the day Patrick had stepped in. He had to. She was heartbroken and lost. Since she didn't have enough money to keep her parents' house, which the O'Connors had mortgaged twice, he suggested she move in with him. He hadn't really expected her to accept the offer of living on a hundred-acre Kentucky horse farm, but to his surprise, she agreed and had been living there ever since.

Much to Patrick's disappointment, Lorraine never dropped her pathetic fiancé. The only thing Patrick liked about the guy was that he couldn't seem to commit to a date, keeping Lorraine on hold until he was ready. Or, as Patrick assumed, until someone better came along.

He unbuckled the worn leather farrier chaps from his waist and calves and hung them up on a hook inside the barn. He stretched his aching muscles in his lower back and removed his cowboy hat by the brim, swiping his sweaty brow with his forearm. After returning Mr. Pride to his stall, he pulled his cell from his pocket. He hated to make this call, but it was necessary. Everything was necessary when it came to Lorraine, even if he had to disappoint his girlfriend—again.

He dialed her number and waited, dreading to hear Beth's voice on the other end.

"Hey, sexy," Beth hummed. "You ready for our ride today?"

Patrick absently kicked at the gravel in his drive as he left the barn and looked up into the bright summer sky, unsure how to respond. "About that…"

"Are you serious? You're canceling on me again?"

"I'm not canceling on you, Beth. I just have to take a rain check." Even as he spoke the words, he cringed at his pathetic excuse. It sounded like something Brad would say.

"Tell me you're not rearranging our date because of Lorraine. Tell me you just got a call for an emergency shoeing in Lexington. Anywhere. Please…"

Patrick stiffened. Blaming this on a high-dollar Thoroughbred sounded pretty good right now, but he wasn't the kind of guy to lie to his girlfriend. "I'm sorry, honey. She just pulled in like a bat outta hell, and evidently, Brad—"

"Why do you care so much?" she interrupted stiffly. "The best thing that could happen to Lorraine is if Brad would just dump her."

"I know that."

"Then let her stew for a while. Let her be pissed off enough to dump his ass for once."

"If I thought it would help, I would. But…" Patrick paced. He knew no matter what he said, Beth wouldn't understand. He cared for her dearly, but when it came to his relationship with Lorraine, he felt obligated to be there for her. He was all she had, especially after she'd lost most of her female friends because of Brad. And even if he kept his plans with Beth, his mind wouldn't be on his girlfriend, but on the fact he deserted Lorraine. It was best to just cancel his date with Beth and move on.

"Are you still here?" he asked.

She sighed. "Yes, I'm still here. But I can't guarantee it'll be for long."

"What does that mean?"

"It means I'm getting tired of being second best, Patrick. And I feel like you and I can't be together like a normal couple because Lorraine is always there. Coming between us. You need to get this sorted out and fast. I shouldn't have to wait at all, but I will, 'cause I love you."

Patrick smiled and hung his head. Those little words made him happy, but he never had the heart to say them back. "How about dinner at my house this Friday? You and me. No one else. We'll ride horses all day, and I'll cook for you when we get back."

"You promise? Just me and you?" Beth asked skeptically.

"Yes…" he replied in a soft whisper. "Just us."

"I'll be there bright and early."

Beth hung up before he could say anything more. He shoved his cell in his back pocket and rubbed the tension from his jaw with a stiff hand, mentally preparing himself for Lorraine.

****

Patrick stepped into the kitchen and slid the door closed behind him. The house was strangely quiet and still.

By now, his rowdy chocolate Lab should've been clumsily traipsing up, all tongue and legs, before he could take one step off the welcome mat. "Raine?" he called tentatively. "You in here?"

"I'm fine, Patrick. Leave me alone."

Lorraine's voice came from her bedroom down the hall. He kicked off his dusty cowboy boots and hung his hat on the hook by the door before making his way. As he expected, her door was shut, and when he gripped the handle, it was locked.

He leaned against the frame. "Raine, open the door."

"I said I'm fine."

There was anger in her voice, but through the gruffness she tried to fake, Patrick heard it crack. His heart melted. "Raine...talk to me."

"I don't feel like talking. I just want to be left alone."

Patrick rolled his eyes. No woman ever meant that. In his experience, *leave me alone* typically meant *be more convincing so I'll feel compelled to share my feelings*.

"Fine," he yielded. "I'll just sit out here and wait till you're ready to talk. I've got all day."

"Aren't you supposed to be horseback riding with Beth this afternoon?"

He rested his forehead on the door. "No, we changed plans."

"She changed plans or you did?"

He grew impatient with talking through the door. "What does it matter?"

"Dammit, Patrick, you can't keep doing that. You can't continue to rearrange your life with her because of me. She already hates me as it is."

Patrick tried the door handle again, to no avail. "Beth

doesn't hate you. She just doesn't understand my relationship with you. Give her time…she'll learn."

"She'll learn to hate you, Patrick. No woman wants to be second, and with me living here, you'll always put me first."

He caught the slight stress on "with me living here" and heard the closet door slide across its tracks, then the sound of her dragging something from inside. He pressed his ear against the door, listening. A furious zipper opened and then a drawer from her dresser. "What are you doing in there? Are you packing?"

She ignored him.

"Raine," he demanded, his voice taking on an urgent tone. "Open this door right now."

She didn't oblige, and the longer he waited, the madder he got. If he knew one thing about Lorraine, it was that she was a determined woman. If she got something in her head, no matter how idiotic it was, she was going to see it through. He feared she'd decided to move out.

He couldn't let her. He cared too much to let her walk out of his life. The only place she could go was Brad's house in Indian Hill—the Beverly Hills of Ohio—and that was the last place he'd want her to run to.

"All right, that's it," Patrick warned. "I'm coming in."

He didn't know why he even gave a warning. It was his house, and he had a right to open any damn door he wanted. He spun around and reached above his bedroom doorframe for the pin key. He drove it in the tiny hole and burst into the room. Lorraine carried an armful of clothes to the edge of the bed, where a heap of unfolded clothes already lay in her suitcase.

His dog, Captain, jumped off the bed and ran to greet him, paws and all. Correcting the dog, he pushed the animal aside and stopped Lorraine. "What are you doing?"

"Patrick, it's bad enough that I'm ruining my relationship with Brad. I'm not going to ruin yours too."

She tried to walk around him, but he stepped in front of her and clasped her face in his hands. "See? This is the shit I'm talking about. Brad has brainwashed you into thinking the reason your relationship is on the rocks is you. Do you know how absurd that is? Raine, it has *never* been your fault. Can't you see that? He doesn't deserve you."

"But Beth deserves you, and I'm not going to stand in your way anymore."

He grabbed her shoulders. "You're not in my way. You're my best friend. And I'm not letting you leave."

Tears welled in her green eyes. Her bottom lip quivered, and he pulled her into his arms, unable to bear the sight of her sorrow. "What happened?" He felt the jerk of quiet sobs in her shoulders as he led her toward the bed so they could sit down. Captain followed and lay down at their feet, his head on his paws.

Patrick took her hands in his. He noticed that the three-carat diamond solitaire she wore on her left, the only impressive thing Brad had ever offered her, was absent. Then again, Patrick never thought for one second that the man actually forked out his own money for it. He'd bet his life that Brad's parents paid for it simply because they didn't want their son to let a good thing slip through his hands.

"Where's your ring?"

Lorraine stared at the floor. "I gave it back to him."

Though her words were music to his ears, he restrained his joy. "Why?"

Lorraine blew out a tremendous sigh, and anger laced

her words. "Because I walked in on him with another woman."

Patrick's heart stopped. "With another woman...doing what?"

Lorraine glared at him. "What do you think, Patrick? They were in bed together, our bed—"

Her tears ran like a faucet now. "Okay, okay..." he consoled, pulling her against him. "I get it. It's okay. Shh...you don't have to say another word. I'm here." He didn't expect her to say anything more, but it was as though his words sparked a need to rant.

"You know what Brad did when I ran out of the house?"

Patrick didn't want to guess. He could only imagine what that scumbag did in the heat of Lorraine finding him screwing another woman.

"He chased me down the sidewalk with a sheet around his waist, saying he could explain. When I continued to run for my car, he actually grabbed me by the arm and said if I gave him just five minutes, he could be ready for our picnic." Lorraine began to laugh hysterically. "Can you believe that? He said he just forgot about our picnic and double booked. Like I'm a flippant appointment he forgot to pencil in and scheduled a necessary fornication session in its place."

Patrick was dumbfounded. "Raine, I am so sorry. I— I..."

Lorraine looked up at him from the pocket of his shoulder. "Oh, don't act so surprised," she snapped, standing up to pace the room.

Patrick jumped up to embrace her again. "I know you can't begin to see it now, but it *is* better this way. You don't have to waste any more time on Brad. You're free to find the man of your dreams, the *right* man of your dreams."

"I don't think he's out there."

"Sure he is," Patrick contended, stroking her long dark hair. "He already visits you in your dreams every night."

Lorraine drew back to look at him. "You're talking about a guy who's a ridiculous figment of my own imagination, mind you, as if he's real."

"You've told me you could feel this man's lips on yours as real as if he were right in bed with you. You've had this dream ever since I've known you. So, how do you explain it?"

"It's called a pathetic girl's wish for her cliché knight in shining armor."

At that, Lorraine's cell phone rang, and she froze with a blank look. On the second ring, she scurried past him and frantically searched her purse on the bed. Pulling it out, she stared at the display.

She didn't have to read the name to Patrick. He already knew it was Brad. Infuriated, he grabbed the cell and threw it out of the room against the hall wall. The phone shattered in pieces, and before she could race out the door to salvage it, Patrick taunted his dog. "You want it? Go get it. Go get it, boy."

Captain jumped to his feet and ran to the plastic fragments lying haphazardly on the floor. Without even sniffing, he chose the biggest scrap and ran away with it in his mouth.

Patrick laughed, until Lorraine turned around with a scowl. She wasn't as pleased as he was with his dog's obedience.

"That was my cell phone. You broke it."

"I'll buy you a new one. With a different number," he

added. "Besides, you have nothing more to say to him."

"Says who?"

"Says me. Now start packing." Suddenly, her idea of leaving was the best thing she'd ever come up with. He was going to make damn sure Brad couldn't find her. "Pack your bags, Raine. You're going on a trip."

"A what?" Lorraine called after him. She watched him disappear into the hall, dumbfounded by what he suggested. *A trip?* Unable to stand there and be ignored, she jetted after him, catching up as he entered his office. He slid into his chair, and his fingers worked like mad over the keys.

Lorraine hovered over his desk and braced her hands on the flat surface. "What's gotten into you? One minute you're begging me to stay, and the next you're giving me orders to leave."

Patrick typed a few more words on his keyboard. "Ah, here we go." He looked up at her. "Would you rather leave from Cincinnati to Chicago to Ireland with a five-hour layover? Or fly into Philly with three hours to kill?"

She blinked repeatedly, her mouth agape.

"You're right," he decided. "Five hours is too long. Let's go with Philly."

"Patrick, you're not listening to me. I'm not going to Ireland."

He looked up from his screen. "Why not? You've always wanted to go there. And you would've by now had it not been for Brad holding you back. You finally have the opportunity to go whenever you want."

Lorraine straightened herself from the desk. "I'm not going to Ireland. I can't afford it."

"I can," Patrick contended.

As he began to click around with his mouse, Lorraine grabbed his hand, jerking his cursor off the screen. "I'm not going, so don't bother booking a flight."

"Give me one good reason why."

"It's too soon. I'm not ready to be on my own. I've just spent four years with a man I thought I was going to marry, and figuring out how to be single again is not something I'm ready to tackle at this point. I don't even like the sound of it. The word 'single' to me means being morbidly alone."

"But you're not alone. You have me."

"It's not the same, and you know it."

Patrick stood and approached her, his face as serious as she'd ever seen it. "No one, at this very moment, cares for you as much as I do. I've sat back and watched you waste your life with Brad for years. I had high hopes for him in the beginning, but even he disappointed me in the span of a couple of dates. You've always known how I felt about him, but once you said 'yes' to his proposal, I figured there was nothing more I could do. You were a grown woman and capable of making your own decisions.

"However, now that you've seen the side of Brad that I've always suspected, you need someone who has a clear head, someone who can make decisions for you that are to your benefit. Believe me, darlin', you need this. You need this trip more than you know—if not just to distance yourself from Brad, then for the sheer enjoyment of it. You can do this. I know you can."

Lorraine stood there and listened to every word Patrick said. He was right about one thing. She definitely needed to distance herself from the man who broke her heart, even though she'd like to go back over to his house and give him a piece of her mind. As grand and exciting as going to Ireland sounded, she still didn't think she had the courage to go on her own. She could hardly stomach the thought of going to a restaurant by herself, much less journey to another country.

Patrick took her hands and folded them in his. "Would you rather I go with you?"

Lorraine rolled her eyes. "Beth would dump your butt for sure, and I'd never forgive myself." She heaved a heavy sigh. She didn't know how she'd gotten so lucky to have Patrick's undying loyalty, and the last thing she wanted to do was leave the only person who cared about her. "I don't know," she muttered. "I'm not up for a vacation right now. And then there's work. I'd have to take off, and who knows if I could on such short notice."

"You bartend at Molly Malone's. I think they can find someone else to serve Guinness for a few weeks."

Lorraine bit her lip.

"Come on, Raine," he encouraged. "What have you got to lose? There's nothing here to hold you back. You're as free as a bird. Grab those daring wings I know you have and soar the skies of Ireland. You never know…you might get lucky there."

"Let's get one thing straight, Patrick Owen O'Rorke. If I go anywhere, it won't be to get lucky."

Patrick's dimples deepened with his smile. "Never say never, Raine." Before she could say more on the subject, he slid back in his chair with his fingers readied on the keys. "So, is that a 'yes'?"

Last-minute jitters crept inside her as she contemplated her final decision. The more she thought about it, the more it sounded like an opportunity she'd be stupid to pass up.

"Only if you let me pay you back."

"Whatever."

When he grabbed the mouse and gave it a click, her stomach instantly twisted in knots.

"It's done. You leave tomorrow."

About Renee Vincent

RENEE VINCENT is a *USA Today* bestselling author of romance and women's fiction. Her books have earned numerous accolades, including a #1 Bestseller for Viking Romance.

She lives on a secluded hundred-acre horse farm in the rolling hills of Kentucky with her husband, two beautiful daughters, and a few fur babies who've managed to weasel their way into a couple of books. When she's not writing, she loves to decorate (and redecorate) her home, knit cozy blankets, send homemade cards to family and friends, and concoct her own versions of recipes to pass down to her girls.

Through the years, Renee has connected with some of the most dedicated and gracious readers who crave unpredictable plot twists, gripping adventure, and undying love. For that, she is most grateful.

www.ReneeVincent.com

Books By Series

Vikings of Honor Series
Sunset Fire, Book 1
Emerald Glory, Book 2
Souls Reborn, Book 3
Tempered Steel, Book 4

Mavericks of Meeteetse Series
Longing for Langston, Brody & Liv, Book 1
Made for McKinley, Jonas & Ava, Book 2
Falling For Forester, Cole & Crys, Book 3

Jamett & Joseph Series
The Start of Something Good, Book 1
The Road to Something Better, Book 2
The Gift of Something Grand, Book 3
Something's Bound to Happen, Books 1 - 3

Stand Alone Novel
Silent Partner

If you enjoyed this book by Renee Vincent, please consider leaving an honest review at your favorite vendor. Reviews not only give credibility to an author's work, they also help other readers find quality books worth reading.

ReneeVincent.com

www.ingramcontent.com/pod-product-compliance
Lightning Source LLC
Chambersburg PA
CBHW020400260626
47156CB00007B/2187